1994

TO KILL
A MAN'S
PRIDE

TO KILL A MAN'S PRIDE

and Other Stories from Southern Africa
edited by Norman Hodge

RAVAN PRESS   JOHANNESBURG

Published by Ravan Press (Pty) Ltd,
P.O. Box 31134, Braamfontein 2017, South Africa
© Copyright: The contributors as listed on the contents page of this book
First impression 1984
Second impression 1985
Third impression 1986
Fourth impression 1987
Fifth impression 1988
Sixth impression 1990
Typesetting: Sandy Parker
Cover Art: Mzwakhe Nhlabatsi
Design: The Graphic Equalizer

ISBN 0 86975 146 8

Printed by Galvin & Sales, Cape Town
              (6534)

ACKNOWLEDGEMENTS

We are grateful to the following for permission to reproduce
copyright material:
ISEA, Grahamstown, for 'The Dog Killers' by RRR Dhlomo
from *English in Africa 2 (1)*; Human and Rousseau Publishers,
Johannesburg, for 'Unto Dust' by H C Bosman from *Unto
Dust*; Mrs Queenie Motsisi for 'Kid Playboy' by Casey Motsisi;
Heinemann Educational Books Ltd., Surrey, for 'The Suit' by
Can Themba from *The Will to Die*, 'The Wind and a Boy' by
Bessie Head from *The Collector of Treasures*, 'Six Feet of the
Country' by Nadine Gordimer from *Some Monday for Sure*;
Jonathan Cape Ltd., London, for 'Ha'penny' by Alan Paton
from *Debbie Go Home*; Weidenfeld and Nicolson Ltd., London,
for 'Beggar My Neighbour' by Dan Jacobson from *Through the
Wilderness*; Ezekiel Mphahlele for 'Mrs Plum' from *African
Stories*; Ad Donker Publisher, Johannesburg, for 'The Visits'
by Richard Rive from *Selected Writings*; Curtis Brown Ltd.,
London, for 'No Witchcraft for Sale' copyright Doris Lessing
1951; Ahmed Essop for 'The Hajji' from *The Hajji and Other
Stories*; Bateleur Press, Johannesburg, for 'The Other
Windows' by Lionel Abrahams from *The Celibacy of Felix
Greenspan*; Mbulelo Mzamane for 'My Other Cousin, Sitha'
from *Mzala*; Mtutuzeli Matshoba for 'To Kill a Man's Pride'
from *Forced Landing* and Njabulo Ndebele for 'The Music of
the Violin' from *Fools and Other Stories*.

CONTENTS

Introduction   1
R.R.R. Dhlomo/*The Dog Killers*   6
H.C. Bosman/*Unto Dust*   11
Casey Motsisi/*Kid Playboy*   18
Can Themba/*The Suit*   22
Alan Paton/*Ha'penny*   36
Dan Jacobson/*Beggar My Neighbour*   42
Ezekiel Mphahlele/*Mrs Plum*   58
Bessie Head/*The Wind and a Boy*   104
Nat Nakasa/*Mr Nakasa Goes to Harlem*   115
Richard Rive/*The Visits*   129
Doris Lessing/*No Witchcraft for Sale*   139
Nadine Gordimer/*Six Feet of the Country*   150
Ahmed Essop/*The Hajji*   166
Lionel Abrahams/*The Other Windows*   185
Mbulelo Mzamane/*My Other Cousin, Sitha*   191
Mtutuzeli Matshoba/*To Kill a Man's Pride*   203
Njabulo Ndebele/*The Music of the Violin*   240

INTRODUCTION

The craft of story-telling is as old as the human community itself and no individual culture can claim an advantage or precedence. Whether one reads Aesop's fables, Xhosa iintsomi, North American Indian legends, ancient Hebrew myths, Persian tales or Norse sagas, the roots are the same and all are equally illustrative of the art of oral narrative and recitation. And common types of stories suggest common interests among untold generations of listeners: the fox who concluded the grapes were sour because he could not reach them, from Aesop's fables; a proud rooster called Chauntecleer who barely escaped being eaten because of his pride, as narrated in Middle English by Chaucer; an Ojibway tale of the famous and frightening Thunderbird, common to that area of Canada where the editor grew up, and that famous creature of so many African stories, Anansi the spider, are all part of the world tradition of the beast fable. Quite simply, there are few if any cultural boundaries in such stories: even today, some of the most popular children's stories in North America originated in Africa. Joel Chandler Harris wrote down the Brer Rabbit tales, which were brought over by the slaves from West Africa and were given in the new world an American flavour, whilst retaining their African heritage.

It is generally accepted that the written form itself reached its first flowering in Europe and America in the early to mid-nineteenth century. Such early craftsmen as Washington Irving, Nathaniel Hawthorne and Edgar Allan Poe in the United States; and Nikolai Gogol, Ivan Turgenev and Gustave Flaubert in Russia and France established a strong base for the genre, popularizing it to such an extent that most major writers now are known for their skills in both novels and stories.

But what is a story? What distinguishes it from, say, a novel, a character portrait, or an essay? The student is very apt to discover that there are as many theories and definitions as there are craftsmen and critics. Only one rather broad description seems sufficient to encompass the varieties:

> A skilful literary artist has constructed a tale. If wise, he has not fashioned his thoughts to accommodate his incidents; but having conceived, with deliberate care, a certain unique or single *effect* to be wrought out, he then invents such incidents — he then combines such events as may best aid him in establishing this preconceived effect . . . the one pre-established design.

The description is by Edgar Allan Poe in his review of Nathaniel Hawthorne's *Twice-Told Tales* in 1842. There is no attempt here to dissect the components of shorter fiction; instead, Poe suggests that the reader focus on the *unity of impression* given by a story. If the writer is good, then all aspects of plot, background, characterization and narrative devices will contribute to the total effect. Further than this general statement one cannot go without finding contradictions. For example, the story is not as long as the novel, but how long or how short? Back in the 1960's, the editor was given a quantitative definition — 50 000 words was the dividing line between a long story and a short novel! This is, we recognize now, absurd: length does not matter. A sketch by Dhlomo and Mphahlele's 'Mrs Plum' are both stories even though the former is but a few hundred words and the latter many thousands; and both function as good stories according to Poe.

In South Africa the story in both its oral and written forms has flourished. A C Jordan's *Tales From Southern Africa,* a collection of oral tales, and Jean Marquard's *A Century of South African Short Stories,* a collection of the written form, show the long history of the genre as well as the genius of its many practitioners.

In its cultural diversity, the clashes and attempts at reconciliation, in the glories and horrors of the land and its social, economic and political histories; in the evolution and transition of its society, Southern Africa has proved a fertile ground for the literary imagination. The reader encounters a distinctly Southern African milieu, whether Bosman's rural world of dusty veld and small dorps, or Can Themba's totally urban world of 'locations' and great cities. Nor is there any borrowed idiom, no language or style of writing that signifies a cultural colonialism — any heritage has been assimilated, not imitated, and there is no particular indebtedness to any alien viewpoint or ideology. A writer like Mphahlele, for example, is both South African and international at the same time: 'Mrs Plum' is distinctly here and now, immediate and applicable to what exists; yet the 'essence' of the story, what it communicates about human nature, has a universal relevance. The American writer, William Faulkner, once wrote that all good literature is about the 'human heart in conflict with itself,' and about what he called the 'eternal verities' of pity and pride, honour and courage — of the need to endure, of the struggle to prevail.

This collection of stories seeks to illustrate both the particular and the general applicability of Southern African shorter fiction — the ways in which writers have looked at their society and shown its 'reality' from a variety of perspectives. All of the stories are modern, the oldest being R R R Dhlomo's 'The Dog Killers' and Herman Charles Bosman's 'Unto Dust', and many are contemporary, representative of the *new* renaissance in shorter fiction here. Selecting one story from any single writer proved most difficult since every author has a number of equally good tales; and the choice of who to leave in and leave out, especially among the craftsmen of the Seventies and early Eighties, came down to personal preference. One hopes that other collections will include selections from those fine writers omitted in this selection.

Many of the stories have also been chosen because they are open to comparison and contrast as groups around a central theme or type. Lionel Abrahams' 'The Other Window', Bessie Head's 'The Wind and a Boy', Dan Jacobson's 'Beggar My Neighbour' and Alan Paton's 'Ha'penny' all focus on the child or youth, the symbol of the future, coming to terms with self and an often incomprehensible adult world.

But the main intention of this collection is to show the fecundity and variety of the genre over the past half-century with the wish that the readers will further explore the rich heritage of Southern African literature. The 'Drum' writers of the 1950s and 1960s — Casey Motsisi, Can Themba, Nat Nakasa and Es'kia Mphahlele — are indicative of the Black Renaissance that preceded the literary movements in East and West Africa, while the newer generation of Mzamane, Matshoba and Ndebele — the 'Staffrider' writers of today — illustrate both the continuity of the tradition and the new directions of Black English. While writers like Nadine Gordimer, Alan Paton, Bessie Head, Dan Jacobson and Doris Lessing simply carry on creating works of major importance, other figures such as Ahmed Essop, Richard Rive and Lionel Abrahams enjoy a steadily growing readership. Most encouraging in the past few years is the increasing interest being shown in African literature by both publishers and booksellers in Southern Africa, Europe and America.

N M HODGE

R.R.R. Dhlomo
THE DOG KILLERS

'I say, Jama, did you hear?'

'Did I hear? What?'

'About the dogs, man. It is said tomorrow they are going out to kill them again.'

'Hau, Muti!' exclaimed Jama, jumping to his feet. 'Are you true? Tell me, man; are you true?'

'I am quite true, Jama. This thing was whispered to me today by Mangena, as we came up from the mine.'

'You did well to come, friend. My dog is also among the dogs here in the compound.'

'Yebo. That is why I ran to tell you, Jama.' And Muti went away to change his wet underground sacks. Jama was left alone very much worried. He loved his dog, Boy. When some police boys in the compound made complaints to the compound manager about dogs, Jama went personally to Mlungu, the native induna, and spoke about his dog. He assured the induna that he would keep him safe.

Hurriedly he changed his wet sacks and ran towards Mlungu's room. He found him surrounded by his police boys.

'Nkosi,' Jama saluted.

'Ya . . . ini?' barked a police boy.

'I have come my father, induna, about my dog, nkos'.'

'Your dog? What about it?' asked Mlungu.

'I hear that there's going to be killing of dogs again.'

'Ya, all the bloody dogs will be killed tomorrow by the order of the Big One.'

'Father, can't you save mine, please?' wailed Jama. 'It troubles no one, father. I care for it.'

'Get away, you!' shouted Mlungu's chief police boy. 'Why do you keep dogs in the compound, hi? You run to induna now, eh? Do you ever put something in Baba's hands when you get your pay? Your dog will die with the others, fool. Hamba-ke! Voetsek!'

Jama picked up his torn hat, and went slowly away towards his frisking and barking dog.

'My Boy,' said Jama, patting it. 'My Boy, I don't know what is to become of you tomorrow.'

The dog wagged its tail and barked joyously. It did not know what was worrying its master.

As he lay on his bunk that night, he decided to take the dog to one of his own friends to look after it until all was over.

Soon after this he fell asleep.

That night word came to Mlungu, and said: 'Mlungu, you heard what I said about the dogs. Take fifty boys and kill all these dogs about the compound.'

'Ya, nkosi,' said Mlungu, so named because of his foolish and sorrowful aping of the white peoples' ways. He smacked his lips in anticipation of the killing.

From the place where the word had come to him he went to one of his chief police boys and told him what was expected of them on the morrow. From the boys' room wild Saturday night brawls and drunken mirth could be heard. These savage joys were now and then rudely interrupted by bloodshed. After these orgies the boys would have no mercy on the dogs.

Mlungu and his police boy then went round the rooms taking care to pick only those boys whose natures would glory in the impending butchery. Boys who knew how to hold their tongues. Boys who had ere now engaged in similar killings and had defied all efforts of the outsiders in getting inside information of the source of these killings.

Jama was roused by a wild yell which came from outside the main gate. Blinking and half-blinded by a strong light just outside his room, he rushed frantically forward with a group of others. 'What is it, man?' he cried.

'Asazi. We don't know even ourselves. But we think they are killing the dogs outside.'

'Wo, the devil take them,' he panted.

Back he dashed to his room. At the back he groped in the dark, shouting: 'Boy! Boy!'

No answering rattle of the chain.

He felt with his hand inside the kennel, but his hand touched nothing. The dog was not there. He rushed again towards the gate. Outside, he could hear now the heart-rending yells and howls of the butchered dogs.

Thud! Bang! Crash!. . .

'Boy! Boy! Boy, my dog!' he called lustily.

The terrified dog heard its master's voice and rushed towards him. As it did so a huge, half-drunken Msutu lifted his stick to dash out its brains. But the dog reached Jama.

Then the infuriated Msutu tried to snatch it from Jama's hold. Jama grasped him by the throat and flung him violently on the ground. Mlungu had seen what happened. He directed another police boy to Jama. This man did not speak a word. With one fierce blow he knocked Jama flat on the sand. As he fell, the boy picked up the growling, snarling dog and deliberately tore its jaws apart.

A frightful yell of pain from the bleeding dog made Jama crawl towards the boy and grasp his leg. But the Shangaan, now half mad with the lust for blood, turned round and kicked Jama full in the face with his heavy mine boots.

'You interfere with me, hi? I am going to show you!' he mouthed thickly, and began to pound the dead dog. He then flung it at its master and joined his fellow hyenas.

One was at that moment clubbing to death a fine collie. Another had got hold of a puppy and was twisting its neck off. In a hollow a group of boys had gathered round a big bulldog, and were busy castrating it.

'I must have these for my medicinal mixture,' laughed one, as he stuffed into his filthy pocket the vitals of the dog.

Pitiful cries pierced the morning as dog after dog died. The mine dump was red with blood. Dogs lay here and there with their bowels scattered all over the place. Others were a mass of blood and sand . . .

For a full hour this went on until the faint light in the east said the day had come. At a word from Mlungu the dead bodies were collected into sacks and burnt in a hollow of the dump. The blood was covered with sand. Then Mlungu thought of Jama. Calling his chief police boy he asked: 'Where is that bloody

Zulu who was fighting for his dog? I told Pakati to go
and help Sam in dealing with him. Call Pakati.'

'Nkosi,' cried Pakati, running up.

'Pakati, where is Jama?'

'I left him lying over there with his dog, nkos'.'

'Run and see if he is still there.'

Pakati came on the spot and then stood rooted.

Lying there where he had left him was Jama, his
face swollen, disfigured, clotted with blood . . . dead!
And just close to his right hand lay his dog, Boy, with
its body mangled out of shape . . .

H.C. Bosman
UNTO DUST

I have noticed that when a young man or woman dies, people get the feeling that there is something beautiful and touching in the event, and that it is different from the death of an old person. In the thought, say, of a girl of twenty sinking into an untimely grave, there is a sweet wistfulness that makes people talk all kinds of romantic words. She died, they say, young, she that was so full of life and so fair. She was a flower that withered before it bloomed, they say, and it all seems so fitting and beautiful that there is a good deal of resentment, at the funeral, over the crude questions that a couple of men in plain clothes from the landdrost's office are asking about cattle-dip.

But when you have grown old, nobody is very much interested in the manner of your dying. Nobody except you yourself, that is. And I think that your past life has got a lot to do with the way you feel when you get near the end of your days. I remember how, when he was lying on his death-bed, Andries Wessels kept on telling us that it was because of the blameless path he had trodden from his earliest years that he could compose himself in peace to lay down his burdens. And I certainly never saw a man breathe his last more tranquilly, seeing that right up to the end he kept on murmuring to us how happy he was, with heavenly hosts and invisible choirs of angels all around him.

Just before he died, he told us that the angels had even become visible. They were medium-sized angels, he said, and they had cloven hoofs and carried forks. It was obvious that Andries Wessels's ideas were getting a bit confused by then, but all the same I never saw a man die in a more hallowed sort of calm.

Once, during the malaria season in the Eastern Transvaal, it seemed to me, when I was in a high fever and like to die, that the whole world was a big burial-ground. I thought it was the earth itself that was a graveyard, and not just those little fenced-in bits of land dotted with tombstones, in the shade of a Western Province oak tree or by the side of a Transvaal koppie. This was a nightmare that worried me a great deal, and so I was very glad, when I recovered from the fever, to think that we Boers had properly marked-out places on our farms for white people to be laid to rest in, in a civilized Christian way, instead of having to be buried just anyhow, along with a dead wild-cat, maybe, or a Bushman with a claypot, and things.

When I mentioned this to my friend, Stoffel Oosthuizen, who was in the Low Country with me at the time, he agreed with me wholeheartedly. There were people who talked in a high-flown way of death as the great leveller, he said, and those high-flown people also declared that everyone was made kin by death. He would still like to see those things proved, Stoffel Oosthuizen said. After all, that was one of the reasons why the Boers trekked away into the Trans-

vaal and the Free State, he said, because the British
Government wanted to give the vote to any Cape
Coloured person walking about with a *kroes* head and
big cracks in his feet.

The first time he heard that sort of talk about
death coming to all of us alike, and making us all
equal, Stoffel Oosthuizen's suspicions were aroused.
It sounded like something out of a speech made by
one of those liberal Cape politicians, he explained.

I found something very comforting in Stoffel
Oosthuizen's words.

Then, to illustrate his contention, Stoffel Oosthuizen told me a story of an incident that took place
in a bygone Transvaal Kafir War. I don't know
whether he told the story incorrectly, or whether it
was just that kind of story, but, by the time he had
finished, all my uncertainties had, I discovered, come
back to me.

'You can go and look at Hans Welman's tombstone
any time you are at Nietverdiend,' Stoffel Oosthuizen
said. 'The slab of red sandstone is weathered by now,
of course, seeing how long ago it all happened. But
the inscription is still legible. I was with Hans Welman
on that morning when he fell. Our commando had
been ambushed by the kafirs and was retreating. I
could do nothing for Hans Welman. Once, when I
looked round, I saw a tall kafir bending over him and
plunging an assegai into him. Shortly afterwards I saw
the kafir stripping the clothes off Hans Welman. A
yellow kafir dog was yelping excitedly around his
black master. Although I was in grave danger myself,
with several dozen kafirs making straight for me on
foot through the bush, the fury I felt at the sight of
what that tall kafir was doing made me hazard a last
shot. Reining in my horse, and taking what aim I

could under the circumstances, I pressed the trigger.
My luck was in. I saw the kafir fall forward beside the
naked body of Hans Welman. Then I set spurs to my
horse and galloped off at full speed, with the fore-
most of my pursuers already almost upon me. The
last I saw was that yellow dog bounding up to his
master — whom I had wounded mortally, as we were
to discover later.

'As you know, that kafir war dragged on for a long
time. There were few pitched battles. Mainly, what
took place were bush skirmishes, like the one in
which Hans Welman lost his life.

'After about six months, quiet of a sort was
restored to the Marico and Zoutpansberg districts.
Then the day came when I went out, in company of a
handful of other burghers, to fetch in the remains of
Hans Welman, at his widow's request, for burial in the
little cemetery plot on the farm. We took a coffin
with us on a Cape-cart.

'We located the scene of the skirmish without
difficulty. Indeed, Hans Welman had been killed not
very far from his own farm, which had been
temporarily abandoned, together with the other
farms in that part, during the time that the trouble
with the kafirs had lasted. We drove up to the spot
where I remembered having seen Hans Welman lying
dead on the ground, with the tall kafir next to him.
From a distance I again saw that yellow dog. He
slipped away into the bush at our approach. I could
not help feeling that there was something rather
stirring about that beast's fidelity, even though it was
bestowed on a dead kafir.

'We were now confronted with a queer situation.
We found that what was left of Hans Welman and the
kafir consisted of little more than pieces of sun-dried

flesh and the dismembered fragments of bleached skeletons. The sun and wild animals and birds of prey had done their work. There was a heap of human bones, with here and there leathery strips of blackened flesh. But we could not tell which was the white man and which the kafir. To make it still more confusing, a lot of bones were missing altogether, having no doubt been dragged away by wild animals into their lairs in the bush. Another thing was that Hans Welman and that kafir had been just about the same size.'

Stoffel Oosthuizen paused in his narrative, and I let my imagination dwell for a moment on that situation. And I realized just how those Boers must have felt about it: about the thought of bringing the remains of a Transvaal burgher home to his widow for Christian burial, and perhaps having a lot of kafir bones mixed up with the burgher — lying with him in the same tomb on which the mauve petals from the oleander overhead would fall.

'I remember one of our party saying that that was the worst of these kafir wars,' Stoffel Oosthuizen continued. 'If it had been a war against the English, and part of a dead Englishman had got lifted into that coffin by mistake, it wouldn't have mattered so much,' he said.

There seemed to me in this story to be something as strange as the African veld. Stoffel Oosthuizen said that the little party of Boers spent almost a whole afternoon with the remains in order to try to get the white man sorted out from the kafir. By the evening they had laid all they could find of what seemed like Hans Welman's bones in the coffin in the Cape-cart.

The rest of the bones and flesh they buried on the spot.

Stoffel Oosthuizen added that, no matter what the difference in the colour of their skin had been, it was impossible to say that the kafir's bones were less white than Hans Welman's. Nor was it possible to say that the kafir's sun-dried flesh was any blacker than the white man's. Alive, you couldn't go wrong in distinguishing between a white man and a kafir. Dead, you had great difficulty in telling them apart.

'Naturally, we burghers felt very bitter about this whole affair,' Stoffel Oosthuizen said, 'and our resentment was something that we couldn't explain, quite. Afterwards, several other men who were there that day told me that they had the same feelings of suppressed anger that I did. They wanted somebody — just once — to make a remark such as "in death they were not divided". Then you would have seen an outburst all right. Nobody did say anything like that, however. We all knew better. Two days later a funeral service was conducted in the little cemetery on the Welman farm, and shortly afterwards the sandstone memorial was erected that you can still see there.'

That was the story Stoffel Oosthuizen told me after I had recovered from the fever. It was a story that, as I have said, had in it features as strange as the African veld. But it brought me no peace in my broodings after that attack of malaria. Especially when Stoffel Oosthuizen spoke of how he had occasion, one clear night when the stars shone, to pass that quiet graveyard on the Welman farm. Something leapt up from the mound beside the sandstone slab. It gave him

quite a turn, Stoffel Oosthuizen said, for the third
time — and in that way — to come across that yellow
kafir dog.

Casey Motsisi
KID PLAYBOY

Everytime a hick job comes around in the office I get
saddled with it. Now the editor pushes this folded
white card at me and says to find out what I can get
out of this here invite. I walk out of the office and
read the card once more. According to the gold-
lettered words a certain Kid Mabothobotho, stays out
Dube, is getting hitched to an Alexandra cherrie.

On Saturday the wedding will take place at the
cherrie's place in Alex. I decide I'd rather wait for it
to come around to Dube on Sunday because I'm
somewhat scared of hopping off to Alex, especially
on weekends on account the bright boys over there
have turned the place into a gunsmoke and knife-
happy township.

On Sunday I haul out my top hat and tails to make
ready to go to Dube. I expect it to be one of those
high society shindigs, as you know how hoity-toity
these Dubeheimers can get when they want to. I get
a good look at myself in my landlord's son's wardrobe mirror as I put on the tie he lent me, and I see
that my eyes are unusually clear — sure sign among
the boozing fraternity that I've been keeping shebeen

queens, especially Aunt Peggy, waiting.

I get to Dube and don't have any difficulty spotting the place where this wedding is taking place on account of the half-a-dozen beribboned convertible cars parked in front of the house. A guy who meets me at the door looks scornfully at my not-too-well pressed trousers, whereupon he gives me the VIP treatment. Only he reckons the 'I' in VIP stands for 'Inconsequential'. He tells me to go and sit in the tent at the back of the house. I tell him who I am, whereupon he smiles and ushers me into the room.

This girl this guy's getting married to is so beautiful that I can't take my eyes off her for a pretty long time. After a while I manage to pull my eyes away from her to look at the groom. Cripes! It's none other than Kid Playboy. I feel the blood revolting in my veins. This is the same Kid Playboy who took away from me some time back the only girl I ever loved. He promised this girl of mine everything in the world and crowned the long list of promises by telling her that he would build a fire under the ocean just so's she can swim in winter.

And like all starry-eyed girls, this girl of mine went and believed every word he told her. Maybe if she hadn't been so gullible she would still have been alive today. As it turns out, Kid Playboy gives her the bird after stringing her for a month on account another foolish cherrie falls for his sweet talk. So what does she do, but commit suicide!

Kid Playboy's eyes meet mine and I pull out my tongue at him. He turns coal black and his adam's apple starts moving up and down like someone who's seen a ghost. The guy looks real scared, and I am just beginning to hate myself for having scared the boy sticking out my tongue at him when I realise that it's not me who's the cause of his sudden jitters. There's a girl who's sitting a few feet behind me who is proving to be the why for Kid's jaded nerves.

I turn around and look at this girl to see what it is about her that can cause so much panic in a satanic soul. But all I can see is that she's an ordinary homely girl, and the small sleeping child she's holding in her arms is the sweetest thing I ever did see.

I'm still busily occupied at looking at this fear-instilling girl and hoping that she's not a ghost, when a voice that sounds like a constipated ostrich's booms: 'Ladies and gentlemen, all those who have presents for the bridal couple may now see the "mabalane" (the MC of the wedding).' The 'mabalane' stands up, breaks into a toothless grin, bows and sits down again.

I thought they had invited us to a wedding, now they want to fleece presents out of us! But seeing as the announcer man said 'ladies and gentlemen', I reckon he has left me out on account nobody ever accused me of being a gentleman, let alone a lady. So I happily ignore him.

A few folk get away from their eats and drinks with parcels of varying sizes beneath their armpits. They stand in line before the 'mabalane', who jots down the name and address of each and every one who dumps a parcel on the table. Some guys who had decided beforehand that it would be much better to save the few pennies they have for paying their rent instead of buying presents for Kid Playboy and his spouse — and perhaps a few others who have a needle against him, like yours truly — suddenly discover that the room is too hot and march out.

After some time the last name and address is written down, and I can see the 'mabalane' hinting at the groom's people for his payment for services duly rendered — a nip of hooch. But he doesn't get the hooch. Instead, the girl with the baby who had so disorganised Kid Playboy a short while ago, stands up and walks to the 'mabalane'. She dumps the child, who is now awake and bawling his young head off, on the table and says, 'Here's my present to the bride and groom. My name is Maisie.' She gives a Mapetla address somewhere in Site and Service. She winds up by saying Kid Playboy's the pop of the child.

All of a sudden, there's a bang of a hulabaloo going on. Kid Playboy is making a hurried exit out of the house, and the bride is tearing at her bridal dress and hurling all sorts of names at Kid Playboy and his family, including the late ones. After every burst of unprintable words she keeps chorusing that she's got a lawyer that's going to show them what makes the grass green.

Up to today nobody ever hears a word about Kid Playboy. But Mr Rumour goes around the townships telling all and sundry that Kid Playboy is in his home-town somewhere in the Tanganyika Territory, although the folks from there pronounce it 'Tananika Torrotoro'.

I reckon the next time the editor tells me to go and cover a wedding, I'm gonna take an advance on my salary and hightail it to Aunt Peggy's joint and cover a bottle of hooch with Kid Playboy's ex-bride on my lap, as she now frequents this place ever since her lawyer proved not to be as hot as she had thought him to be.

Can Themba
THE SUIT

Five-thirty in the morning, and the candlewick bed-spread frowned as the man under it stirred. He did not like to wake his wife lying by his side — as yet — so he crawled up and out by careful peristalsis. But before he tiptoed out of his room with shoes and socks under his arm, he leaned over and peered at the sleeping serenity of his wife: to him a daily matutinal miracle.

He grinned and yawned simultaneously, offering his wordless Te Deum to whatever gods for the goodness of life; for the pure beauty of his wife; for the strength surging through his willing body; for the even, unperturbed rhythms of his passage through days and months and years — it must be — to heaven.

Then he slipped soundlessly into the kitchen. He flipped aside the curtain of the kitchen window, and saw outside a thin drizzle, the type that can soak one to the skin, and that could go on for days and days. He wondered, head aslant, why the rain in Sophiatown always came in the morning when workers had to creep out of their burrows; and then at how blistering heatwaves came during the day when

messengers had to run errands all over; and then at
how the rain came back when workers knocked off
and had to scurry home.

He smiled at the odd caprice of the heavens, and
tossed his head at the naughty incongruity, as if, 'Ai,
but the gods!'

From behind the kitchen door, he removed an old
rain cape, peeling off in places, and swung it over his
head. He dashed for the lavatory, nearly slipping in a
pool of muddy water, but he reached the door. Aw,
blast, someone had made it before him. Well, that is
the toll of staying in a yard where twenty . . . thirty
other people have to share the same lean-to. He was
dancing and burning in that climactic moment when
trouser-fly will not come wide soon enough. He
stepped round the lavatory and watched the streamlets
of rainwater quickly wash away the jet of tension
that spouted from him. That infinite after-relief.
Then he dashed back to his kitchen. He grabbed the
old baby-bathtub hanging on a nail under the slight
shelter of the gutterless roof-edge. He opened a large
wooden box and quickly filled the bathtub with coal.
Then he inched his way back to the kitchen door and
inside.

He was huh-huh-huhing one of those fugitive tunes
that cannot be hidden, but often just occur and linger
naggingly in the head. The fire he was making soon
licked up cheerfully, in mood with his contentment.

He had a trick for these morning chores. While the
fire in the old stove warmed up, the water kettle
humming on it, he gathered and laid ready the things
he would need for the day: briefcase and the files
that go with it; the book that he was reading currently; the letters of his lawyer boss which he usually
posted before he reached the office; his wife's and his

own dry-cleaning slips for the Sixty-Minutes; his lunch
tin solicitously prepared the night before by his
attentive wife; and, today, the battered rain cape. By
the time the kettle on the stove sang (before it actually
boiled), he poured water from it into a washbasin,
refilled and replaced it on the stove. Then he washed
himself carefully: across the eyes, under, in and out
the armpits, down the torso and in between the legs.
This ritual was thorough, though no white man a-
complaining of the smell of wogs knows anything
about it. Then he dressed himself fastidiously. By this
time he was ready to prepare breakfast.

Breakfast! How he enjoyed taking in a tray of
warm breakfast to his wife, cuddled in bed. To appear
there in his supremest immaculacy, tray in hand when
his wife comes out of ether to behold him. These
things we blacks want to do for our own ... not
fawningly for the whites for whom we bloody-well
got to do it. He wasn't one of those who believed in
putting his wife in her place even if she was a good
wife. Not he.

Matilda, too, appreciated her husband's kindness,
and only put her foot down when he offered to wash
up also.

'Off with you,' she scolded him on his way.

At the bus-stop he was a little sorry to see that
jovial old Maphikela was in a queue for a bus ahead of
him. He would miss Maphikela's raucous laughter and
uninhibited, bawdy conversations in fortissimo. Maphikela hailed him nevertheless. He thought he noticed
hesitation in the old man, and a slight clouding of his
countenance, but the old man shouted back at him,
saying that he would wait for him at the terminus in
town.

Philemon considered this morning trip to town

with garrulous old Maphikela as his daily bulletin. All
the township news was generously reported by loud-
mouthed heralds, and spiritedly discussed by the bus
at large. Of course, 'news' included views on bosses
(scurrilous), the Government (rude), Ghana and Russia
(idolatrous), America and the West (sympathetically
ridiculing), and boxing (bloodthirsty). But it was
always stimulating and surprisingly comprehensive
for so short a trip. And there was no law of libel.

Maphikela was standing under one of those token
bus-stop shelters that never keep out rain nor wind
nor sun-heat. Philemon easily located him by his
noisy ribbing of some office boys in their khaki-green
uniforms. They walked together into town, but from
Maphikela's suddenly subdued manner, Philemon
gathered that there was something serious coming up.
Maybe a loan.

Eventually, Maphikela came out with it.

'Son,' he said sadly, 'if I could've avoided this,
believe you me I would, but my wife is nagging the
spice out of my life for not talking to you about it.'

It just did not become blustering old Maphikela to
sound so grave and Philemon took compassion upon
him.

'Go ahead, dad,' he said generously. 'You know
you can talk to me about anything.'

The old man gave a pathetic smile. 'We-e-ell, it's
not really any of our business ... er ... but my wife
felt ... you see. Damn it all! I wish these women
would not snoop around so much.' Then he rushed it.
'Anyway, it seems there's a young man who's going
to visit your wife every morning ... ah ... for these
last bloomin' three months. And that wife of mine
swears by her heathen gods you don't know a thing
about it.'

It was not quite like the explosion of a devastating bomb. It was more like the critical breakdown in an infinitely delicate piece of mechanism. From outside, the machine just seemed to have gone dead. But deep in its innermost recesses, menacing electrical flashes were leaping from coil to coil, and hot, viscous, molten metal was creeping up on the fuel tanks . . .

Philemon heard gears grinding and screaming in his head . . .

'Dad,' he said hoarsely, 'I . . . I have to go back home.'

He turned round and did not hear old Maphikela's anxious, 'Steady, son. Steady, son.'

The bus ride home was a torture of numb dread and suffocating despair. Though the bus was now emptier Philemon suffered crushing claustrophobia. There were immense washerwomen whose immense bundles of soiled laundry seemed to baulk and menace him. From those bundles crept miasmata of sweaty intimacies that sent nauseous waves up and down from his viscera. Then the wild swaying of the bus as it negotiated Mayfair Circle hurtled him sickeningly from side to side. Some of the younger women shrieked delightedly to the driver, '*Fuduga!* . . . Stir the pot!' as he swung his steering-wheel this way and that. Normally, the crazy tilting of the bus gave him a prickling exhilaration. But now . . .

He felt like getting out of there, screaming, elbowing everything out of his way. He wished this insane trip were over, and then again, he recoiled at the thought of getting home. He made a tremendous resolve to gather in all the torn, tingling threads of his nerves contorting in the raw. By a merciless act of will, he kept them in subjugation as he stepped out of the bus back in the Victoria Road terminus,

Sophiatown.

The calm he achieved was tense . . . but he could think now . . . he could take a decision . . .

With almost boyishly innocent urgency, he rushed through his kitchen into his bedroom. In the lightning flash that the eye can whip, he saw it all . . . the man beside his wife . . . the chestnut arm around her neck . . . the ruffled candlewick bedspread . . . the suit across the chair. But he affected not to see.

He opened the wardrobe door, and as he dug into it, he cheerfully spoke to his wife: 'Fancy, Tilly, I forgot to take my pass. I had already reached town, and was going to walk up to the office. If it hadn't been for wonderful old Mr Maphikela.'

A swooshing noise of violent retreat and the clap of his bedroom window stopped him. He came from behind the wardrobe door and looked out from the open window. A man clad only in vest and under-pants was running down the street. Slowly, he turned round and contemplated . . . the suit.

Philemon lifted it gingerly under his arm and looked at the stark horror in Matilda's eyes. She was now sitting up in bed. Her mouth twitched, but her throat raised no words.

'Ha,' he said, 'I see we have a visitor,' indicating the blue suit. 'We really must show some of our hospitality. But first, I must phone my boss that I can't come to work today . . . mmmm-er, my wife's not well. Be back in a moment, then we can make arrangements.' He took the suit along.

When he returned he found Matilda weeping on the bed. He dropped the suit beside her, pulled up the chair, turned it round so that its back came in front of him, sat down, brought down his chin onto his folded arms before him, and waited for her.

After a while the convulsions of her shoulders
ceased. She saw a smug man with an odd smile and
meaningless inscrutability in his eyes. He spoke to her
with very little noticeable emotion; if anything, with
a flutter of humour.

'We have a visitor, Tilly.' His mouth curved ever so
slightly. 'I'd like him to be treated with the greatest
of consideration. He will eat every meal with us and
share all we have. Since we have no spare room, he'd
better sleep in here. But the point is, Tilly, that you
will meticulously look after him. If he vanishes or
anything else happens to him . . . ' A shaft of evil shot
from his eye . . . 'Matilda, I'll kill you.'

He rose from the chair and looked with incongruous
supplication at her. He told her to put the fellow in
the wardrobe for the time being. As she passed him to
get the suit, he turned to go. She ducked frantically,
and he stopped.

'You don't seem to understand me, Matilda.
There's to be no violence in this house if you and I
can help it. So, just look after that suit.' He went out.

He went out to the Sophiatown Post Office, which
is placed on the exact line between Sophiatown and
the white man's surly Westdene. He posted his boss's
letters, and walked to the beerhall at the tail end of
Western Native Township. He had never been inside it
before, but somehow the thunderous din laved his
bruised spirit. He stayed there all day.

He returned home for supper . . . and surprise. His
dingy little home had been transformed, and the air
of stern masculinity it had hitherto contained had
been wiped away, to be replaced by anxious feminine
touches here and there. There were even gay, colourful curtains swirling in the kitchen window. The old-
fashioned coal stove gleamed in its blackness. A clean,

chequered oil cloth on the table. Supper ready.

Then she appeared in the doorway of the bedroom. Heavens! Here was the woman he had married; the young, fresh, cocoa-coloured maid who had sent rushes of emotion shuddering through him. And the dress she wore brought out all the girlishness in her, hidden so long beneath German print. But no hint of coquettishness, although she stood in the doorway and slid her arm up the jamb, and shyly slanted her head to the other shoulder. She smiled weakly.

What makes a woman like this experiment with adultery, he wondered.

Philemon closed his eyes and gripped the seat of his chair on both sides as some overwhelming, un-disciplined force sought to catapult him towards her. For a moment some essence glowed fiercely within him, then sank back into itself and died . . .

He sighed and smiled sadly back at her. 'I'm hungry, Tilly.'

The spell snapped, and she was galvanized into action. She prepared his supper with dexterous hands that trembled a little only when they hesitated in mid-air. She took her seat opposite him, regarded him curiously, clasped her hands waiting for his prayer, but in her heart she murmured some other, much more urgent prayer of her own.

'Matilda!' he barked. 'Our visitor!' The sheer savagery with which he cracked at her jerked her up, but only when she saw the brute cruelty in his face did she run out of the room, toppling the chair behind her.

She returned with the suit on a hanger, and stood there quivering like a feather. She looked at him with helpless dismay. The demoniacal rage in his face was evaporating, but his heavy breathing still rocked his thorax above the table, to and fro.

'Put a chair, there.' He indicated with a languid gesture of his arm. She moved like a ghost as she drew a chair to the table.

'Now seat our friend at the table . . . no, no, not like that. Put him in front of the chair, and place him on the seat so that he becomes indeed the third person.'

Philemon went on relentlessly: 'Dish up for him. Generously. I imagine he hasn't had a morsel all day, the poor devil.'

Now, as consciousness and thought seeped back into her, her movements revolved so that always she faced this man who had changed so spectacularly. She started when he rose to open the window and let in some air.

She served the suit. The act was so ridiculous that she carried it out with a bitter sense of humiliation. He came back to sit down and plunge into his meal. No grace was said for the first time in this house. With his mouth full, he indicated by a toss of his head that she should sit down in her place. She did so. Glancing at her plate, the thought occurred to her that someone, after a long famine, was served a sumptuous supper, but as the food reached her mouth it turned to sawdust. Where had she heard it?

Matilda could not eat. She suddenly broke into tears.

Philemon took no notice of her weeping. After supper, he casually gathered the dishes and started washing up. He flung a dry cloth at her without saying a word. She rose and went to stand by his side drying up. But for their wordlessness, they seemed a very devoted couple.

After washing up, he took the suit and turned to

her. 'That's how I want it every meal, every day.'
Then he walked into the bedroom.

So it was. After that first breakdown, Matilda
began to feel that her punishment was not too severe,
considering the heinousness of the crime. She tried to
put a joke into it, but by slow, unconscious degrees,
the strain nibbled at her. Philemon did not harass her
much more, so long as the ritual with the confounded
suit was conscientiously followed.

Only once, he got one of his malevolent brainwaves.
He got it into his head that 'our visitor' needed an
outing. Accordingly the suit was taken to the dry-
cleaners during the week, and, come Sunday, they
had to take it out for a walk. Both Philemon and
Matilda dressed for the occasion. Matilda had to carry
the suit on its hanger over her back and the three of
them strolled leisurely along Ray Street. They passed
the church crowd in front of the famous Anglican
Mission of Christ the King. Though the worshippers
saw nothing unusual in them, Matilda felt, searing
through her, red-hot needles of embarrassment, and
every needle-point was a public eye piercing into her
degradation.

But Philemon walked casually on. He led her down
Ray Street and turned into Main Road. He stopped
often to look into shop windows or to greet a friend
passing by. They went up Toby Street, turned into
Edward Road, and back home. To Philemon the
outing was free of incident, but to Matilda it was one
long, excruciating incident.

At home, he grabbed a book on abnormal psycho-
logy, flung himself into a chair and calmly said to her,
'Give the old chap a rest, will you, Tilly?'

In the bedroom, Matilda said to herself that things
could not go on like this. She thought of how she

could bring the matter to a head with Philemon; have
it out once and for all. But the memory of his face
that first day she had forgotten to entertain the suit,
stayed her. She thought of running away, but where
to? Home? What could she tell her old-fashioned
mother had happened between Philemon and her? All
right, run away clean then. She thought of many
young married girls who were divorcees now, who
had won their freedom.

What had happened to Staff Nurse Kakile? The
woman drank heavily now, and when she got drunk,
the boys of Sophiatown passed her around and called
her the Cesspot.

Matilda shuddered.

An idea struck her. There were still decent, married
women around Sophiatown. She remembered how
after the private schools had been forced to close
with the advent of Bantu Education, Father Harringay
of the Anglican Mission had organized cultural clubs.
One, she seemed to remember, was for married
women. If only she could lose herself in some cultural
activity, find absolution for her conscience in some
doing good; that would blur her blasted home life,
would restore her self-respect. After all, Philemon had
not broadcast her disgrace abroad . . . nobody knew;
not one of Sophiatown's slander-mongers suspected
how vulnerable she was. She must go and see
Mrs Montjane about joining a cultural club. She must
ask Philemon now if she might . . . she must ask him
nicely.

She got up and walked into the other room where
Philemon was reading quietly. She dreaded disturbing
him, did not know how to begin talking to him . . .
they had talked so little for so long. She went and
stood in front of him, looking silently upon his deep

concentration. Presently, he looked up with a frown on his face.

Then she dared, 'Phil, I'd like to join one of those cultural clubs for married women. Would you mind?'

He wrinkled his nose and rubbed it between thumb and index finger as he considered the request. But he had caught the note of anxiety in her voice and thought he knew what it meant.

'Mmm,' he said, nodding. 'I think that's a good idea. You can't be moping around here all day. Yes, you may, Tilly.' Then he returned to his book.

The cultural club idea was wonderful. She found women like herself with time (if not with tragedy) on their hands, engaged in wholesome refreshing activities. The atmosphere was cheerful and cathartic. They learned things and they did things. They organized fêtes, bazaars, youth activities, sport, music, self-help and community projects. She got involved in committees, meetings, debates, conferences. It was for her a whole new venture into humancraft, and her personality blossomed. Philemon gave her all the rein she wanted.

Now, abiding by that silly ritual at home seemed a little thing . . . a very little thing . . .

Then one day she decided to organize a little party for her friends and their husbands. Philemon was very decent about it. He said it was all right. He even gave her extra money for it. Of course, she knew nothing of the strain he himself suffered from his mode of castigation.

There was a week of the most hectic preparation. Philemon stepped out of its cluttering way as best he could. So many things seemed to be taking place simultaneously. New dresses were made. Cakes were baked; three different orders of meat prepared; beef for the uninvited chancers; mutton for the normal guests; turkey and chicken for the inner pith of the club's core. To Philemon, it looked as if Matilda planned to feed the multitude on the Mount with no aid of miracles.

On the Sunday of the party, Philemon saw Matilda's guests. He was surprised by the handsome grace with which she received them. There was a long table with enticing foods and flowers and serviettes. Matilda placed all her guests round the table, and the party was ready to begin in the mock-formal township fashion. Outside a steady rumble of conversation went on where the human odds and ends of every Sophiatown party had their 'share'.

Matilda caught the curious look on Philemon's face. He tried to disguise his edict when he said, 'Er . . . the guest of honour.'

But Matilda took a chance. She begged, 'Just this once, Phil.'

He became livid. 'Matilda!' he shouted. 'Get our visitor!' Then with incisive sarcasm, 'Or are you ashamed of him?'

She went ash-grey; but there was nothing for it but to fetch her albatross. She came back and squeezed a chair into some corner, and placed the suit on it. Then she slowly placed a plate of food before it. For a while the guests were dumbfounded. Then curiosity flooded in. They talked at the same time. 'What's happening?' Some just giggled in a silly way. Philemon carelessly swung his head towards Matilda. 'You better ask my wife. She knows the fellow best.'

All interest beamed upon poor Matilda. For a moment she could not speak, all enveloped in misery. Then she said, unconvincingly, 'It's just a game that my husband and I play at mealtime.' They roared with laughter. Philemon let her get away with it.

The party went on, and every time Philemon's glare sent Matilda scurrying to serve the suit each course; the guests were no-end amused by the persistent mock-seriousness with which this husband and wife played out their little game. Only, to Matilda, it was no joke; it was a hot poker down her throat. After the party, Philemon went off with one of the guests who had promised to show him a joint 'that sells genuine stuff, boy, genuine stuff.'

Reeling drunk, late that sabbath, he crashed through his kitchen door, onwards to his bedroom. Then he saw her.

They have a way of saying in the argot of Sophiatown, 'Cook out of the head!' signifying that someone was impacted with such violent shock that whatever whiffs of alcohol still wandered through his head were instantaneously evaporated and the man stood sober before stark reality.

There she lay, curled as if just before she died she begged for a little love, implored some implacable lover to cuddle her a little . . . just this once . . . just this once more.

In screwish anguish, Philemon cried, 'Tilly!'

Alan Paton
HA'PENNY

Of the six hundred boys at the reformatory, about one hundred were from ten to fourteen years of age. My Department had from time to time expressed the intention of taking them away, and of establishing a special institution for them, more like an industrial school than a reformatory. This would have been a good thing, for their offences were very trivial, and they would have been better by themselves. Had such a school been established I should have liked to be Principal of it myself, for it would have been an easier job; small boys turn instinctively towards affection, and one controls them by it, naturally and easily.

Some of them, if I came near them, either on parade or in school or at football, would observe me watchfully, not directly or fully, but obliquely and secretly; sometimes I would surprise them at it, and make some small sign of recognition, which would satisfy them so that they would cease to observe me, and would give their full attention to the event of the moment. But I knew that my authority was thus confirmed and strengthened.

The secret relations with them were a source of

continuous pleasure to me. Had they been my own children I would no doubt have given a greater expression to it. But often I would move through the silent and orderly parade, and stand by one of them. He would look straight in front of him with a little frown of concentration that expressed both childish awareness of and manly indifference to my nearness. Sometimes I would tweak his ear, and he would give me a brief smile of acknowledgement, or frown with still greater concentration. It was natural, I suppose, to confine these outward expressions to the very smallest, but they were taken as symbolic, and some older boys would observe them and take themselves to be included. It was a relief, when the reformatory was passing through times of turbulence and trouble, amd when there was danger of estrangement between authority and boys, to make these simple and natural gestures, which were reassurances to both me and them that nothing important had changed.

On Sunday afternoons when I was on duty I would take my car to the reformatory and watch the free boys being signed out at the gate. This simple operation was also watched by many boys not free, who would tell each other, 'in so many weeks I'll be signed out myself.' Among the watchers were always some small boys, and these I would take by turns in the car. We would go out to the Potchefstroom Road with its ceaseless stream of traffic, and to the Baragwanath crossroads, and come back by the Van Wyksrus road to the reformatory. I would talk to them about their families, their parents, their sisters and brothers, and I would pretend to know nothing of Durban, Port Elizabeth, Potchefstroom and Clocolan, and ask them if these places were bigger than Johannesburg.

One of the small boys was Ha'penny, and he was about twelve years old. He came from Bloemfontein and was the biggest talker of them all. His mother worked in a white person's house, and he had two brothers and two sisters. His brothers were Richard and Dickie, and his sisters Anna and Mina.

'Richard and Dickie?' I asked.

'Yes, meneer.'

'In English,' I said, 'Richard and Dickie are the same name.'

When we returned to the reformatory, I sent for Ha'penny's papers; there it was plainly set down; Ha'penny was a waif, with no relatives at all. He had been taken in from one home to another, but he was naughty and uncontrollable, and eventually had taken to pilfering at the market.

I then sent for the Letter Book, and found that Ha'penny wrote regularly, or rather that others wrote for him till he could write himself, to Mrs Betty Maarman, of 48 Vlak Street, Bloemfontein. But Mrs Maarman had never once replied to him. When questioned, he had said, perhaps she is sick. I sat down and wrote at once to the Social Welfare Officer at Bloemfontein, asking him to investigate.

The next time I had Ha'penny out in the car I questioned him again about his family. And he told me the same as before, his mother, Richard and Dickie, Anna and Mina. But he softened the 'D' of Dickie, so that it sounded now like Tickie.

'I thought you said Dickie,' I said.

'I said Tickie,' he said.

He watched me with concealed apprehension, and I came to the conclusion that this waif of Bloemfontein was a clever boy, who had told me a story that was all imagination, and had changed one single

letter of it to make it safe from any question. And I
thought I understood it all too, that he was ashamed
of being without a family and had invented them all,
so that no one might discover that he was fatherless
and motherless and that no one in the world cared
whether he was alive or dead. This gave me a strong
feeling for him, and I went out of my way to
manifest towards him that fatherly care that the State,
though not in those words, had enjoined upon me by
giving me this job.

Then the letter came from the Social Welfare
Officer in Bloemfontein, saying that Mrs Betty Maarman of 48 Vlak Street was a real person, and that she
had four children, Richard and Dickie, Anna and
Mina, but that Ha'penny was no child of hers, and
she knew him only as a derelict of the streets. She
had never answered his letters, because he wrote to
her as 'Mother', and she was no mother of his, nor did
she wish to play any such role. She was a decent
woman, a faithful member of the church, and she had
no thought of corrupting her family by letting them
have anything to do with such a child.

But Ha'penny seemed to me anything but the usual
delinquent; his desire to have a family was so strong,
and his reformatory record was so blameless, and his
anxiety to please and obey so great, that I began to
feel a great duty towards him. Therefore I asked him
about his 'mother'.

He could not speak enough of her, nor with too
high praise. She was loving, honest, and strict. Her
home was clean. She had affection for all her children.
It was clear that the homeless child, even as he had
attached himself to me, would have attached himself
to her; he had observed her even as he had observed
me, but did not know the secret of how to open her

heart, so that she would take him in, and save him from the lonely life that he led.

'Why did you steal when you had such a mother?' I asked.

He could not answer that; not all his brains nor his courage could find an answer to such a question, for he knew that with such a mother he would not have stolen at all.

'The boy's name is Dickie,' I said, 'not Tickie.'

And then he knew the deception was revealed. Another boy might have said, 'I told you it was Dickie,' but he was too intelligent for that; he knew that if I had established that the boy's name was Dickie, I must have established other things too. I was shocked by the immediate and visible effect of my action. His whole brave assurance died within him and he stood there exposed, not as a liar, but as a homeless child who had surrounded himself with mother, brothers, and sisters, who did not exist. I had shattered the very foundations of his pride and his sense of human significance.

He fell sick at once, and the doctor said it was tuberculosis. I wrote at once to Mrs Maarman, telling her the whole story, of how this small boy had observed her, and had decided that she was the person he desired for his mother. But she wrote back saying that she could take no responsibility for him. For one thing, Ha'penny was a Mosuto, and she was a coloured woman; for another, she had never had a child in trouble, and how could she take such a boy?

Tuberculosis is a strange thing; sometimes it manifests itself suddenly in the most unlikely host, and swiftly sweeps to the end. Ha'penny withdrew himself from the world, from all Principals and mothers, and the doctor said there was little hope. In desperation I sent money for Mrs Maarman to come.

She was a decent, homely woman, and seeing that the situation was serious, she, without fuss or embarrassment, adopted Ha'penny for her own. The whole reformatory accepted her as his mother. She sat the whole day with him, and talked to him of Richard and Dickie, Anna and Mina, and how they were all waiting for him to come home. She poured out her affection on him, and had no fear of his sickness, nor did she allow it to prevent her from satisfying his hunger to be owned. She talked to him of what they would do when he came back, and how he would go to the school, and what they would buy for Guy Fawkes night.

He in his turn gave his whole attention to her, and when I visited him he was grateful, but I had passed out of his world. I felt judged in that I had sensed only the existence and not the measure of his desire. I wished I had done something sooner, more wise, more prodigal.

We buried him on the reformatory farm, and Mrs Maarman said to me, 'When you put up the cross, put he was my son.'

'I'm ashamed,' she said, 'that I wouldn't take him.'

'The sickness,' I said, 'the sickness would have come.'

'No,' she said, shaking her head with certainty. 'It wouldn't have come. And if it had come at home, it would have been different.'

So she left for Bloemfontein, after her strange visit to a reformatory. And I was left too, with the resolve to be more prodigal in the task that the State, though not in so many words, had enjoined on me.

Dan Jacobson
BEGGAR MY NEIGHBOUR

Michael saw them for the first time when he was
coming home from school one day. One moment the
street had been empty, glittering in the light from the
sun behind his back, with no traffic on the roadway
and apparently no pedestrians on the broad sandy
pavement; the next moment these two were before
him, their faces raised to his. They seemed to emerge
directly in front of him, as if the light and shade of
the glaring street had suddenly condensed itself into
two little piccanins with large eyes set in their round,
black faces.

'*Stukkie brood?*' the elder, a boy, said in a plain-
tive voice. A piece of bread. At Michael's school the
slang term for any African child was just that: *stukkie
brood*. That was what African children were always
begging for.

'*Stukkie brood?*' the little girl said. She was
wearing a soiled white dress that was so short it
barely covered her loins; there seemed to be nothing
at all beneath the dress. She wore no socks, no shoes,
no cardigan, no cap or hat. She must have been about
ten years old. The boy, who was dressed in a torn

khaki shirt and a pair of grey shorts much too large for him, was about Michael's age, about twelve, though he was a little smaller than the white boy. Like the girl, he was barefoot. Their limbs were painfully thin; their wrists and ankles stood out in knobs, and the skin over these protruding bones was rougher than elsewhere. The dirt on their skin showed up as a faint greyness against the black.

'I've got no bread,' the white boy said. He had halted in surprise at the suddenness of their appearance before him. They must have been hiding behind one of the trees that were planted at intervals along the pavement. 'I don't bring bread from school.'

They did not move. Michael shifted his school case from one hand to the other and took a pace forward. Silently, the African children stood aside. As he passed them, Michael was conscious of the movement of their eyes; when he turned to look back he saw that they were standing still to watch him go. The boy was holding one of the girl's hands in his.

It was this that made the white child pause. He was touched by their dependence on one another, and disturbed by it too, as he had been by the way they had suddenly come before him and by their watchfulness and silence after they had uttered their customary, begging request. Michael saw again how ragged and dirty they were, and thought of how hungry they must be. Surely he could give them a piece of bread. He was only three blocks from home.

He said, 'I haven't any bread here. But if you come home with me, I'll see that you get some bread. Do you understand?'

They made no reply; but they obviously understood what he had said. The three children moved down the pavement. Only Michael's shod feet crunched

on the sand; the footfalls of the others were silent.
They walked a little behind Michael, and to one side
of him. Once he asked them if they went to school,
and the boy shook his head; when he asked them if
they were brother and sister, the boy nodded.

When they reached Michael's house, he went inside
and told Dora, the cook-girl, that there were two
piccanins in the lane outside, and that he wanted her
to cut some bread and jam for them. Dora grumbled
that she was not supposed to look after every little
beggar in town, and Michael answered her angrily,
'We've got lots of bread. Why shouldn't we give them
some?' He was particularly indignant because he felt
that Dora, being of the same race as the two outside,
should have been even readier than he was to help
them. When Dora was about to take the bread out to
the back gate, where the children waited, he stopped
her. 'It's all right, Dora,' he said in a tone of reproof,
'I'll take it,' and he went out into the sunlight,
carrying the plate in his hand.

'Stukkie brood,' he called out to them. 'Here's
your *stukkie brood.'*

The children stretched their hands out eagerly, and
Michael let them take the inch-thick slices from the
plate. He was pleased to see that Dora had put a
scraping of apricot jam on the bread. Each of them
held the bread in both hands, as if afraid of dropping
it. The girl's mouth worked a little, but she kept her
eyes fixed on the white boy.

'What do you say?' Michael asked.

They replied in high, clear voices, 'Thank you, baas.'

'That's better. Now you can eat.' He wanted to see
them eat it; he wanted to share their pleasure in
satisfying their strained appetites. But without saying
a word to him, they began to back away, side by side.

They took a few paces, and then they turned and ran along the lane towards the main road they had walked down earlier. The little girl's dress fluttered behind her, white against her black body. At the corner they halted, looked back once, and then ran on, out of sight.

A few days later, at the same time and in the same place, Michael saw them again, on his way home from school. They were standing in the middle of the pavement, and he saw them from a long way off. They were obviously waiting for him to come. Michael was the first to speak, as he approached them.

'What? Another piece of bread?' he called out from a few yards away.

'Yes, baas,' they answered together. They turned immediately to join him as he walked by. Yet they kept a respectful pace or two behind.

'How did you know I was coming?'

'We know the baas is coming from school.'

'And how do you know that I'm going to give you bread?'

There was no reply; not even a smile from the boy, in response to Michael's. They seemed to him, as he glanced casually at them, identical in appearance to a hundred, a thousand, other piccanins, from the peppercorns on top of their heads to their wide, calloused, sand-grey feet.

When they reached the house, Michael told Dora, 'Those *stukkie broods* are waiting outside again. Give them something, and they can go.'

Dora grumbled once again, but did as she was told. Michael did not go out with the bread himself; he was in a hurry to get back to work on a model car he was making, and was satisfied to see, out of his bedroom window, Dora coming from the back gate a few

minutes later with an empty plate in her hand. Soon
he had forgotten all about the two children. He did
not go out of the house until a couple of hours had
passed; by then it was dusk, and he took a torch with
him to help him find a piece of wire for his model in
the darkness of the lumber-shed. Handling the torch
gave Michael a feeling of power and importance, and
he stepped into the lane with it, intending to shine
it about like a policeman on his beat. Immediately he
opened the gate, he saw the two little children
standing in the half-light, just a few paces away from
him.

'What are you doing here?' Michael exclaimed in
surprise.

The boy answered, holding his hand up, as if
warning Michael to be silent. 'We were waiting to say
thank you to the baas.'

'What!' Michael took a step towards them both,
and they stood their ground, only shrinking together
slightly.

For all the glare and glitter there was in the streets
of Lyndhurst by day, it was winter, midwinter; and
once the sun had set, the air turned bitterly cold as
swiftly as the light disappeared. The cold at night
wrung deep notes from the contracting iron roofs of
the houses, and froze the fish-ponds in all the gardens
of the white suburbs. Already Michael could feel its
sharp touch on the tips of his ears and fingers. And
the two African children stood there barefoot, in a
flimsy dress and torn shirt, waiting to thank him for
the bread he had sent out to them.

'You mustn't wait,' Michael said. In the half-
darkness he saw the white dress on the girl more
clearly than the boy's clothing; and he remembered
the nakedness and puniness of her black thighs. He

stretched his hand out, with the torch in it. 'Take it,' he said. The torch was in his hand, and there was nothing else that he could give to them. 'It's nice,' he said. 'It's a torch. Look.' He switched it on and saw in its beam of light a pair of startled eyes, darting desperately from side to side. 'You see how nice it is,' Michael said, turning the beam upwards, where it lost itself against the light that lingered in the sky. 'If you don't want it, you can sell it. Go on, take it.'

A hand came up and took the torch from him. Then the two children ran off, in the same direction they had taken on the first afternoon. When they reached the corner all the street lights came on, as if at a single touch, and the children stopped and stared at them, before running again. Michael saw the torch glinting in the boy's hand, and only then did it occur to him that despite their zeal to thank him for the bread they hadn't thanked him for the torch. The size of the gift must have surprised them into silence, Michael decided; and the thought of his own generosity helped to console him for the regret he couldn't help feeling when he saw the torch being carried away from him.

Michael was a lonely child. He had neither brothers nor sisters; both his parents worked during the day, and he had made few friends at school. But he was not unhappy in his loneliness. He was used to it, in the first place; and then, because he was lonely, he was all the better able to indulge himself in his own fantasies. He played for hours, by himself, games of his own invention — games of war, of exploration, of seafaring, of scientific invention, of crime, of espionage, of living in a house beneath or above his

real one. It was not long before the two African
children, who were now accosting him regularly,
appeared in some of his games, for their weakness,
poverty, and dependence gave Michael ample scope
to display in fantasy his kindness, generosity, courage
and decisiveness. Sometimes in his games Michael
saved the boy's life, and was thanked for it in broken
English. Sometimes he saved the girl's, and then she
humbly begged his pardon for having caused him so
much trouble. Sometimes he was just too late to save
the life of either, though he tried his best, and then
there were affecting scenes of farewell.

But in real life, Michael did not play with the
children at all: they were too dirty, too ragged, too
strange, too persistent. Their persistence eventually
drove Dora to tell Michael's mother about them; and
his mother did her duty by telling Michael that on no
account should he play with the children, nor should
he give them anything of value.

'Play with them!' Michael laughed at the idea. And
apart from bread and the torch he had given them
nothing but a few old toys, a singlet or two, a pair of
old canvas shoes. No one could begrudge them those
gifts. Michael's mother certainly didn't. What she was
anxious to do was simply to prevent her son playing
with the piccanins, fearing that he would pick up
germs, bad language, and 'Kaffir ways' generally from
them. Hearing both from Michael and Dora that he
did not play with them, and that he had never even
asked them into the backyard, let alone the house,
she was satisfied.

They came to Michael about once a week, meeting
him as he walked back from school, or simply waiting
for him outside the back gate. The spring winds had
already blown the cold weather away, almost over-

night, and still the children came. Their words of thanks never varied, whatever Michael gave them; but they had revealed, in response to his questions, that the boy's name was Frans and the girl's name was Annie, that they lived in Green Point Location, and that their mother and father were both dead. During all this time Michael had not touched them, except for the fleeting contact of their hands when he passed a gift to them. Yet sometimes Michael wished that they were more demonstrative in their expressions of gratitude to him; he thought that they could, for instance, seize his hand and embrace it; or go down on their knees and weep, just once. As it was, he had to content himself with fantasies of how they spoke of him among their friends, when they returned to the tumbled squalor of Green Point Location; of how incredulous their friends must be to hear their stories about the kind white *kleinbaas* who gave them food and toys and clothing.

One day Michael came out to them carrying a possession he particularly prized — an elaborate pen and pencil set which had been given to him for a recent birthday. He had no intention of giving the outfit to the African children, and he did not think that he would be showing off with it in front of them. He merely wanted to share his pleasure in it with someone who had not already seen it. But as he noticed the way the children were looking at the open box, Michael knew the mistake he had made. 'This isn't for you,' he said abruptly. The children blinked soundlessly, staring from the box to Michael and back to the box again. 'You can just look at it,' Michael said. He held the box tightly in his hand stretching it forward, the pen and the propelling pencils shining inside the velvet-lined case. The two heads of the children came together over the box; they stared deeply into it.

At last the boy lifted his head. 'It's beautiful,' he breathed out. As he spoke, his hand slowly came up towards the box.

'No,' Michael said, and snatched the box away.

'Baas?'

'No.' Michael retreated a little from the beseeching eyes and uplifted hand.

'Please, baas, for me?'

And his sister said, 'For me also, baas.'

'No, you can't have this.' Michael attempted to laugh, as if at the absurdity of the idea. He was annoyed with himself for having shown them the box, and at the same time shocked at them for having asked for it. It was the first time they had asked for anything but bread.

'Please, baas. It's nice.' The boy's voice trailed away on the last word, in longing; then his sister repeated the work, like an echo, her own voice trailing away too. 'Ni-ce.'

'No! I won't give it to you! I won't give you anything if you ask for this. Do you hear?'

Their eyes dropped, their hands came together, they lowered their heads. Being sure now that they would not again ask for the box, Michael relented. He said, 'I'm going in now, and I'll tell Dora to bring you some bread.'

But Dora came to him in his room a few minutes later. 'The little Kaffirs are gone.' She was holding the plate of bread in her hand. Dora hated the two children, and Michael thought there was some kind of triumph in her voice and manner as she made the announcement.

He went outside to see if she was telling the truth.

The lane was empty. He went to the street, and looked up and down its length, but there was no sign of them there either. They were gone. He had driven them away. Michael expected to feel guilty; but to his own intense surprise he felt nothing of the kind. He was relieved that they were gone, and that was all.

When they reappeared a few days later, Michael felt scorn towards them for coming back after what had happened on the last occasion. He felt they were in his power. 'So you've come back?' he greeted them. 'You like your *stukkies brood,* hey? You're hungry, so today you'll wait, you won't run away.'

'Yes, baas,' they said, in their low voices.

Michael brought the bread out to them; when they reached for it he jokingly pulled the plate back and laughed at their surprise. Then only did he give them the bread.

'Thank you, baas.'

'Thank you, baas.'

They ate the bread in Michael's presence; watching them, he felt a little more kindly disposed towards them. 'All right, you can come another day, and there'll be some more bread for you.'

'Thank you, baas.'

'Thank you, baas.'

They came back sooner than Michael had expected them to. He gave them their bread and told them to go. They went off, but again did not wait for the usual five or six days to pass, before approaching him once more. Only two days had passed, yet here they were with their eternal request — '*Stukkie brood,* baas?'

Michael said, 'Why do you get hungry so quickly now?' But he gave them their bread.

When they appeared in his games and fantasies, Michael no longer rescued them, healed them, casually presented them with kingdoms and motor-cars. Now he ordered them about, sent them away on disastrous missions, picked them out to be shot for cowardice in the face of the enemy. And because something similar to these fantasies was easier to enact in the real world than his earlier fantasies, Michael soon was ordering them about unreasonably in fact. He deliberately left them waiting; he sent them away and told them to come back on days when he knew he would be in town; he told them there was no bread in the house. When he did give them anything, it was bread only now; never old toys or articles of clothing.

So, as the weeks passed, Michael's scorn gave way to impatience and irritation, irritation to anger. What angered him most was that the two piccanins seemed too stupid to realize what he now felt about them, and instead of coming less frequently, continued to appear more often than ever before. Soon they were coming almost every day, though Michael shouted at them and teased them, left them waiting for hours, and made them do tricks and sing songs for their bread. They did everything he told them to do; but they ignored his instruction as to which days they should come. Invariably, they would be waiting for him in the shade of one of the trees that grew along-side the main road from school, or standing at the gate behind the house with sand scuffed up about their bare toes. They were as silent as before; but more persistent, inexorably persistent. Michael took to walking home by different routes, but they were not to be so easily discouraged. They simply waited at the back gate, and whether he went into the house by the front or the back gate he could not avoid seeing their upright, unmoving figures.

Finally, he told them to go and never come back at all. Often he had been tempted to do this, but some shame or pride had always prevented him from doing it; he had always weakened previously, and named a date, a week or two weeks ahead, when they could come again. But now he shouted at them, 'It's finished! No more bread — nothing! Go on, *voetsak!* If you come back I'll tell the garden-boy to chase you away.'

From then on they came every day. They no longer waited right at the back gate, but squatted in the sand across the lane. Michael was aware of their eyes following him when he went by, but they did not approach him. They did not even get up from the ground when he passed. A few times he shouted at them to go, and stamped his foot, but he shrank from hitting them. He did not want to touch them. Once he sent out Jan, the garden-boy, to drive them away; but Jan, who had hitherto always shared Dora's views on the children, came back muttering angrily and incomprehensibly to himself; when Michael peeped into the lane he saw that they were still there. Michael tried to ignore them, to pretend he did not see them. He hated them now; even more, he began to dread them.

But he did not know how much he hated and feared the two children until he fell ill with a cold, and lay feverish in bed for a few days. During those days the two children were constantly in his dreams, or in his half-dreams, for even as he dreamed he knew he was turning in his bed; he was conscious of the sun shining outside by day, and at night of the passage-light that had been left on inside the house. In these dreams he struck and struck again at the children with weapons he found in his hands; he fled in fear from them down lanes so thick with sand his feet could barely move through it; he committed lewd, cruel acts upon the bare-thighed girl, and her brother shrieked to tell the empty street what he was doing. Michael struck out at him with a piece of heavy cast-iron guttering. Its edge dug sharply into his hands as the blow fell, and when he lifted the weapon he saw the horror he had made of the side of the boy's head, and how the one remaining eyeball still stared un-winkingly at him.

Michael thought he was awake, and suddenly calm. The fever seemed to have left him. It was as though he had slept deeply, for days, after that last dream of violence; yet his impression was that he had woken directly from it. The bedclothes felt heavy on him and he threw them off. The house was quite silent. He got out of bed and went to look at the clock in the kitchen: it was early afternoon. Dora and Jan were resting in their rooms across the yard, as they always did after lunch. Outside, the light of the sun was unremitting, a single golden glare. He walked back to his bedroom; there, he put on his dressing-gown and slippers, feeling the coolness inside his slippers on his bare feet. He went through the kitchen again and on to the stoep, and then across the yard. The sun seemed to seize the back of his neck as firmly as a hand grasping, and its light was so bright he was aware of it only as a darkness beyond the little stretch of ground he looked down upon. He opened the back gate. Inevitably, as he had known they would be, the two were waiting.

He did not want to go beyond the gate in his pyjamas and dressing-gown, so, shielding his eyes from the glare with one hand, he beckoned them to him with the other. Together, in silence, they rose and crossed the lane. It seemed to take them a long time to come to him, but at last they stood in front of him, with their hands interlinked. Michael stared into their dark faces, and they stared into his.

'What are you waiting for?' he asked.

'For you.' First the boy answered; then the girl repeated, 'For you.'

Michael looked from the one to the other, and he remembered what he had been doing to them in his dreams. Their eyes were fathomlessly black to look into. Staring forward, Michael understood what he should have understood long before: that they came to him not in hope or appeal or even in reproach, but in hatred. What he felt towards them, they felt towards him; what he had done to them in his dreams, they did to him in theirs.

The sun, their staring eyes, his own fear came together in a sound that seemed to hang in the air of the lane — a cry, the sound of someone weeping. Then Michael knew that he was the one who was crying. He felt the heat of the tears in his eyes, their moisture running down his cheeks. With the same fixity of decision that had been his in his dreams of violence and torture, Michael knew what he must do. He beckoned them forward, closer. They came. He stretched out his hands, he felt under his fingers the springy hair he had looked at so often before from the distance between himself and them; he felt the smooth skin of their faces; their frail, rounded shoulders, their hands. Their hands were in his, and he led them inside the gate.

He led them into the house, through the kitchen, down the passage, into his room, where they had never been before. They looked about at the pictures on the walls, the toys on top of the low cupboard, the twisted white sheets and tumbled blankets on the bed. They stood on both sides of him, and for the first time since he had met them, their lips parted into slow, grave smiles. Michael knew that what he had to give them was not toys or clothes or bread, but something more difficult. Yet it was not difficult at all, for there was nothing else he could give them. He took the girl's face in his hands and pressed his lips to hers. He was aware of the darkness of her skin, and of the smell of it, and of the faint movement of her lips, a single pulse that beat momentarily against his own. Then it was gone. He kissed the boy, too, and let them go. They came together, and grasped each other by the hand, staring at him.

'What do you want now?' he asked.

A last anxiety flickered in Michael and left him, as the boy slowly shook his head. He began to step back pulling his sister with him. When he was through the door he turned his back on Michael and they walked away down the passage. Michael watched them go. At the door of the kitchen, on their way out of the house, they paused, turned once more, and lifted their hands, the girl copying the boy, in a silent, tentative gesture of farewell.

Michael did not follow them. He heard the back gate swing open and then bang when it closed. He went wearily back to his bed, and as he fell upon it, his relief and gratitude that the bed should be there to receive him, changed suddenly into grief at the knowledge that he was already lying upon it — that he had never left it.

His cold grew worse, turned into bronchitis, kept him in bed for several weeks. But his dreams were no longer of violence; they were calm, spacious, empty of people. As empty as the lane was, when he was at last allowed out of the house, and made his way there immediately, to see if the children were waiting for him.

He never saw them again, though he looked for them in the streets and lanes of the town. He saw a hundred, a thousand, like them, but not the two he hoped to find.

Ezekiel Mphahlele
MRS PLUM

My madam's name was Mrs Plum. She loved dogs and Africans and said that everyone must follow the law even if it hurt. These were three big things in Madam's life.

I came to work for Mrs Plum in Greenside, not very far from the centre of Johannesburg, after leaving two white families. The first white people I worked for as a cook and laundry woman were a man and his wife in Parktown North. They drank too much and always forgot to pay me. After five months I said to myself, No. I am going to leave these drunks. So that was it. That day I was as angry as a red-hot iron when it meets water. The second house I cooked and washed for had five children who were badly brought up. This was in Belgravia. Many times they called me You Black Girl and I kept quiet. Because their mother heard them and said nothing. Also I was only new from Phokeng my home, very far away, near Rustenburg. I wanted to learn and know the white people before I knew how far to go with the others I would work for afterwards. The thing that drove me mad and made me pack and go was a man who came to visit them often. They said he was a cousin or something like that. He came to the kitchen many times and tried to make me laugh. He patted me on the buttocks. I told the master. The man did it again and I asked the madam that very day to give me my money and let me go.

These were the first nine months after I had left Phokeng to work in Johannesburg. There were many of us girls and young women from Phokeng, from Zeerust, from Shuping, from Koster, and many other places who came to work in the cities. So the suburbs were full of blackness. Most of us had already passed Standard Six and so we learned more English where we worked. None of us likes to work for white farmers, because we know too much about them on the farms near our homes. They do not pay well and they are cruel people.

At Easter time so many of us went home for a long weekend to see our people and to eat chicken and sour milk and *morogo* — wild spinach. We also took home sugar and condensed milk and tea and coffee and sweets and custard powder and tinned foods.

It was a home-girl of mine, Chimane, who called me to take a job in Mrs Plum's house, just next door to where she worked. This is the third year now. I have been quite happy with Mrs Plum and her daughter Kate. By this I mean that my place as a servant in Greenside is not as bad as that of many others. Chimane too does not complain much. We are paid six pounds a month with free food and free servant's room. No one can ever say that they are well paid, so we go on complaining somehow. Whenever we meet on Thursday afternoons, which is time-off for all of us black women in the suburbs, we talk and

talk and talk: about our people at home and their
letters; about their illnesses; about bad crops; about a
sister who wanted a school uniform and books and
school fees; about some of our madams and masters
who are good, or stingy with money or food, or
stupid or full of nonsense, or who kill themselves and
each other, or who are dirty — and so many things I
cannot count them all.

Thursday afternoons we go to town to look at the
shops, to attend a women's club, to see our boy
friends, to go to bioscope some of us. We turn up
smart, to show others the clothes we bought from the
black men who sell soft goods to servants in the
suburbs. We take a number of things and they come
round every month for a bit of money until we finish
paying. Then we dress the way of many white
madams and girls. I think we look really smart.
Sometimes we catch the eyes of a white woman
looking at us and we laugh and laugh and laugh until
we nearly drop onto the ground because we feel good
inside ourselves.

What did the girl next door call you, Mrs Plum asked
me the first day I came to her. Jane, I replied. Was
there not an African name? I said yes, Karabo. All
right, Madam said. We'll call you Karabo, she said.
She spoke as if she knew a name is a big thing. I
knew so many whites who did not care what they
called black people as long as it was all right for their
tongue. This pleased me, I mean Mrs Plum's use of
Karabo; because the only time I heard the name was
when I was at home or when my friends spoke to me.
Then she showed me what to do: meals, meal times,
washing, and where all the things were that I was
going to use.

My daughter will be here in the evening, Madam said. She is at school. When the daughter came, she added, she would tell me some of the things she wanted me to do for her every day.

Chimane, my friend next door, had told me about the daughter Kate, how wild she seemed to be, and about Mr Plum who had killed himself with a gun in a house down the street. They had left the house and come to this one.

Madam is a tall woman. Not slender, not fat. She moves slowly, and speaks slowly. Her face looks very wise, her forehead seems to tell me she has a strong liver: she is not afraid of anything. Her eyes are always swollen at the lower eyelids like a white person who has not slept for many many nights or like a large frog. Perhaps it is because she smokes too much, like wet wood that will not know whether to go up in flames or stop burning. She looks me straight in the eyes when she talks to me, and I know she does this with other people too. At first this made me fear her, now I am used to her. She is not a lazy woman, and she does many things outside, in the city and in the suburbs.

This was the first thing her daughter Kate told me when she came and we met. Don't mind mother, Kate told me. She said, She is sometimes mad with people for very small things. She will soon be all right and speak nicely to you again.

Kate, I like her very much, and she likes me too. She tells me many things a white woman does not tell a black servant. I mean things about what she likes and does not like, what her mother does or does not do, all these. At first I was unhappy and wanted to stop her, but now I do not mind.

Kate looks very much like her mother in the face. I

think her shoulders will be just as round and strong-
looking. She moves faster than Madam. I asked her
why she was still at school when she was so big. She
laughed. Then she tried to tell me that the school
where she was was for big people, who had finished
with lower school. She was learning big things about
cooking and food. She can explain better, me I
cannot. She came home on weekends.

Since I came to work for Mrs Plum Kate has been
teaching me plenty of cooking. I first learned from
her and Madam the word *recipes*. When Kate was at
the big school, Madam taught me how to read
cookery books. I went on very slowly at first, slower
than an ox-wagon. Now I know more. When Kate
came home, she found I had read the recipe she left
me. So we just cooked straightaway. Kate thinks I am
fit to cook in a hotel. Madam thinks so too. Never
never, I thought. Cooking in a hotel is like feeding
oxen. No one can say thank you to you. After a few
months I could cook the Sunday lunch and later I
could cook specials for Madam's or Kate's guests.

Madam did not only teach me cooking. She taught
me how to look after guests. She praised me when I
did very very well, not like the white people I had
worked for before. I do not know what runs crooked
in the heads of other people. Madam also had classes
in the evenings for servants to teach them how to
read and write. She and two other women in Greenside taught in a church hall.

As I say, Kate tells me plenty of things about
Madam. She says to me she says, My mother goes to
meetings many times. I ask her I say, What for? She
says to me she says, For your people. I ask her I say,
My people are in Phokeng far away. They have got
mouths, I say. Why does she want to say something

for them? Does she know what my mother and what
my father want to say? They can speak when they
want to. Kate raises her shoulders and drops them
and says, How can I tell you Karabo? I don't say your
people — your family only. I mean all the black
people in this country. I say Oh! What do the black
people want to say? Again she raises her shoulders
and drops them, taking a deep breath.

I ask her I say, With whom is she in the meeting?

She says, With other people who think like her.

I ask her I say, Do you say there are people in the
world who think the same things?

She nods her head.

I ask, What things?

So that a few of your people should one day be
among those who rule this country, get more money
for what they do for the white man and — what did
Kate say again? Yes, that Madam and those who
think like her also wanted my people who have been
to school to choose those who must speak for them
in the — I think she said it looks like a *Kgotla* at
home who rule the villages.

I say to Kate I say, Oh I see now. I say, Tell me
Kate why is madam always writing on the machine,
all the time everyday nearly?

She replies she says, Oh my mother is writing
books.

I ask, You mean a book like those? — pointing at
the books on the shelves.

Yes, Kate says.

And she told me how Madam wrote books and
other things for newspapers and she wrote for the
newspapers and magazines to say things for the black
people who should be treated well, be paid more
money, for the black people who can read and write

many things to choose those who want to speak for them.

Kate also told me she said, My mother and other women who think like her put on black belts over their shoulders when they are sad and they want to show the white government they do not like the things being done by whites to blacks. My mother and the others go and stand where the people in government are going to enter or go out of a building.

I ask her I say, Does the government and the white people listen and stop their sins? She says No. But my mother is in another group of white people.

I ask, Do the people of the government give the women tea and cakes? Kate says, Karabo, how stupid! oh!

I say to her I say, Among my people if someone comes and stands in front of my house I tell him to come in and I give him food. You white people are wonderful. But they keep standing there and the government people do not give them anything.

She replies, You mean strange. How many times have I taught you not to say *wonderful* when you mean *strange!* Well, Kate says with a short heart and looking cross and she shouts, Well they do not stand there the whole day to ask for tea and cakes stupid. Oh dear!

Always when Madam finished to read her newspapers she gave them to me to read to help me speak and write better English. When I had read she asked me to tell her some of the things in it. In this way, I did better and better and my mind was opening and opening and I was learning and learning many things about the black people inside and outside the towns which I did not know in the least. When I found words that were too difficult or I did not understand

some of the things I asked Madam. She always told
me You see this, you see that, eh? with a heart that
can carry on a long way. Yes, Madam writes many
letters to the papers. She is always sore about the way
the white police beat up black people; about the way
black people who work for whites are made to sit at
the Zoo Lake with their hearts hanging, because the
white people say our people are making noise on
Sunday afternoon when they want to rest in their
houses and gardens; about many ugly things that
happen when some white people meet black man on
the pavement or street. So madam writes to the
papers to let others know, to ask the government to
be kind to us.

In the first year Mrs Plum wanted me to eat at
table with her. It was very hard, one because I was
not used to eating at table with a fork and knife, two
because I heard of no other kitchen worker who was
handled like this. I was afraid. Afraid of everybody,
of Madam's guests if they found me doing this.
Madam said I must not be silly. I must show that
African servants can also eat at table. Number three, I
could not eat some of the things I loved very much:
mealie-meal porridge with sour milk or *morogo*,
stamped mealies mixed with butter beans, sour
porridge for breakfast and other things. Also, except
for morning porridge, our food is nice when you eat
with the hand. So nice that it does not stop in the
mouth or the throat to greet anyone before it passes
smoothly down.

We often had lunch together with Chimane next-
door and our garden boy — Ha! I must remember
never to say *boy* again when I talk about a man. This
makes me think of a day during the first few weeks in
Mrs Plum's house. I was talking about Dick her

garden man and I said 'garden boy'. And she says to
me she says Stop talking about a 'boy', Karabo. Now
listen here, she says, you Africans must learn to
speak properly about each other. And she says White
people won't talk kindly about you if you look down
upon each other.

I say to her I say Madam, I learned the word from
the white people I worked for, and all the kitchen
maids say 'boy'.

She replies she says to me, Those are white people
who know nothing, just low-class whites. I say to her
I say I thought white people know everything.

She said, You'll learn my girl and you must start in
this house, hear? She left me there thinking, my mind
mixed up.

I learned. I grew up.

If any woman or girl does not know the Black Crow
Club in Bree Street, she does not know anything. I
think nearly everything takes place inside and outside
that house. It is just where the dirty part of the City
begins, with factories and the market. After the
market is the place where Indians and 'coloured'
people live. It is also at the Black Crow that the buses
turn round and go back to the black townships.
Noise, noise, noise all the time. There are women who
sell hot sweet potatoes and fruit and monkey nuts
and boiled eggs in the winter, boiled mealies and the
other things in the summer, all these on the pavements. The streets are always full of potato and fruit
skins and monkey nut shells. There is always a strong
smell of roast pork. I think it is because of Piel's cold
storage down Bree Street.

Madam said she knew the black people who work
in the Black Crow. She was happy that I was spending

my afternoon on Thursdays in such a club. You will learn sewing, knitting, she said, and other things that you like. Do you like to dance? I told her I said, Yes, I want to learn. She paid the two shillings fee for me each month.

We waited on the first floor, we were the ones who were learning sewing; waiting for the teacher. We talked and laughed about madams and masters, and their children and their dogs and birds and whispered about our boy friends.

Sies! My Madam you do not know — *mojuta oa'nete* — a real miser . . .

Jo — jo — jo! you should see our new dog. A big thing like this. People! Big in a foolish way . . .

What! Me, I take a master's bitch by the leg, me, and throw it away so that it keeps howling, *tjwe — tjwe! ngo — wu ngo — wy!* I don't play about with them, me . . .

Shame, poor thing! God sees you, true . . . !

They wanted me to take their dog out for a walk every afternoon and I told them I said It is not my work in other houses the garden man does it. I just said to myself I said they can go to the chickens. Let them bite their elbow before I take out a dog, I am not so mad yet . . .

Hei! It is not like the child of my white people who keeps a big white rat and you know what? He puts it on his bed when he goes to school. And let the blankets just begin to smell of urine and all the nonsense and they tell me to wash them. *Hei,* people!

Did you hear about Rebone, people? Her Madam put her out, because her master was always tapping her buttocks with his fingers. And yesterday the madam saw the master press Rebone against himself . . .

Jo — jo — jo! people . . . !

Dirty white man!

No, not dirty. The madam smells too old for him.

Hei! Go and wash your mouth with soap, this girl's mouth is dirty . . .

Jo, Rebone, daughter of the people! We must help her to find a job before she thinks of going back home.

The teacher came. A woman with strong legs, a strong face, and kind eyes. She had short hair and dressed in a simple but lovely floral frock. She stood well on her legs and hips. She had a black mark between the two top front teeth. She smiled as if we were her children. Our group began with games, and then Lilian Ngoyi took us for sewing. After this she gave a brief talk to all of us from the different classes.

I can never forget the things this woman said and how she put them to us. She told us that the time had passed for black girls and women in the suburbs to be satisfied with working, sending money to our people and going to see them once a year. We were to learn, she said, that the world would never be safe for black people until they were in the government with the power to make laws. The power should be given by the Africans who were more than whites.

We asked her questions and she answered them with wisdom. I shall put some of them down in my own words as I remember them.

Shall we take the place of the white people in the government?

Some yes. But we shall be more than they as we are more in the country. But also the people of all colours will come together and there are good white men we can choose and there are Africans some white people will choose to be in the government.

There are good madams and masters and bad ones. Should we take the good ones for friends?

A master and a servant can never be friends. Never, so put that out of your head, will you! You are not even sure if the ones you say are good are not like that because they cannot breathe or live without the work of your hands. As long as you need their money, face them with respect. But you must know that many sad things are happening in our country and you, all of you, must always be learning, adding what you already know, and obey us when we ask you to help us.

At other times Lilian Ngoyi told us she said, Remember your poor people at home and the way in which the whites are moving them from place to place like sheep and cattle. And at other times again she told us she said, Remember that a hand cannot wash itself, it needs another to do it.

I always thought of Madam when Lilian Ngoyi spoke. I asked myself, What would she say if she knew that I was listening to such words. Words like: A white man is looked after by his black nanny and his mother when he is a baby. When he grows up the white government looks after him, sends him to school, makes it impossible for him to suffer from the great hunger, keeps job ready and open for him as soon as he wants to leave school. Now Lilian Ngoyi asked she said, How many white people can be born in a white hospital, grow up in white streets, be clothed in lovely cotton, lie on white cushions; how many whites can live all their lives in a fenced place away from people of other colours and then, as men and women learn quickly the correct ways of thinking, learn quickly to ask questions in their minds, big questions that will throw over all the nice

things of a white man's life? How many? Very very
few! For those who have begun and are joining us
with both feet in our house, we can only say
Welcome!

I was learning. I was growing up. Every time I
thought of Madam, she became more and more like a
dark forest which one fears to enter, and which one
will never know. But there were several times when I
thought, This woman is easy to understand, she is like
all the other white women.

What else are they teaching you at the Black Crow,
Karabo?

I tell her I say, nothing, Madam. I ask her I say
Why does Madam ask?

You are changing.

What does Madam mean?

Well, you are changing.

But we are always changing Madam.

And she left me standing in the kitchen. This was a
few days after I had told her that I did not want to
read more than one white paper a day. The only
magazines I wanted to read, I said to her, were those
from overseas, if she had them. I told her that white
papers had pictures of white people most of the time.
They talked mostly about white people and their
gardens, dogs, weddings and parties. I asked her if she
could buy me a Sunday paper that spoke about my
people. Madam bought it for me. I did not think that
she would do it.

There were mornings when, after hanging the white
people's washing on the line Chimane and I stole a
little time to stand at the fence and talk. We always
stood where we could be hidden by our rooms.

Hei, Karabo, you know what? That was Chimane.

No — what? Before you start, tell me, has Timi

come back to you?

Ach, I do not care. He is still angry. But boys are fools they always come back dragging themselves on their empty bellies. *Hei* you know what?

Yes?

The Thursday past I saw Moruti K.K. I laughed until I dropped on the ground. He is standing in front of the Black Crow. I believe his big stomach was crying from hunger. Now he has a small dog in his armpit, and is standing before a woman selling boiled eggs and — *hei* home-girl! — tripe and intestines are boiling in a pot — oh, — the smell, you could fill a hungry belly with it, the way it was good. I think Moruti K.K. is waiting for the woman to buy a boiled egg. I do not know what the woman was still doing. I am standing nearby. The dog keeps wriggling and pushing out its nose, looking at the boiling tripe. Moruti keeps patting it with his free hand, not so? Again the dog wants to spill out of Moruti's hand and it gives a few sounds through the nose. *Hei* man, home-girl! One two three the dog spills out to catch some of the good meat! It misses falling into the hot gravy in which the tripe is swimming I do not know how. Moruti K.K. tries to chase it. It has tumbled on to the women's eggs and potatoes and all are in the dust. She stands up and goes after K.K. She is shouting to him to pay, not so? Where am I at that time? I am nearly dead with laughter the tears are coming down so far.

I was myself holding tight on the fence so as not to fall through laughing. I held my stomach to keep back a pain in the side.

I ask her I say, Did Moruti K.K. come back to pay for the wasted food?

Yes, he paid.

The dog?

He caught it. That is a good African dog. A dog must look for its own food when it is not time for meals. Not these stupid spoiled angels the whites keep giving tea and biscuits.

Hmm.

Dick our garden man joined us, as he often did. When the story was repeated to him the man nearly rolled on the ground laughing.

He asks who is Reverend K.K.?

I say he is the owner of the Black Crow.

Oh!

We reminded each other, Chimane and I, of the round minister. He would come into the club, look at us with a smooth smile on his smooth round face. He would look at each one of us, with that smile on all the time, as if he had forgotten that it was there. Perhaps he had, because as he looked at us, almost stripping us naked with his watery shining eyes — funny — he could have been a farmer looking at his ripe corn, thinking many things.

K.K. often spoke without shame about what he called ripe girls — *matjitjana* — with good firm breasts. He said such girls were pure without any nonsense in their heads and bodies. Everybody talked a great deal about him and what they thought he must be doing in his office whenever he called in so-and-so.

The Reverend K.K. did not belong to any church. He baptised, married, and buried people for a fee, who had no church to do such things for them. They said he had been driven out of the Presbyterian Church. He had formed his own, but it did not go far. Later he came and opened the Black Crow. He knew just how far to go with Lilian Ngoyi. She said

although she used his club to teach us things that
would help us in life, she could not go on if he was
doing any wicked things with the girls in his office.
Moruti K.K. feared her, and kept his place.

When I began to tell my story I thought I was going
to tell you mostly about Mrs Plum's two dogs. But I
have been talking about people. I think Dick is right
when he says What is a dog! And there are so many
dogs cats and parrots in Greenside and other places
that Mrs Plum's dogs do not look special. But there
was something special in the dog business in Madam's
house. The way in which she loved them, maybe.

Monty is a tiny animal with long hair and small
black eyes and a face nearly like that of an old
woman. The other, Malan, is a bit bigger, with brown
and white colours. It has small hair and looks naked
by the side of his friend. They sleep in two separate
baskets which stay in Madam's bedroom. They are to
be washed often and brushed and sprayed and they
sleep on pink linen. Monty has a pink ribbon which
stays on his neck most of the time. They both carry a
cover on their backs. They make me fed up when I
see them in their baskets, looking fat, and as if they
knew all that was going on everywhere.

It was Dick's work to look after Monty and Malan,
to feed them, and to do everything for them. He did
this together with garden work and cleaning of the
house. He came at the beginning of this year. He just
came, as if from nowhere, and Madam gave him the
job as she had chased away two before him, she told
me. In both those cases, she said that they could not
look after Monty and Malan.

Dick had a long heart, even although he told me
and Chimane that European dogs were stupid,

spoiled. He said, one day those white people will put ear rings and toe rings and bangles on their dogs. That would be the day he would leave Mrs Plum. For, he said, he was sure that she would want him to polish the rings and bangles with Brasso.

Although he had a long heart, Madam was still not sure of him. She often went to the dogs after a meal or after a cleaning and said to them Did Dick give you food sweethearts? Or, Did Dick wash you sweethearts? Let me see. And I could see that Dick was blowing up like a balloon with anger. These things called white people! he said to me. Talking to dogs!

I say to him I say, People talk to oxen at home do I not say so?

Yes, he says, but at home do you not know that a man speaks to an ox because he wants to make it pull the plough or the wagon or to stop or to stand still for a person to inspan it. No one simply goes to an ox looking at him with eyes far apart and speaks to it. Let me ask you, do you ever see a person where we come from take a cow and press it to his stomach or his cheek? Tell me!

And I say to Dick I say, We were talking about an ox, not a cow.

He laughed with his broad mouth until tears came out of his eyes. At a certain point I laughed aloud too.

One day when you have time, Dick says to me, he says, you should look into Madam's bedroom when she has put a notice outside her door.

Dick, what are you saying, I ask.

I do not talk, me. I know deep inside me.

Dick was about our age, I and Chimane. So we always said *moshiman'o* when we spoke about his tricks. Because he was not too big to be a boy to us.

He also said to us *Hei, lona banyana kelona* — Hey you girls, you! His large mouth always seemed to be making ready to laugh. I think Madam did not like this. Many times she would say What is there to make you laugh here? Or in the garden she would say This is a flower and when it wants water that is not funny! Or again, If you did more work and stopped trying to water my plants with your smile you would be more useful. Even when Dick did not mean to smile. What Madam did not get tired of saying was, If I left you to look after my dogs without anyone to look after you at the same time you would drown the poor things.

Dick smiled at Mrs Plum. Dick hurt Mrs Plum's dogs? Then cows can fly. He was really — really afraid of white people, Dick. I think he tried very hard not to feel afraid. For he was always showing me and Chimane in private how Mrs Plum walked, and spoke. He took two bowls and pressed them to his chest, speaking softly to them as Madam speaks to Monty and Malan. Or he sat at Madam's table and acted the way she sits when writing. Now and again he looked back over his shoulder, pulled his face long like a horse's making as if he were looking over his glasses while telling me something to do. Then he would sit on one of the armchairs, cross his legs and act the way Madam drank her tea; he held the cup he was thinking about between his thumb and pointing finger, only letting their nails meet. And he laughed after every act. He did these things, of course, when Madam was not home. And where was I at such times? Almost flat on my stomach, laughing.

But oh how Dick trembled when Mrs Plum scolded him! He did his house-cleaning very well. Whatever mistake he made, it was mostly with the dogs; their

linen, their food. One white man came into the house
one afternoon to tell Madam that Dick had been very
careless when taking the dogs out for a walk. His own
dog was waiting on Madam's stoep. He repeated that
he had been driving down our street and Dick had let
loose Monty and Malan to cross the street. The white
man made plenty of noise about this and I think
wanted to let Madam know how useful he had been.
He kept on saying Just one inch, *just* one inch. It was
lucky I put on my brakes quick enough . . . But your
boy kept on smiling — Why? Strange. My boy would
only do it twice and only twice and then . . . ! His
pass. The man moved his hand like one writing, to
mean that he would sign his servant's pass for him to
go and never come back. When he left, the white man
said Come on Rusty, the boy is waiting to clean you.
Dogs with names, men without, I thought.

Madam climbed on top of Dick for this, as we say.

Once one of the dogs, I don't know which — Malan
or Monty — took my stocking — brand new, you hear
— and tore it with its teeth and paws. When I told
Madam about it, my anger as high as my throat, she
gave me money to buy another pair. It happened
again. This time she said she was not going to give me
money because I must also keep my stockings where
the two gentlemen would not reach them. Mrs Plum
did not want us ever to say *Voetsek* when we wanted
the dogs to go away. Me I said this when they came
sniffing at my legs or fingers. I hate it.

In my third year in Mrs Plum's house, many things
happened, most of them all bad for her. There was
trouble with Kate; Chimane had big trouble; my heart
was twisted by two loves; and Monty and Malan
became real dogs for a few days.

Madam had a number of suppers and parties. She

invited Africans to some of them. Kate told me the
reasons for some of the parties. Like her mother's
books when finished, a visitor from across the seas
and so on. I did not like the black people who came
here to drink and eat. They spoke such difficult
English like people who were full of all the books in
the world. They looked at me as if I were right down
there whom they thought little of — me a black
person like them.

One day I heard Kate speak to her mother. She
says I don't know why you ask so many Africans to
the house. A few will do at a time. She said something about the government which I could not hear
well. Madam replies she says to her You know some
of them do not meet white people often, so far away
in their dark houses. And she says to Kate that they
do not come because they want her as a friend but
they just want a drink for nothing.

I simply felt that I could not be the servant of
white people and of blacks at the same time. At my
home or in my room I could serve them without a
feeling of shame. And now, if they were only coming
to drink!

But one of the black men and his sister always
came to the kitchen to talk to me. I must have looked
unfriendly the first time, for Kate talked to me about
it afterwards as she was in the kitchen when they
came. I know that at that time I was not easy at all. I
was ashamed and I felt that a white person's house
was not the place for me to look happy in front of
other black people while the white man looked on.

Another time it was easier. The man was alone. I
shall never forget that night, as long as I live. He
spoke kind words and I felt my heart grow big inside
me. It caused me to tremble. There were several other

visits. I knew that I loved him, I could never know
what he really thought of me, I mean as a woman and
he as a man. But I loved him, and I still think of him
with a sore heart. Slowly I came to know the pain of
it. Because he was a doctor and so full of knowledge
and English I could not reach him. So I knew he
could not stoop down to see me as someone who
wanted him to love me.

Kate turned very wild. Mrs Plum was very much
worried. Suddenly it looked as if she were a new
person, with new ways and new everything. I do not
know what was wrong or right. She began to play the
big gramophone aloud, as if the music were for the
whole of Greenside. The music was wild and she
twisted her waist all the time, with her mouth half
open. She did the same things in her room. She left
the big school and every Saturday night now she went
out. When I looked at her face, there was something
deep and wild there on it, and when I thought she
looked young she looked old, and when I thought she
looked old she was young. We were both 22 years of
age. I think that I could see the reason why her mother
was so worried, why she was suffering.

Worse was to come.

They were now openly screaming at each other.
They began in the sitting room and went upstairs
together, speaking fast hot biting words, some of
which I did not grasp. One day Madam comes to me
and says You know Kate loves an African, you know
the doctor who comes to supper here often. She says
he loves her too and they will leave the country and
marry outside. Tell me, Karabo, what do your people
think of this kind of thing between a white woman
and a black man? It *cannot* be right is it?

I reply and I say to her We have never seen it

happen before where I come from.

That's right, Karabo, it is just madness.

Madam left. She looked like a hunted person.

These white women, I say to myself I say these white women, why do not they love their own men and leave us to love ours!

From that minute I knew that I would never want to speak to Kate. She appeared to me as a thief, as a fox that falls upon a flock of sheep at night. I hated her. To make it worse, he would never be allowed to come to the house again.

Whenever she was home there was silence between us. I no longer wanted to know anything about what she was doing, where or how.

I lay awake for hours on my bed. Lying like that, I seemed to feel parts of my body beat and throb inside me, the way I have seen big machines doing, pounding and pounding and pushing and pulling and pouring some water into one hole which came out at another end. I stretched myself so many times so as to feel tired and sleepy.

When I did sleep, my dreams were full of painful things.

One evening I made up my mind, after putting it off many times. I told my boy-friend that I did not want him any longer. He looked hurt, and that hurt me too. He left.

The thought of the African doctor was still with me and it pained me to know that I should never see him again, unless I met him in the street on a Thursday afternoon. But he had a car. Even if I did meet him by luck, how could I make him see that I loved him? Ach, I do not believe he would even stop to think what kind of woman I am. Part of that winter was a time of longing and burning for me. I

say part because there are always things to keep
servants busy whose white people go to the sea for
the winter.

To tell the truth, winter was the time for servants;
not nannies, because they went with their madams so
as to look after the children. Those like me stayed
behind to look after the house and dogs. In winter so
many families went away that the dogs remained the
masters and madams. You could see them walk like
white people in the streets. Silent but with plenty of
power. And when you saw them you knew that they
were full of more nonsense and fancies in the house.

There was so little work to do.

One week word was whispered round that a home-
boy of ours was going to hold a party in his room on
Saturday. I think we all took it for a joke. How could
the man be so bold and stupid? The police were
always driving about at night looking for black
people; and if the whites next door heard the party
noise — *oho!* But still, we were full of joy and wanted
to go. As for Dick, he opened his big mouth and
nearly fainted when he heard of it and that I was
really going.

During the day on the big Saturday Kate came.

She seemed a little less wild. But I was not ready to
talk to her. I was surprised to hear myself answer her
when she said to me Mother says you do not like a
marriage between a white girl and a black man,
Karabo.

Then she was silent.

She says But I want to help him, Karabo.

I ask her I say You want to help him to do what?

To go higher and higher, to the top.

I knew I wanted to say so much that was boiling in
my chest. I could not say it. I thought of Lilian Ngoyi

at the Black Crow, what she said to us. But I was
mixed up in my head and in my blood.

You still agree with my mother?

All I could say was I said to your mother I had
never seen a black man and a white woman marrying,
you hear me? What I think about it is my business.

I remembered that I wanted to iron my party dress
and so I left her. My mind was full of the party again
and I was glad because Kate and the doctor would
not worry my peace that day. And the next day the
sun would shine for all of us, Kate or no Kate,
doctor or no doctor.

The house where our home-boy worked was
hidden from the main road by a number of trees. But
although we asked a number of questions and
counted many fingers of bad luck until we had no
more hands for fingers, we put on our best pay-while-
you-wear dresses and suits and clothes bought from
boys who had stolen them, and went to our home-
boy's party. We whispered all the way while we
climbed up to the house. Someone who knew told us
that the white people next door were away for the
winter. Oh, so that is the thing, we said.

We poured into the garden through the back and
stood in front of his room laughing quietly. He came
from the big house behind us, and were we not struck
dumb when he told us to go into the white people's
house! Was he mad? We walked in with slow foot-
steps that seemed to be sniffing at the floor, not sure
of anything. Soon we were standing and sitting all
over on the nice warm cushions and the heaters were
on. Our home-boy turned the lights low. I counted
fifteen people inside. We saw how we loved one
another's evening dress. The boys were smart too.

Our home-boy's girl-friend Naomi was busy in the

kitchen preparing food. He took out glasses and cold
drinks — fruit juice, tomato juice, ginger beers, and so
many other kinds of soft drink. It was just too nice.
The tarts, the biscuits, the snacks, the cakes, *woo*,
that was a party, I tell you. I think I ate more ginger
cake than I had ever done in my life. Naomi had
baked some of the things. Our home-boy came to me
and said I do not want the police to come here and
have reason to arrest us, so I am not serving hot
drinks, not even beer. There is no law that we cannot
have parties, is there? So we can feel free. Our use of
this house is the master's business. If I had asked him
he would have thought me mad.

I say to him I say, You have a strong liver to do
such a thing.

He laughed.

He played pennywhistle music on gramophone
records — Miriam Makeba, Dorothy Masuka and other
African singers and players. We danced and the party
became more and more noisy and more happy. *Hai*,
those girls Miriam and Dorothy, they can sing, I tell
you! We ate more and more and told more stories. In
the middle of the party, our home-boy called us to
listen to what he was going to say. Then he told us
how he and a friend of his in Orlando collected
money to bet on a horse for the July Handicap in
Durban. They did this each year but lost. Now they
had won two hundred pounds. We all clapped hands
and cheered. Two hundred pounds *woo!*

You should go and sit at home and just eat time, I
say to him. He laughs and says You have no understanding not one little bit.

To all of us he says Now my brothers and sisters
enjoy yourselves. At home I should slaughter a goat
for us to feast and thank our ancestors. But this is

town life and we must thank them with tea and cake and all those sweet things. I know some people think I must be so bold that I could be midwife to a lion that is giving birth, but enjoy yourselves and have no fear.

Madam came back looking strong and fresh.

The very week she arrived the police had begun again to search servants' rooms. They were looking for what they called loafers and men without passes who they said were living with friends in the suburbs against the law. Our dog's meat boys became scarce because of the police. A boy who had a girl-friend in the kitchens, as we say, always told his friends that he was coming for dog's meat when he meant he was visiting his girl. This was because we gave our boy-friends part of the meat the white people bought for the dogs and us.

One night a white and a black policeman entered Mrs Plum's yard. They said they had come to search. She says no, they cannot. They say Yes, they must do it. She answers No. They forced their way to the back, to Dick's room and mine. Mrs Plum took the hose that was running in the front garden and quickly went round to the back. I cut across the floor to see what she was going to say to the men. They were talking to Dick, using dirty words. Mrs Plum did not wait, she just pointed the hose at the two policemen. This seemed to surprise them. They turned round and she pointed it into their faces. Without their seeing me I went to the tap at the corner of the house and opened it more. I could see Dick, like me, was trying to keep down his laughter. They shouted and tried to wave the water away, but she kept the hose pointing at them, now moving it up and down. They turned and ran through the back gate, swearing the while.

That fixes them, Mrs Plum said.

The next day the morning paper reported it.

They arrived in the afternoon — the two policemen
— with another. They pointed out Mrs Plum and she
was led to the police station. They took her away to
answer for stopping the police while they were doing
their work.

She came back and said she had paid bail.

At the magistrate's court, Madam was told that she
had done a bad thing. She would have to pay a fine or
else go to prison for fourteen days. She said she
would go to jail to show that she felt she was not in
the wrong.

Kate came and tried to tell her that she was doing
something silly going to jail for a small thing like that.
She tells Madam she says This is not even a thing to
take to the high court. Pay the money. What is £5?

Madam went to jail.

She looked very sad when she came out. I thought
of what Lilian Ngoyi often said to us: You must be
ready to go to jail for the things you believe are true
and for which you are taken by the police. What did
Mrs Plum really believe about me, Chimane, Dick and
all the other black people, I asked myself. I did not
know. But from all those things she was writing for
the papers and all those meetings she was going to
where white people talked about black people and
the way they are treated by the government, from
what those white women with black bands over their
shoulders were doing standing where a white government man was going to pass, I said to myself I said
This woman, *hai*, I do not know she seems to think
very much of us black people. But why was she so
sad?

Kate came back home to stay after this. She still played the big gramophone loud-loud-loud and twisted her body at her waist until I thought it was going to break. Then I saw a young white man come often to see her. I watched them through the opening near the hinges of the door between the kitchen and the sitting room where they sat. I saw them kiss each other for a long long time. I saw him lift up Kate's dress and her white-white legs begin to tremble, and — oh I am afraid to say more, my heart was beating hard. She called him Jim. I thought it was funny because white people in the shops call black men Jim.

Kate had begun to play with Jim when I met a boy who loved me and I loved. He was much stronger than the one I sent away and I loved him more, much more. The face of the doctor came to my mind often, but it did not hurt me so any more. I stopped looking at Kate and her Jim through openings. We spoke to each other, Kate and I, almost as freely as before but not quite. She and her mother were friends again.

Hello, Karabo, I heard Chimane call me one morning as I was starching my apron. I answered. I went to the line to hang it. I saw she was standing at the fence, so I knew she had something to tell me. I went to her.

Hello!

Hello, Chimane!

O kae?

Ke teng. Wena?

At that moment a woman came out through the back door of the house where Chimane was working.

I have not seen that one before, I say, pointing with my head.

Chimane looked back. Oh, that one. *Hei*, daughter-of-the-people, *Hei*, you have not seen miracles. You

know this is Madam's mother-in-law as you see her
there. Did I never tell you about her?

White people, nonsense. You know what? That
poor woman is here now for two days. She has to
cook for herself and I cook for the family.

On the same stove?

Yes, she comes after me when I have finished.

She had her own food to cook?

Yes, Karabo. White people have no heart no sense.

What will eat them up if they share their food?

Ask me, just ask me. God! She clapped her hands
to show that only God knew, and it was His business,
not ours.

Chimane asks me she says, Have you heard from
home?

I tell her I say, Oh daughter-of-the-people, more
and more deaths. Something is finishing the people at
home. My mother has written. She says they are all
right, my father too and my sisters, except for the
people who have died. Malebo, the one who lived
alone in the house I showed you last year, a white
house, he is gone. Then teacher Sedimo. He was very
thin and looked sick all the time. He taught my sisters
not me. His mother-in-law you remember I told you
died last year — *no*, the year before. Mother says also
there is a woman she does not think I remember
because I last saw her when I was a small girl she
passed away in Zeerust she was my mother's greatest
friend when they were girls. She would have gone
to her burial if it was not because she has swollen
feet.

How are the feet?

She says they are still giving her trouble. I ask
Chimane, How are your people at Nokaneng? They
have not written?

She shook her head.

I could see from her eyes that her mind was on another thing and not her people at that moment.

Wait for me Chimane eh, forgive me, I have scones in the oven, eh! I will just take them out and come back, eh!

When I came back to her Chimane was wiping her eyes. They were wet.

Karabo, you know what?

$E - e$. I shook my head.

I am heavy with child.

Hau!

There was a moment of silence.

Who is it, Chimane?

Timi. He came back only to give me this.

But he loves you. What does he say have you told him?

I told him yesterday. We met in town.

I remembered I had not seen her at the Black Crow.

Are you sure, Chimane? You have missed a month?

She nodded her head.

Timi himself — he did not use the thing?

I only saw after he finished, that he had not.

Why? What does he say?

He tells me he says I should not worry I can be his wife.

Timi is a good boy, Chimane. How many of these boys with town ways who know too much will even say Yes it is my child?

Hai, Karabo, you are telling me other things now. Do you not see that I have not worked long enough for my people? If I marry now who will look after them when I am the only child?

Hm. I hear your words. It is true. I tried to think

of something soothing to say.

Then I say You can talk it over with Timi. You can go home and when the child is born you look after it for three months and when you are married you come to town to work and can put your money together to help the old people while they are looking after the child.

What shall we be eating all the time I am at home? It is not like those days gone past when we had land and our mother could go to the fields until the child was ready to arrive.

The light goes out in my mind and I cannot think of the right answer. How many times have I feared the same thing! Luck and the mercy of the gods that is all I live by. That is all we live by — all of us.

Listen, Karabo. I must be going to make tea for Madam. It will soon strike half-past ten.

I went back to the house. As Madam was not in yet, I threw myself on the divan in the sitting-room. Malan came sniffing at my legs. I put my foot under its fat belly and shoved it up and away from me so that it cried *tjunk — tjunk — tjunk* as it went out. I say to it I say Go and tell your brother what I have done to you and tell him to try it and see what I will do. Tell your grandmother when she comes home too.

When I lifted my eyes he was standing in the kitchen door, Dick. He says to me he says *Hau!* now you have also begun to speak to dogs!

I did not reply. I just looked at him, his mouth ever stretched out like the mouth of a bag, and I passed to my room.

I sat on my bed and looked at my face in the mirror. Since the morning I had been feeling as if a black cloud were hanging over me, pressing on my

head and shoulders. I do not know how long I sat
there. Then I smelled Madam. What was it? Where
was she? After a few moments I knew what it was.
My perfume and scent. I used the same cosmetics as
Mrs Plum's. I should have been used to it by now. But
this morning — why did I smell Mrs Plum like this?
Then, without knowing why, I asked myself I said,
Why have I been using the same cosmetics as Madam?
I wanted to throw them all out. I stopped. And then I
took all the things and threw them into the dustbin. I
was going to buy other kinds on Thursday; finished!

I could not sit down. I went out and into the white
people's house. I walked through and the smell of the
house made me sick and seemed to fill up my throat.
I went to the bathroom without knowing why. It was
full of the smell of Madam. Dick was cleaning the
bath. I stood at the door and looked at him cleaning
the dirt out of the bath, dirt from Madam's body.
Sies! I said aloud. To myself I said, Why cannot
people wash the dirt of their own bodies out of the
bath? Before Dick knew I was near I went out. Ach, I
said again to myself, why should I think about it now
when I have been doing their washing for so long and
cleaned the bath many times when Dick was ill. I had
held worse things from her body times without
number . . .

I went out and stood midway between the house
and my room, looking into the next yard. The three-
legged grey cat next door came to the fence and our
eyes met. I do not know how long we stood like that
looking at each other. I was thinking, Why don't you
go and look at your grandmother like that, when it
turned away and mewed hopping on the three legs.
Just like someone who feels pity for you.

In my room I looked into the mirror on the chest

of drawers. I thought, is this Karabo this?

Thursday came, and the afternoon off. At the Black Crow I did not see Chimane. I wondered about her. In the evening I found a note under my door. It told me if Chimane was not back that evening I should know that she was at 660 3rd Avenue, Alexandra Township. I was not to tell the white people.

I asked Dick if he could not go to Alexandra with me after I had washed the dishes. At first he was unwilling. But I said to him I said, Chimane will not believe that you refused to come with me when she sees me alone. He agreed.

On the bus Dick told me much about his younger sister whom he was helping with money to stay at school until she finished, so that she could become a nurse and a midwife. He was very fond of her, as far as I could find out. He said he prayed always that he should not lose his job, as he had done many times before, after staying a few weeks only at each job; because of this he had to borrow money from people to pay his sister's school fees, to buy her clothes and books. He spoke of her as if she were his sweetheart. She was clever at school, pretty (she was this in the photo Dick had shown me before). She was in Orlando Township. She looked after his old people, although she was only thirteen years of age. He said to me he said Today I still owe many people because I keep losing my job. You must try to stay with Mrs Plum, I said.

I cannot say that I had all my mind on what Dick was telling me. I was thinking of Chimane: what could she be doing? Why that note?

We found her in bed. In that terrible township where night and day are full of knives and bicycle chains and guns and the barking of hungry dogs and of people in trouble. I held my heart in my hands. She was in pain and her face, even in the candlelight, was grey. She turned her eyes on me. A fat woman was sitting in a chair. One arm rested on the other and held her chin in its palm. She had hardly opened the door for us after we had shouted our names when she was on her bench again as if there were nothing else to do.

She snorted, as if to let us know that she was going to speak. She said There is your friend. There she is my own-own niece who comes from the womb of my sister, my sister who was make to spit out my mother's breast to give way for me. Why does she go and do such an evil thing. *Ao!* you young girls of today you do not know children die so fast these days that you have to thank God for sowing a seed in your womb to grow into a child. If she had let the child be born I should have looked after it or my sister would have been so happy to hold a grandchild on her lap, but what does it help? She has allowed a worm to cut the roots, I don't know.

Then I saw that Chimane's aunt was crying. Not once did she mention her niece by her name, so sore her heart must have been. Chimane only moaned.

Her aunt continued to talk, as if she was never going to stop for breath, until her voice seemed to move behind me, not one of the things I was thinking: trying to remember signs, however small, that could tell me more about this moment in a dim little room in a cruel township without street lights, near Chimane. Then I remembered the three-legged cat, its grey-green eyes, its *miau*. What was this shadow that seemed to walk about us but was not coming right in front of us?

I thanked the gods when Chimane came to work at the end of the week. She still looked weak, but that shadow was no longer there. I wondered Chimane had never told me about her aunt before. Even now I did not ask her.

I told her I told her white people that she was ill and had been fetched to Nokaneng by a brother. They would never try to find out. They seldom did, these people. Give them any lie, and it will do. For they seldom believe you whatever you say. And how can a black person work for white people and be afraid to tell them lies. They are always asking the questions, you are always the one to give the answers.

Chimane told me all about it. She had gone to a woman who did these things. Her way was to hold a sharp needle, cover the point with the finger, and guide it into the womb. She then fumbled in the womb until she found the egg and then pierced it. She gave you something to ease the bleeding. But the pain, spirits of our forefathers!

Mrs Plum and Kate were talking about dogs one evening at dinner. Every time I brought something to table I tried to catch their words. Kate seemed to find it funny, because she laughed aloud. There was a word I could not hear well which began with *sem* —: whatever it was, it was to be for dogs. This I understood by putting a few words together. Mrs Plum said it was something that was common in the big cities of America, like New York. It was also something Mrs Plum wanted and Kate laughed at the thought. Then later I was to hear that Monty and Malan could be sure of a nice burial.

Chimane's voice came up to me in my room the next morning, across the fence. When I come out she tells me she says *Hei* child-of-my-father, here is some-

thing to tickle your ears. You know what? What? I
say. She says, These white people can do things that
make the gods angry. More godless people I have not
seen. The madam of our house says the people of
Greenside want to buy ground where they can bury
their dogs. I heard them talk about it in the sitting
room when I was giving them coffee last night. *Hei*,
people, let our forefathers come and save us!

Yes, I say, I also heard the madam of our house
talk about it with her daughter. I just heard it in
pieces. By my mother one day these dogs will sit at
table and use knife and fork. These things are to be
treated like people now, like children who are never
going to grow up.

Chimane sighed and she says *Hela batho*, why do
they not give me some of that money they will spend
on the ground and on gravestones to buy stockings! I
have nothing to put on, by my mother.

Over her shoulder I saw the cat with three legs. I
pointed with my head. When Chimane looked back
and saw it she said *Hm*, even *they* live like kings. The
mother-in-law found it on a chair and the madam said
the woman should not drive it away. And there was
no other chair, so the woman went to her room.

Hela!

I was going to leave when I remembered what I
wanted to tell Chimane. It was that five of us had
collected £1 each to lend her so that she could pay
the woman of Alexandra for having done that thing
for her. When Chimane's time came to receive money
we collected each month and which we took in turns,
she would pay us back. We were ten women and each
gave £2 at a time. So one waited ten months to
receive £20. Chimane thanked us for helping her.

I went to wake up Mrs Plum as she had asked me.

She was sleeping late this morning. I was going to
knock at the door when I heard strange noises in the
bedroom. What is the matter with Mrs Plum, I asked
myself. Should I call her, in case she is ill? No, the
noises were not those of a sick person. They were
happy noises but like those a person makes in a
dream, the voice full of sleep. I bent a little to peep
through the keyhole. What is this? I kept asking
myself. Mrs Plum! Malan! What is she doing this one?
Her arm was round Malan's belly and pressing its back
against her stomach at the navel, Mrs Plum's body in
a nightdress moving in jerks like someone in fits . . .
her leg rising and falling . . . Malan silent like a thing
to be owned without any choice it can make to
belong to another.

The gods save me, I heard myself saying, the words
sounding like wind rushing out of my mouth. So this
is what Dick said I would find out for myself!

No one could say where it all started; who talked
about it first; whether the police wanted to make a
reason for taking people without passes and people
living with servants and working in town or not
working at all. But the story rushed through
Johannesburg that servants were going to poison the
white people's dogs. Because they were too much
work for us: that was the reason. We heard that
letters were sent to the newspapers by white people
asking the police to watch over the dogs to stop any
wicked things. Some said that we the servants were
not really bad, we were being made to think of doing
these things by evil people in town and in the
locations. Others said the police should watch out lest
we poison madams and masters because black people
did not know right from wrong when they were
angry. We were still children at heart, others said.

Mrs Plum said that she had also written to the papers.

Then it was the police came down on the suburbs like locusts on a cornfield. There were lines and lines of men who were arrested hour by hour in the day. They liked this very much, the police. Everybody they took, everybody who was working was asked, Where's the poison eh? Where did you hide it? Who told you to poison the dogs eh? If you tell us we'll leave you to go free, you hear? And so many other things.

Dick kept saying It is wrong this thing they want to do to kill poor dogs. What have these things of God done to be killed for? Is it the dogs that make us carry passes? Is it dogs that make the laws that give us pain? People are just mad they do not know what they want, stupid! But when white policemen spoke to him, Dick trembled and lost his tongue and the things he thought. He just shook his head. A few moments after they had gone through his pockets he still held his arms stretched out, like the man of straw who frightens away birds in a field. Only when I hissed and gave him a sign did he drop his arms. He rushed to a corner of the garden to go on with his work.

Mrs Plum had put Monty and Malan in the sitting room, next to her. She looked very much worried. She called me. She asked me she said Karabo, you think Dick is a boy we can trust? I did not know how to answer. I did not know whom she was talking about when she said *we*. Then I said I do not know, Madam. You know, she said. I looked at her. I said I do not know what Madam thinks. She said she did not think anything, that was why she asked. I nearly laughed because she was telling a lie this time and not I.

At another time I should have been angry if she lied to me, perhaps. She and I often told each other lies, as Kate and I also did. Like when she came back from jail, after that day when she turned a hosepipe on two policemen. She said life had been good in jail. And yet I could see she was ashamed to have been there. Not like our black people who are always being put in jail and only look at it as the white man's evil game. Lilian Ngoyi often told us this, and Mrs Plum showed me how true those words are. I am sure that we have kept to each other by lying to each other.

There was something in Mrs Plum's face as she was speaking which made me fear her and pity her at the same time. I had seen her when she had come from prison; I had seen her when she was shouting at Kate and the girl left the house; now there was this thing about dog poisoning. But never had I seen her face like this before. The eyes, the nostrils, the lips, the teeth seemed to be full of hate, tired, fixed on doing something bad; and yet there was something on that face that told me she wanted me on her side.

Dick is all right madam, I found myself saying. She took Malan and Monty in her arms and pressed them to herself, running her hands over their heads. They looked so safe, like a child in a mother's arms.

Mrs Plum said All right you may go. She said Do not tell anybody what I have asked about Dick eh?

When I told Dick about it, he seemed worried.

It is nothing, I told him.

I had been thinking before that I did not stand with those who wanted to poison the dogs, Dick said. But the police have come out, I do not care what happens to the dumb things, now.

I asked him I said Would you poison them if you were told by someone to do it?

No. But I do not care, he replied.

The police came again and again. They were having a good holiday, everyone could see that. A day later Mrs Plum told Dick to go because she would not need his work any more.

Dick was almost crying when he left. Is madam so unsure of me, he asked. I never thought a white person could fear me! And he left.

Chimane shouted from the other yard. She said, *Hei ngoana'rona*, the boers are fire-hot eh!

Mrs Plum said she would hire a man after the trouble was over.

A letter came from my parents in Phokeng. In it they told me my uncle had passed away. He was my mother's brother. The letter also told me of other deaths. They said I would not remember some, I was sure to know the others. There were also names of sick people.

I went to Mrs Plum to ask her if I could go home. She asks she says When did he die? I answer I say It is three days, madam. She says So that they have buried him? I reply Yes Madam. Why do you want to go home then? Because my uncle loved me very much madam. But what are you going to do there? To take my tears and words of grief to his grave and to my aunt, madam. No you cannot go, Karabo. You are working for me you know? Yes, madam. I, and not your people pay you. I must go madam, that is how we do it among my people, madam. She paused. She walked into the kitchen and came out again. If you want to go, Karabo, you must lose the money for the days you will be away. Lose my pay, madam? Yes, Karabo.

The next day I went to Mrs Plum and told her I was leaving for Phokeng and was not coming back to her. Could she give me a letter to say that I worked for her. She did, with her lips shut tight. I could feel that something between us was burning like raw chillies. The letter simply said that I had worked for Mrs Plum for three years. Nothing more. The memory of Dick being sent away was still an open sore in my heart.

The night before the day I left, Chimane came to see me in my room. She had her own story to tell me. Timi, her boyfriend, had left her — for good. Why? Because I killed his baby. Had he not agreed that you should do it? No. Did he show he was worried when you told him you were heavy? He was worried, like me as you saw me, Karabo. Now he says if I kill one I shall eat all his children up when we are married. You think he means what he says? Yes, Karabo. He says his parents would have been very happy to know that the woman he was going to marry can make his seed grow.

Chimane was crying, softly.

I tried to speak to her, to tell her that if Timi left her just like that, he had not wanted to marry her in the first place. But I could not, no, I could not. All I could say was do not cry, my sister, do not cry. I gave her my handkerchief.

Kate came back the morning I was leaving, from somewhere very far I cannot remember where. Her mother took no notice of what Kate said asking her to keep me, and I was not interested either.

One hour later I was on the Railway bus to Phokeng. During the early part of the journey I did not feel anything about the Greenside house I had worked in. I was not really myself, my thoughts dancing between Mrs Plum, my uncle, my parents, and Phokeng, my home. I slept and woke up many times during the bus ride. Right through the ride I seemed to see, sometimes in sleep, sometimes between sleep and waking, a red car passing our bus, then running behind us. Each time I looked out it was not there.

Dreams came and passed. He tells me he says You have killed my seed I wanted my mother to know you are a woman in whom my seed can grow . . . Before you make the police take you to jail make sure that it is for something big you should go to jail for, otherwise you will come out with a heart and mind that will bleed inside you and poison you . . .

The bus stopped for a short while, which made me wake up.

The Black Crow, the club women . . . *Hei*, listen! I lie to the madam of our house and I say I had a telegram from my mother telling me she is very very sick. I show her a telegram my sister sent me as if mother were writing. So I went home for a nice weekend . . .

The laughter of the women woke me up, just in time for me to stop a line of saliva coming out over my lower lip. The bus was making plenty of dust now as it was running over part of the road they were digging up. I was sure the red car was just behind us, but it was not there when I woke.

Any one of you here who wants to be baptized or has a relative without a church who needs to be can come and see me in the office . . . A round man with a fat tummy and sharp hungry eyes, a smile that goes a long, long way . . .

The bus was going uphill, heavily and noisily.

I kick a white man's dog, me, or throw it there if it has not been told the black people's law . . . This is Mister Monty and this is Mister Malan. Now get up

you lazy boys and meet Mister Kate. Hold out your
hands and say hello to him ... Karabo, bring two
glasses there ... Wait a bit — What will you chew
boys while Mister Kate and I have a drink? Nothing?
Sure?

We were now going nicely on a straight tarred road
and the trees rushed back. Mister Kate. What
nonsense, I thought.

Look Karabo, madam's dogs are dead. What?
Poison. I killed them. She drove me out of a job did
she not? For nothing. Now I want her to feel she
drove me out for something. I came back when you
were in your room and took the things that poisoned
them ... And you know what? She has buried them
in clean pink sheets in the garden. *Ao,* clean clean
good sheets. I am going to dig them out and take one
sheet do you want the other one? Yes, give me the
other one I will send it to my mother ... *Hei,*
Karabo, see here they come. Monty and Malan. The
bloody fools they do not want to stay in their hole.
Go back you silly fools. Oh you do not want to move
eh? Come here, now I am going to throw you in the
big pool. No, Dick! No Dick! No, No! Dick! They
cannot speak do not kill things that cannot speak.
Madam can speak for them she always does. No!
Dick ...

I woke up with a jump after I had screamed Dick's
name, almost hitting the window. My forehead was
full of sweat. The red car also shot out of my sleep
and was gone. I remembered a friend of ours who
told us how she and the garden man had saved two
white sheets in which their white master had buried
their two dogs. They went to throw the dogs in a
dam.

When I told my parents my story Father says to

me he says, So long as you are in good health my
child, it is good. The worker dies, work does not.
There is always work. I know when I was a boy a
strong sound body and a good mind were the biggest
things in life. Work was always there, and the lazy
man could never say there was no work. But today
people see work as something bigger than everything
else, bigger than health, because of money.

I reply I say, Those days are gone Papa. I must go
back to the city after resting a little to look for work.
I must look after you. Today people are too poor to
be able to help you.

I knew when I left Greenside that I was going to
return to Johannesburg to work. Money was little,
but life was full and it was better than sitting in
Phokeng and watching the sun rise and set. So I told
Chimane to keep her eyes and ears open for a job.

I had been at Phokeng for one week when a red car
arrived. Somebody was sitting in front with the
driver, a white woman. At once I knew it to be that
of Mrs Plum. The man sitting beside her was showing
her the way, for he pointed towards our house in
front of which I was sitting. My heart missed a few
beats. Both came out of the car. The white woman
said 'Thank you' to the man after he had spoken a
few words to me.

I did not know what to do and how to look at her
as she spoke to me. So I looked at the piece of cloth I
was sewing pictures on. There was a tired but soft
smile on her face. Then I remembered that she might
want to sit. I went inside to fetch a low bench for
her. When I remembered it afterwards, the thought
came to me that there are things I never think white
people can want to do at our homes when they visit
for the first time: like sitting, drinking water or

entering the house. This is how I thought when the white priest came to see us. One year at Easter Kate drove me home as she was going to the north. In the same way I was at a loss what to do for a few minutes.

Then Mrs Plum says, I have come to ask you to come back to me, Karabo. Would you like to?

I say I do not know, I must think about it first.

She says, Can you think about it today? I can sleep at the town hotel and come back tomorrow morning, and if you want to you can return with me.

I wanted her to say she was sorry to have sent me away, I did not know how to make her say it because I know white people find it too much for them to say sorry to a black person. As she was not saying it, I thought of two things to make it hard for her to get me back and maybe even lose me in the end.

I say, You must ask my father first, I do not know, should I call him?

Mrs Plum says, Yes.

I fetched both father and mother. They greeted her while I brought benches. Then I told them what she wanted.

Father asks mother and mother asks father. Father asks me. I say if they agree, I will think about it and tell her the next day.

Father says, It goes by what you feel my child.

I tell Mrs Plum I say, If you want me to think about it I must know if you will want to put my wages up from £6 because it is too little.

She asks me, How much will you want?

Up by £4.

She looked down for a few moments.

And then I want two weeks at Easter and not just the weekend. I thought if she really wanted me she would want to pay for it. This would also show how sorry she was to lose me.

Mrs Plum says, I can give you one week. You see you already have something like a rest when I am in Durban in the winter.

I tell her I say I shall think about it.

She left.

The next day she found me packed and ready to return with her. She was very much pleased and looked kinder than I had ever known her. And me, I felt sure of myself, more than I had ever done.

Mrs Plum says to me, You will not find Monty and Malan.

Oh?

Yes, they were stolen the day after you left. The police have not found them yet. I think they are dead myself.

I thought of Dick . . . my dream. Could he? And she . . . did this woman come to ask me to return because she had lost two animals she loved?

Mrs Plum says to me she says, You know, I like your people, Karabo, the Africans.

And Dick and me, I wondered.

Bessie Head
THE WIND AND A BOY

Like all the village boys, Friedman had a long wind
blowing for him, but perhaps the enchanted wind
that blew for him, filled the whole world with magic.

Until they became ordinary, dull grown men, who
drank beer and made babies, the little village boys
were a special set all on their own. They were kings
whom no one ruled. They wandered where they
willed from dawn to dusk and only condescended to
come home at dusk because they were afraid of the
horrible things in the dark that might pounce on
them. Unlike the little girls who adored household
chores and drawing water, it was only now and then
that the boys showed themselves as useful attach-
ments to any household. When the first hard rains of
summer fell, small dark shapes, quite naked except
for their loin-cloths, sped out of the village into the
bush. They knew that the first downpour had drowned
all the wild rabbits, moles and porcupines in their
burrows in the earth. As they crouched down near
the entrances to the burrows, they would see a
small drowned nose of an animal peeping out; they
knew it had struggled to emerge from its burrow,

flooded by the sudden rush of storm water, and as
they pulled out the animal, they would say, pityingly:
'Birds have more sense than rabbits, moles and porcupines. They build their homes in trees.' But it was
hunting made easy, for no matter how hard a boy and
his dog ran, a wild rabbit ran ten times faster; a
porcupine hurled his poisonous quills into the body;
and a mole stayed where he thought it was safe —
deep under the ground. So it was with inordinate
pride that the boys carried home armfuls of dead
animals for their families to feast on for many days.
Apart from that, the boys lived very much as they
pleased, with the wind and their own games.

Now and then, the activities of a single family
could captivate the imagination and heart of all the
people of their surroundings; for years and years, the
combination of the boy, Friedman, and his grandmother, Sejosenye, made the people of Ga-Sefete-
Molemo ward, smile, laugh, then cry.

They smiled at his first two phases. Friedman came
home as a small bundle from the hospital, a bundle
his grandmother nursed carefully near her bosom and
crooned to day and night with extravagant care and
tenderness.

'She is like that,' people remarked, 'because he
may be the last child she will ever nurse. Sejosenye is
old now and will die one of these days; the child is a
gift to keep her heart warm.'

Indeed, all Sejosenye's children were grown, married
and had left home. Of all her children, only her last-
born daughter was unmarried and Friedman was the
result of some casual mating she had indulged in, in a
town a hundred miles away where she had a job as a
typist. She wanted to return to her job almost
immediately, so she handed the child over to her

mother and that was that; she could afford to forget him as he had a real mother now. During all the time that Sejosenye haunted the hospital awaiting her bundle, a friendly foreign doctor named Friedman took a fancy to her maternal, grandmotherly ways. He made a habit of walking out of his path to talk to her. She never forgot it and on receiving her bundle she called the baby, Friedman.

They smiled at his second phase, a small dark shadow who toddled silently and gravely beside a very tall grandmother; wherever the grandmother went, there went Friedman. Most women found this phase of the restless, troublesome toddler tedious; they dumped the toddler onto one of their younger girls and were off to weddings and visits on their own.

'Why can't you leave your handbag at home sometimes, granny?' they said.

'Oh, he's no trouble,' Sejosenye would reply.

They began to laugh at his third phase. Almost overnight he turned into a tall, spindly-legged, graceful gazelle with large, grave eyes. There was an odd, musical lilt to his speech and when he teased, or was up to mischief, he moved his head on his long thin neck from side to side like a cobra. It was he who became the king of kings of all the boys in his area; he could turn his hand to anything and made the best wire cars with their wheels of shoe polish tins. All his movements were neat, compact, decisive, and for his age he was a boy who knew his own mind. They laughed at his knowingness and certainty on all things, for he was like the grandmother who had had a flaming youth all her own too. Sejosenye had scandalized the whole village in her days of good morals by leaving her own village ward to live with a married man in Ga-Sefete-Molemo ward. She had won him from his wife and married him and then lived down the scandal in the way only natural queens can. Even in old age, she was still impressive. She sailed through the village, head in the air, with a quiet, almost expressionless face. She had developed large buttocks as time went by and they announced their presence firmly in rhythm with her walk.

Another of Sejosenye's certainties was that she was a woman who could plough, but it was like a special gift. Each season, in drought or hail or sun, she removed herself to her lands. She not only ploughed but nursed and brooded over her crops. She was there all the time till the corn ripened and the birds had to be chased off the land, till harvesting and threshing were done; so that even in drought years with their scanty rain, she came home with some crops. She was the envy of all the women of the surroundings.

'Sejosenye always eats fine things in her house,' they said. 'She ploughs and then sits down for many months and enjoys the fruits of her labour.'

The women also envied her beautiful grandson. There was something special there, so that even when Friedman moved into his bad phase, they forgave him crimes other boys received a sound thrashing for. The small boys were terrible thieves who harassed people by stealing their food and money. It was all a part of the games they played but one which people did not like. Of them all, Friedman was the worst thief, so that his name was mentioned more and more in any thieving that had been uncovered.

'But Friedman showed us how to open the window with a knife and string,' the sobbing, lashed boys would protest.

'Friedman isn't as bad as you,' the parents would reply, irrationally. They were hypnotised by a beauti-

ful creature. The boy Friedman, who had become a
real nuisance by then, also walked around as though
he were special. He couldn't possibly be a thief and
he added an aloof, offended, disdainful expression to
his pretty face. He wasn't just an ordinary sort of boy
in Ga-Sefete-Molemo ward. He was . . .

It happened, quite accidentally, that his grandmother told him all those stories about the hunters,
warriors, and emissaries of old. She was normally a quite
absentminded woman, given to dreaming by herself,
but she liked to sing the boy a little song now and then
as they sat by the outdoor fire. A lot of them were
church songs and rather sad; they more or less passed
as her bed-time prayer at night — she was one of the
old church-goers. Now and then she added a quaint
little song to her repertoire and as the night-time, fire-
light flames flicked between them, she never failed to
note that this particular song was always well-received
by the boy. A little light would awaken in his eyes
and he would bend forward and listen attentively.

'Welcome, Robinson Crusoe, welcome,' she would
sing, in clear, sweet tones. 'How could you stay, so
long away, Robinson, how could you do so?'

When she was very young, Sejosenye had attended
the mission school of the village for about a year;
made a slight acquaintance with the ABC and one,
two, three, four, five, and the little song about
Robinson Crusoe. But girls didn't need an education
in those days when ploughing and marriage made up
their whole world. Yet Robinson Crusoe lived on as a
gay and out-of-context memory of her school-days.
One evening the boy leaned forward and asked:
'Is that a special praise-poem song for Robinson
Crusoe, grandmother?'

'Oh yes,' she replied, smiling.

'It appears that the people liked Robinson Crusoe much,' the boy observed. 'Did he do great things for them?'

'Oh yes,' she said, smiling.

'What great things did he do?' the boy asked, pointedly.

'They say he was a hunter who went by Gweta side and killed an elephant all by himself,' she said, making up a story on the spot. 'Oh! In those days, no man could kill an elephant by himself. All the regiments had to join together and each man had to thrust his sword into the side of the elephant before it died. Well, Robinson Crusoe was gone many days and people wondered about him: "Perhaps he has been eaten by a lion," they said. "Robinson likes to be a solitary person and do foolish things. We won't ever go out into the bush by ourselves because we know it is dangerous." Well, one day, Robinson suddenly appeared in their midst and people could see that he had a great thing on his mind. They all gathered around him. He said: "I have killed an elephant for all the people." The people were surprised: "Robinson!" they said. "It is impossible! How did you do it? The very thought of an elephant approaching the village makes us shiver!" And Robinson said: "Ah, people, I saw a terrible sight! I was standing at the feet of the elephant. I was just a small ant. I could not see the world any more. Elephant was above me until his very head touched the sky and his ears spread out like great wings. He was angry but I only looked into one eye which was turning round and round in anger. What to do now? I thought it better to put that eye out. I raised my spear and threw it at the angry eye. People! It went right inside. Elephant said not a word and he fell to

one side. Come, I will show you what I have done."
Then the women cried in joy: "Loo-loo-loo!" They
ran to fetch their containers as some wanted the meat
of the elephant; some wanted the fat. The men made
their knives sharp. They would make shoes and many
things from the skin and bones. There was something
for all the people in the great work Robinson Crusoe
did.'

All this while, as he listened to the story, the boy's
eyes had glowed softly. At the end of it, he drew in a
long breath.

'Grandmother,' he whispered, adroitly stepping
into the role of Robinson Crusoe, the great hunter.
'One day, I'm going to be like that. I'm going to be a
hunter like Robinson Crusoe and bring meat to all the
people.' He paused for breath and then added tensely:
'And what other great thing did Robinson Crusoe
do?'

'Tsaa!' she said, clicking her tongue in exhaustion.
'Am I then going away that I must tell *all* the stories
at once?'

Although his image of Robinson Crusoe, the great
hunter, was never to grow beyond his everyday
boyish activities of pushing wire cars, hunting in the
fields for wild rabbits, climbing trees to pull down
old birds' nests and yelling out in alarm to find that a
small snake now occupied the abandoned abode, or
racing against the wind with the spoils of his latest
theft, the stories awakened a great tenderness in him.
If Robinson Crusoe was not churning up the dust in
deadly hand-to-hand combat with an enemy, he was
crossing swollen rivers and wild jungles as the great
messenger and ambassador of the chief — all his
activities were touchingly in aid of or in defence of
the people. One day Friedman expressed this awakened

compassion for life in a strange way. After a particularly violent storm, people found their huts invaded by
many small mice and they were hard-pressed to rid
themselves of these pests. Sejosenye ordered Friedman
to kill the mice.

'But grandmother,' he protested. 'They have come
to us for shelter. They lost all their homes in the
storm. It's better that I put them in a box and carry
them out into the fields again once the rains are over.'

She had laughed in surprise at this and spread the
story around among her women friends, who smiled
tenderly then said to their own offspring: 'Friedman
isn't as bad as you.'

Life and its responsibilities began to weigh down
heavily on Friedman as he approached his fourteenth
year. Less time was spent in boyish activities. He grew
more and more devoted to his grandmother and
concerned to assist her in every way. He wanted a
bicycle so that he might run up and down to the
shops for her, deliver messages, or do any other chore
she might have in mind. His mother, who worked in a
town far away, sent him the money to purchase the
bicycle. The gift brought the story of his life abruptly
to a close.

Towards the beginning of the rainy season, he
accompanied his grandmother to her lands which
were some twenty miles outside the village. They
sowed seed together after the hired tractor had
turned up the land but the boy's main chore was to
keep the household pot filled with meat. Sometimes
they ate birds Friedman had trapped, sometimes they
ate fried tortoise-meat or wild rabbit; but there was
always something as the bush abounded with animal
life. Sejosenye only had to take a bag of mealie meal,
packets of sugar, tea, and powdered milk as provisions

for their stay at the lands; meat was never a problem. Mid-way through the ploughing season, she began to run out of sugar, tea, and milk.

'Friedman,' she said that evening, 'I shall wake you early tomorrow morning. You will have to take the bicycle into the village and purchase some more sugar, tea, and milk.'

He was up at dawn with the birds, a solitary figure cycling on a pathway through the empty bush. By nine, he had reached the village and first made his way to Ga-Sefete-Molemo ward and the yard of a friend of his grandmother, who gave him a cup of tea and a plate of porridge. Then he put one foot on the bicycle and turned to smile at the woman with his beautiful gazelle eyes. His smile was to linger vividly before her for many days as a short while later, hard pounding feet came running into her yard to report that Friedman was dead.

He pushed the bicycle through the winding, sandy pathway of the village ward, reached the high embankment of the main road, pedalled vigorously up it and out of the corner of his eye saw a small green truck speeding towards him. In the devil-may-care fashion of all the small boys, he cycled right into its path, turned his head and smiled appealingly at the driver. The truck caught him on the front bumper, squashed the bicycle and dragged the boy along at a crazy speed for another hundred yards, dropped him and careered on another twenty yards before coming to a halt. The boy's pretty face was a smear all along the road and he only had a torso left.

People of Ga-Sefete-Molemo ward never forgot the last coherent words Sejosenye spoke to the police. A number of them climbed into the police truck and accompanied it to her lands. They saw her walk

slowly and enquiringly towards the truck, they heard
the matter-of-fact voice of the policeman announce
the death, then they heard Sejosenye say piteously:
'Can't you return those words back?'

She turned away from them, either to collect her
wits or the few possessions she had brought with her.
Her feet and buttocks quivered anxiously as she
stumbled towards her hut. Then her feet tripped her
up and she fell to the ground like a log.

The people of Ga-Sefete-Molemo ward buried the
boy Friedman but none of them would go near the
hospital where Sejosenye lay. The stories brought to
them by way of the nurses were too terrible for
words. They said the old woman sang and laughed
and talked to herself all the time. So they merely asked
each other: 'Have you been to see Mma-Sejosenye?'
'I'm afraid I cannot. It would kill my heart.' Two
weeks later, they buried her.

As was village habit, the incident was discussed
thoroughly from all sides till it was understood. In
this timeless, sleepy village, the goats stood and
suckled their young ones on the main road or lay
down and took their afternoon naps there. The
motorists either stopped for them or gave way. But
it appeared that the driver of the truck had neither
brakes nor a driving licence. He belonged to the
new, rich civil-servant class whose salaries had become
fantastically high since independence. They had
to have cars in keeping with their new status; they
had to have any car, as long as it was a car; they
were in such a hurry about everything that they
couldn't be bothered to take driving lessons. And
thus progress, development, and a pre-occupation
with status and living-standards first announced
themselves to the village. It looked like being an

ugly story with many decapitated bodies on the main
road.

Nat Nakasa
MR NAKASA GOES TO HARLEM

Harlem, like all New York, is the most indescribable place I have ever seen. It humbles the visitor by its size alone. After weeks of being there, I was still trying to understand and describe it to myself.

Before coming here, I had read stories by Langston Hughes and powerful essays by James Baldwin. They often made Harlem sound like one of the townships in Johannesburg. When Baldwin spoke of the ghetto, I likened Harlem to Sophiatown.

I had visions of private homes turned into shebeens — illegal drinking clubs. Here I would find the drinking fraternity and be welcomed like a long-missed cousin. But Harlem drinks in night clubs and bars, like the white fold. In Harlem I missed the sense of danger which characterized our drinking sessions, many of which were so rudely interrupted by the Johannesburg police.

Harlem has a facade of respectability, the kind I associate with white suburbia. Many people here chew cigars, while others read newspapers on the back seats of licensed taxis. I am more accustomed to the overloaded pirate taxis which used to find their

way into Johannesburg through devious routes. None
of these were driven by whites.

Harlem even has its banks in the community,
despite all the talk about how rough it is. Now,
nobody ever risked opening a bank in Sophiatown or
Edenvale. Those were outfits of the sedate, more
secure white world.

The townships in Johannesburg were neatly separated from the white area, in accordance with the
official policy of apartheid. Some were fenced in like
game reserves, which is what we called them. Harlem
is not like that. My friends had difficulty in showing
me where it began. Besides, I hear there are whites
living there as well, which would not be tolerated
where I come from.

Yet, at the same time, Harlem is quite different
from white or integrated New York — that is, those
few parts of both places that I saw. I felt more at
home in Harlem than I could ever be in the plush
hotels downtown. A lot of Harlem's battles and pre-
occupations are no different from mine. The people
here are still fighting for a place in the sun, just like
me.

I saw filth and squalor and saw people climb from
plush cars into disgusting hovels — their homes. For,
even though Harlem had its cigars, I did not see
poodles and fox terriers in the place. I did not see
housewives take dogs for afternoon walks, a practice
I know only as having something to do with white
affluence.

When I asked if the community had its poodle-
raising set, I was told a story about the last riot.
Apparently, someone swiped yards of sausage from a
shop during the riot lootings, only to be besieged by
Harlem's dogs as he went down the sidewalk. The

dogs, it is said, forced the man to the ground and made off with much of his loot. I can well imagine the same thing happening in Edenvale, Johannesburg.

Finally, the white folks downtown seem to be somewhat apprehensive about going uptown. Taximen kept turning me down on many occasions when I wanted a ride to my hotel in Harlem. Some would slow down on seeing my raised hand then sweep past me without stopping. One cab driver left me in the rain after stopping. When I mentioned Harlem, he said: 'I thought you were going downtown. I would take you if you were going the right way.' Negroes told me this was something I would have to expect a good deal of the time.

Some whites drive through Harlem, but take care not to stop any place. It is worse for Southern motorists. A friend from Alabama, a white journalist, had to use a false registration plate on his car in order to drive through Harlem. In this respect, as in many others, Harlem is reminiscent of Johannesburg. The few whites who do go to our townships do so at their peril. Our drunken brawls and weekend brutalities, as well as anti-white feelings, have long put God's fear into them.

So much for invidious comparisons. The most I can do is put down my reactions to Harlem, just how it felt to be there . . .

I lived at the Hotel Theresa, apparently the Negro Waldorf of yesteryear. This is the tall, ageing building where 7th Avenue meets 125th Street. From my room, I could see Harlem Square, where the local soapbox men hold forth in the summer.

The Theresa was built in 1895, strictly for whites. As Harlem went black, however, it was taken over by Negro celebrities. Joe Louis, Ella Fitzgerald and other personages have lived there. More recently, its guests included Fidel Castro and Cassius Clay. The world champion gave instructions that all walls and furniture in his suite be painted pink.

But there were no celebrities in the Theresa when I checked in. Even Malcolm X, who had an office there, spent most of his time elsewhere. I never saw him there, although I tried many times.

The Theresa has survived three riots and, last summer, a group of young men moved into the place carrying rifles. The police were called in, but they could make no arrests as the rifles turned out to be unloaded.

The police were among the most fascinating people to speak with in Harlem. They are a lonely crowd, and people stare coldly at them with accusing eyes. I never saw anybody talk with them. One of them, white, smiled like a schoolboy when I introduced myself as a stranger from South Africa.

'You're a long ways from home,' he said.

Across the street, advertising a book, stood a weatherbeaten placard. It proclaimed in bold lettering: THE GODDAM WHITE MAN. This made me uneasy, but the policeman seemed to take no notice of it.

Nervously, I lit a cigarette and offered the policeman one. 'Can't take it,' he said. 'Not allowed to smoke in uniform.' I should have known better, I thought. But then I don't have much experience of chatting with policemen on the sidewalks.

'This is a bad neighbourhood,' he warned, almost confidentially, 'you must be careful.'

'But why? The people seem to be nice and harmless to me.'

'Yes, you're looking at the church people. This is Sunday and the bad ones aren't up yet,' he said.

'What places do you think I should go and see?' I asked.

'The museum downtown. Been there yet?'

'No. But I went to the Solomon Guggenheim.'

'Right. That's a good one. What about the Empire State Building?'

'Yes, I went there, but I got scared before we reached the top . . . Tell me, were you here during the last riot?'

'What do they call it?'

'Disturbance.'

In this officer's view, the junkies and the hoodlums of Harlem were responsible for the disturbance. The good folks had nothing to do with the whole business. It was true that many people were badly housed, but that was their own fault. They did not look after their apartments properly.

'Who owns the apartments?' I asked.

The officer explained that most of the people in Harlem did not own the apartments. But then they lived in them, sublet them and overcrowded the place. He himself did not live there and his parents did not like him working in the neighbourhood.

I could have talked to the policeman much longer. But I soon noticed that our chat was slowly stirring the crowd in Harlem Square. Passers-by stared fiercely, directly at us, apparently suspecting impending trouble. Another policeman joined us, and I thought it was curious that the Harlem police were almost always in pairs. Meanwhile, teen-age boys snuggled close to us, obviously to listen in without asking what was going on. Harlem has obviously not forgotten the shooting of Jimmy Powell by a policeman, shortly before the last riot.

I got the feeling in Harlem that people are not

always amused by outsiders coming to write about the community. Like Jews, they seem to resent the situation being turned into party conversation or tourist-story material.

Also, like white Americans, Negroes do not like outsiders lashing out at the United States, especially as foreigners almost always get their facts and local nuances mixed up. This is nothing peculiar to the United States. I have seen Africans get irritated in Johannesburg when white and black foreigners begin to assail South Africa and get their facts mixed up.

Harlem loves America dearly, bitterly. Its people will stop at nothing to change America and make it a better home for themselves. But they do not want to see the country hurt or disparaged unduly. Not by outsiders, anyway. Harlemites are like the South African refugees who are desperate for a change back home, but remain irrevocably in love with the country.

My relationship with Harlem is largely what Joe Louis meant to me when he rocked the myth of white supremacy in the ring. To this day, Africans in South Africa would fork out their last cents to see the Brown Bomber, even without his gloves. I think, in turn, when Africans arrive at the United Nations, Negroes identify with them and see a new dawn in their own lives.

The same Harlemites, however, do not like too much interference with the details of their situation. 'I really think it is presumptuous for people to come here for a short while and go writing about Harlem,' a young, talented novelist said to me. Another person, a Negro woman, put it more frankly. 'You know,' she said, 'you really have no right to write about Harlem. You don't know anything about it.'

A bearded Negro actor — I'll call him Vos — took a slightly different attitude. He welcomed me into his studio with the warm greetings of Negro-African brotherhood. Vos answered my questions diligently until I told him I was writing for the *New York Times*.

'Give me that notebook,' he said, suddenly, firmly. 'I don't want to have anything to do with white papers.' For a moment I felt like a spy in Harlem. I tore off the pages which contained the actor's comments and gave them to him. I also told him I failed to see the logic of his thinking. But the matter did not end there.

I was to meet more nationalists. Vos and the others invited me and a friend to a party, adding bitterly, 'But please don't bring any white folks with you.' Vos had recently fought with a Nigerian student who brought a white date to one of Harlem's parties.

I got the impression that Vos belonged to a new world in Harlem, the world beyond Malcom X, if such is possible. For Malcolm now stands for brotherhood to those who offer friendship, and enmity to those who threaten the black man's cause. He has conceded, time and again, publicly, that not all whites are the same. But Vos and his fellow nationalists want no truck with whites, however good they may be.

Time moves fast, even for the Malcolms, although most whites I met regarded Malcolm as the worst in Negro extremism. If anything, my own guess is that Malcolm, like Martin Luther King, may yet be charged with 'cooling it' too soon with the white folks. I can see the younger nationalists sneering at him for his appearances at Harvard and in the pages of the *Saturday Evening Post* which carried his biography.

This aspect of Harlem's many faces left me a little frightened. I am, by nature, somewhat easy to scare. But this was something else, something quite apart from my unbrave makeup. It was a brand of black-manship such as I had not met anywhere else before.

Harlem has this element of resilient, unapologising blackmanship and not all of it is negative. I saw this at the Schomburg Library in Harlem where, for the first time in my life, I saw a collection of writings by distinguished black men. Here, again for the first time, I saw busts of black men.

This came as a thrill to me. For, where I come from, all great men are whites. The heroes in our schoolbooks and films and all the statues in our capitals are those of white men. The only black statue I ever saw was that of the great Zulu king, uShaka. Even that lies out of the way, far from the cities, and we were taught to despise the statue as a relic from our savage past.

Like any other place Harlem has its great contra-dictions. I met Negroes who sat at my feet and listened for hours to the clicks in my Zulu language. Some asked me to teach them the language. I also met Negroes who wished to have little or nothing to do with me. I think that this was partly because of a sense of embarrassment which many Negroes still feel in being associated with Africans.

There was the churchman I met in the cafeteria at the basement of his church. I told him I was a journalist from South Africa and that I wished to talk with anybody who had some time. There were many people in the cafeteria, all engaged in the chit-chats which make Sunday a great social occasion in Harlem. The churchman led me to an empty table and gave me coffee. I thought he would sit with me and talk, but he went to join the rest of the chatting crowd. He later returned to ask how I was enjoying my coffee. I said, lamely, that I was doing fine and would like to have a chat with anyone. Now the man offered me some food, but I told him I did not want to eat. At this stage, he went to the kitchen and fetched half of a roasted chicken and six or eight buns. I was to take that away with me, he said. 'That's the best I can do for you, my friend,' he said.

Thus, minus my chat, I left the place clutching a parcel of roasted chicken in one hand, plus half a dozen buns in the other. My next interviews that night were to be conducted with the splendid smell of chicken under my arm.

Rightly or unfairly, I drew certain inferences from this incident. There can be no doubt that there are many Negroes in Harlem who look down on Africans in the same way that many Johannesburg Africans foolishly despise other Africans, or the English condescend, insufferably, to Americans.

It's no use saying the churchman misunderstood me. If anything, Negroes are forever telling me how clearly I speak English. Besides, there are several similar incidents I know of. Not so long ago, an African girl was proposed to by a Negro boy. Yet, shortly before the two met for the first time, the young man had told his uncle that he might not know what to do with the girl when she appeared. 'Is she going to come with those spears and African drums, Uncle?' he had asked. I myself have been asked by Negroes if we still eat people where I come from.

Now, for this sort of thing, I am inclined to blame the white world more than anyone else. For years now, white cartoonists have been churning out stereotypes of Africans putting white hunters into black pots and boiling them. I have never lunched on anybody's ribs, and it's no use pointing at the Congo. The cartoons I speak of were done scores of years before the Congo erupted. I wonder how London or Rome or New York would feel if Africans began producing caricatures, based on true stories, of whites lynching black men or cutting their hands off as was done by the Belgians.

But there is another side to the story of Negro-African relations. A lot of people complained, for instance, that many Africans who came to New York remained downtown where the 'white girls show them a good time.' It was said that few Africans ever came among the people in Harlem.

A man recalled that some of the African politicians used to live in Africa House in Harlem when they were students. The same man charged that these Africans now spent most of their time with whites, having acquired a new status as diplomats. He said that, until recently, Africans employed white secretaries and white clerks in their embassies and no Negroes.

When Sekou Touré came to Harlem, he apparently brought a white girl to interpret from French for him. This was evidently unsatisfactory for Harlem and a Negro interpreter was hurriedly produced to replace the white one.

Yet, whatever the current feelings may be between Africans and Negroes, it would be a mistake to under-estimate the sentiments of kinship between the two.

Even *Ebony,* while peddling wigs and skin-bleaching creams, is currently running a series on 'Africa's Golden Past'. The magazine feeds Harlem constantly on stories of progress and success by Africans.

Perhaps the people I met came to life most when

they spoke of the ways in which they continuously survived and beat the odds against them. There was the young, college-trained businessman who told of the difficulties he had trying to get a job. 'They just wouldn't hire me,' he said, 'so I borrowed money and opened my own business. I figured the best thing to do was to hire them, and send them to places where my black skin would not be welcomed.'

A woman traced this attitude to a Jewish source. 'If the Jews go into a shop and get discriminated against,' she quipped, 'they buy the joint.' This seemed an attractive philosophy to me, although, heaven knows, there are too many who never reach college or know where to borrow cash to open shop.

Lewis Michaux, a bookstore owner at Harlem Square, made it the hard way. A former labourer, he 'took' and sold three pigs from his boss's farm before going into the book business. Now he is one of the pillars of Harlem.

A small man, Mr Michaux has been a nationalist of the Marcus Garvey breed for decades now. His bookstore is filled with books and magazines by and about black men all over the world. 'The House of Common Sense and the Home of Proper Propaganda' his store is called.

This is where Dr W E B Du Bois, the late Negro scholar, first met his wife, Shirley Graham. In the back room, Mr Michaux keeps something like a hall of fame. The walls of this room are covered with big and small portraits of former American Presidents.

Mr Michaux believes that Jesus was a black man. 'They lynched Jesus,' he said, 'and they don't lynch white folks!'

Old Michaux had made this claim to many groups of students from white universities, some of whom come to the shop to hear him talk. He is now writing a biography of a former American President who, Mr Michaux is satisfied, had a Negro mother.

On the Negroes in Harlem, Mr Michaux said: 'The so-called Negro has been woke up for years now, but he never got up yet. It's not enough to open your eyes and stay in bed. You got to get up and go to work as well.'

I suppose few people would go to Harlem and take no interest in the churches there. For some of the people of Harlem, the church is the very core of their lives, something which has to do with their day-to-day survival. I remember clearly the power of the organ and the singing inside those storefront churches. At times it was tragic and yet beautiful. At no time was it comical.

I saw a girl take a position behind the mike while the rest of the congregation clapped to her song, and somebody pumped the organ. At first there was a suggestion of suffering and self-pity in her voice. Then this transformed into pain, agony, which almost drove me out of the place. The handclapping took on a faster pace and more people said, 'Amen, praise the Lord, Sister!' Then, as if in a trance, the girl let out some gibberish and moaned and twisted her body and contorted her face until I thought she would smash her head on the floor. Finally, the congregation switched to a new, cheerful tune and the girl began to swing and sing the gospel blues like Mahalia Jackson.

I understood this because I used to preach in the street myself. In those few moments, the girl told the long story of misery, pain and an unbending will to survive. I visited other churches, Daddy Grace's for instance, and found people going through the same experience. Beautiful, ebony-black women rose in

turn to the mike and unleashed gospel blues, sometimes with a jazzy beat, transforming the service into
a great jazz festival.

The odd men out in Harlem are the businessmen,
the white shopkeepers. I saw them straining to be
polite and friendly to unresponsive black customers.
Some of them were aware of the disadvantages at
which Harlem is placed inside those decaying tene-
ments, with all the dope-peddling and the numbers
business. They even conceded that something ought
to be done, perhaps by the Negroes themselves. Yet
they seemed so removed from Harlem that I wondered
if they had any intimate understanding of its problems.

The most sympathetic businessman said to me:
'But for the grace of God, I could also have been born
black.' He told me about a number of Negro organisations which he supported financially and in many
other ways. I had no way of explaining effectively to
him that what he had just said might annoy a lot of
black men. For I doubt that there are many black
men who enjoy being pitied in this way.

One of the things which Le Roi Jones says in his
play *The Slave* is about just this. The central character
in the play, a Negro, says to his ex-wife, a white
woman: ' . . . you were certain, my God, so certain . . .
emotionally and intellectually, that you were right
until the only idea you had about me was to pity
me . . . '

This does not mean, however, that all Harlem is
suspicious or resentful of all whites. There are white
people who have good names in certain quarters of
Harlem. One of them was President Kennedy. A
number of people had a good word for him. 'He was
one of the few Presidents that ever came to Harlem,'
one man said, 'and he really cared about civil rights.'

Yet even Kennedy had his critics. I remember the large Harlem housewife who said: 'I never trusted him. I don't like nothin' Irish. That dirty Irishman stole the idea of the Peace Corps from us. We was going to do it ourselves.' This lady, I gathered later, was an ardent Republican.

I asked a seasoned newspaperman in Harlem to name six top Negro leaders in the order of their importance according to his judgement. He listed Martin Luther King, Roy Wilkins, Whitney Young, James Farmer, Dorothy Height and A Philip Randolph.

Of Malcolm X he said: 'I know Malcolm. He's a friend of mine. Malcolm X is a necessary evil. As long as our society is as twisted as it is, there will always be a place for the Malcolm X's. If you want to get rid of Malcolm X, begin by getting rid of the imperfections in our society.'

I did not meet any of the six leaders listed above, but I developed a deep respect for their work from what I heard people say. Harlem functions on a vast, complex scale, comprising innumerable fronts, some of which appear to be in desperate competition with each other. Harlem has its branch of the NAACP, Mobilisation for Youth, Har-you-Act and other groups. Somewhere, somehow, all these organisations as well as many others, find a common focal point where most of their pressure converges, all in the business of finding a place in the sun for black America. This is the only way I could explain finding a drawing of Du Bois, Martin Luther King and Ralph Bunche in Malcolm X's head office.

Richard Rive
THE VISITS

It was on the evening The Student had gone out that
The Woman had first arrived. It wasn't actually a
visit, but that was the nearest he could come to it. He
remembered it very clearly. First the phone call for
The Student, some girl or other (the ringing sounded
brazen and adolescent), then the front-door banging.
The Student revving his engine and the tortured
whine as the Honda gathered speed up the driveway.

He was distinctly annoyed. He went to the front-
door, opened it, peered out from long habit, then
closed the door gently as if to make up to it for The
Student's treatment. He returned to his study and sat
down at the cluttered desk. Should he read or mark
books? He was busy fighting his way through *A
Century of South African Verse in English*. What a
bore. What a boring bore. Should he mark the
Standard Ten compos instead? Mark books?

There was a quietness which settled over the flat. It
was like that whenever The Student went out and he
took the phone off the cradle. The silence surging
softly . . . but first the storm before the calm. The
phone, then the revving of that damn engine, then

peace. Mark books. Standard Ten compos. Remember,
dearest children, the word *can* denotes ability,
whereas *may* denotes possibility. Ability and possibility. Can ability. May possibility. Can-ability, may-
possibility. He repeated it mentally until a rhythm
formed. May-possibility sounded clumsy, so he
changed it to canability, mayability. But that was
wrong. Sacrificing meaning for rhythm. Maybe he
could use it on his seniors. His students. The Student?

He got up, uncomfortable at the triviality of his
ideas. Must be getting old. Mr Chips. Old at forty-
five. Young at forty-five. He walked to the kitchen to
make some tea and turned on the tap for hot water.
The gurgle echoed through the flat. How vacant the
place sounded without The Student. How empty
when he wasn't there. How empty when he was there.
A different kind of emptiness.

Impossible to speak to him any longer. He was too
. . . too physical. Throwing his weight and looks
around. Girls, the telephone and the Honda. Looks
and muscle. A student of rags and tatters. He switched
on the stove reflectively, and put on the water. Mayability, canability. Canability, mayability.

It was then that he heard the knocking at the
door. Not loudly but it could be heard throughout
the flat. Who could it be? He was curious but didn't
answer the door at once. He fussed loudly in the
kitchen to show that he was in (he knew he could be
heard at the entrance), until the knocking was repeated. He coughed and said, 'Coming.'

When he opened the door he was surprised and dis-
appointed to see the African woman standing there.

'Yes?' he asked somewhat annoyed.

She said nothing, just stood there, her eyes downcast. He took in her appearance. She was extremely

unattractive, seemed all of a heap from her doughy bosom to her thick ankles hanging over her shoes.

'Yes?' he repeated, showing his impatience.

She looked at him for the first time and he noticed a mixture of shyness and aggression. He felt like shutting the door on her, but was incapable of such behaviour. He braced himself and became the teacher. (For God's sake boy, open your mouth when you recite. Can denotes ability. May possibility.)

Then she said in a half-whisper, 'I want food.' And as an afterthought, 'Please.'

It was the way she said it that made him look at her more closely. Although she whispered, her tone was not servile or pleading. She spoke almost as if the asking for food was hers by right. Not quite a demand, more a taking for granted. He wanted her to go, but there was something about her he didn't quite understand. He couldn't see her eyes very clearly but sensed they were laughing and mocking him. When he tried to see she cast them down.

'Food?' he repeated, and knew he sounded foolish. She maintained her silence, not looking him in the face.

'Wait here, I'll see.' He realized that this was a sign of defeat. But why should he be defeated? There was no contest, or was there? What he knew was that he had to get away from her. He wished The Student was there. He could deal physically with the situation. But this was so different. He went back to the kitchen and stood for some time staring at the water boiling over on the stove and hissing on the plate. Then he opened the provisions cupboard and started filling an empty carrier bag. Sugar, rice, a tin of mushrooms. There was some apricot jam left over, a bottle of pickles, stuffed olives. What the hell could she do with stuffed olives? He opened the fridge and removed cheese, butter and two pints of milk. Then he opened the bread bin. He stared at the bulging carrier on the kitchen table.

He seemed afraid to face her and hoped she would be gone by the time he returned to the door. He decided to have a cup of tea while playing for time. Should he invite her in? He smiled and decided against the tea. Then resolutely he took the paper carrier. Give her the food and tell her to get the hell away.

When he handed over the provisions she made a slight, old-fashioned bow. It seemed comical because he estimated she could not be more than forty. Still, one could never tell with these people. Or could one?

'Thank you,' she said in the same whisper. Then she was gone. He returned to the kitchen and felt relieved, and for no reason at all, he felt completely exhausted.

The second time The Woman came it was almost like her first visit. Had she visited him? One did not visit and ask for food. The Student was out again (flexing his muscles at some giddy fresher in a coffee bar). He had been in his study for some time reading the book on South African verse. It wasn't quite as boring as he had thought at first.

Roy Campbell. *Upon a dark and gloomy night.* Yes it was a dark and gloomy night. Outside it was dark with squalls of north-wester. *Upon a gloomy night with nobody in sight, I went abroad when all my house was hushed.* To waste the poetry of that great Spanish mystic St John of the Cross upon the snot-nosed brats in his matriculation class. (For goodness sake, try to feel what the poet is trying to get at.

Feel the *brio*.) They lived for Hondas and girls and pop. Telephones and screaming singers. The Animals. The Insecticides.

He settled down for more Roy Campbell. *In safety, in disguise, in darkness up the secret stair I crept . . .* he recognized the knock at once when it came and was afraid to answer.

She stood halfway in the shadow of the entrance but he had no difficulty recognizing the dumpy figure, the heavy legs and the downcast eyes. This time he was determined that she should speak first. She had the empty carrier bag with her. He didn't want to break the silence. Somehow he seemed afraid of his own voice. She held out the bag without saying anything.

'What is it this time?' he said in his schoolmaster voice. Then he regretted his tone and felt his attitude was wrong, far too aggressive. There was certainly no cause for aggression.

'More food?' he asked, hoping he sounded friendly.

'Yes, please,' she said at last.

He went into the kitchen and half-filled the bag with all the left-overs he could find. By the time he returned he felt more at ease, more in control of himself, and was determined to speak.

'Tell me,' he said without handing over the bag, 'what is your name? Who are you?'

She mumbled something which sounded like Edith. The surname was inaudible. He didn't bother to ask her to repeat it.

'Now look here, Edith or whoever you are.' He spoke faster than usual, his voice a trifle raspy. 'Now look here. You're a grown woman. You should be working instead of begging like this. Take the carrier but don't come back here again. Do you understand?'

She nodded slightly and took the food with the same old-fashioned bow. Then, like the first time, she was gone.

He went back to his study and slumped down in the chair. He took up his book but had no further interest in Roy Campbell. Edith something or other. For God's sake why must she come to him? What had he done to her? What had he done for her? He felt guilty but there was nothing he could think of to feel guilty about. He had given her food. He had done his duty. What was his duty and why should he do it? Again the nagging feeling of guilt. Well, he had to tell her not to come again. Couldn't keep giving food away. Not a charitable institution. He wished The Student would come home earlier so that they could talk. No, not about The Woman necessarily. Only just talk.

He sat in the dark until well after eleven o'clock when he heard The Student's Honda whining up the driveway. Then he went to bed.

Even after her third visit he said nothing to The Student about it. They seldom spoke and communicated only when it was necessary. (The Student was in sometimes now because examinations were pressing.) The night of her third visit, however, The Student was out, and he was alone in the flat, although himself on the verge of going out. He was going out more frequently now. He sometimes visited two members of his staff with whom he was quite intimate, and his one married sister. Most times he sat in the Public Library reading until closing time. He even went to cinemas although he detested them. What he seemed afraid of was being alone in the flat. The loneliness got him down. Or was it the aloneness. He used to enjoy it before. The silence, his books, his

pipe. A cup of tea and a small brandy with water
before turning in for the night. He couldn't stand the
sameness any longer. And the loneliness. One tired
of too much routine.

He had put on his overcoat and prepared himself
mentally for the brisk walk to the library. The dark
shadows of the trees lining the avenue, the smell of
rain. He was about to pick up his books when the
knock came. He looked around for possible escape
routes but there was only the bathroom window and
he realized how absurd it was for him to climb
through that.

She stood in the doorway holding the same empty
carrier.

'But I told you not to come back!' He tried to
control himself. 'I told you not to come again.'

She maintained her silence, her eyes, as usual,
downcast. He clenched the library books till he could
feel the edges cutting into his palm.

'Do you understand me?'

She nodded slightly.

'I told you to stay away! Do you understand? Stay
away!' She stood dumbly, not looking at him.

'If you come again I'll be forced to call the police.
Police!' he repeated.

She started slightly and cast a quick glance at him.
He felt it was hostile.

'Police!' he repeated. 'Police!'

There was a pause that lasted longer than it should
have done.

'Hell,' he said, dropping the books on the table.
'Hell, what do I do now?' He decided to try to be
reasonable and sat down wearily. 'Where you from?'

She kept her eyes down, not replying.

'Look,' he said frustratedly, 'I'll give you food for

the last time. For the last time. You understand? You must never come again. If you do come I'll call the police. Then you'll go to jail! Understand?'

She stared at him, her eyes no longer downcast.

'Jail! Police! Jail!'

Then he noticed, almost with a start, that she was crying. Two tears rolled down her cheeks but her face remained immobile. The tears did not seem part of her. He felt the sense of guilt again, felt like assuring her that he would not call the police. That he was only pretending. But she must not come again.

He went into the kitchen, and when he returned she took the carrier with the same quaint bow. He watched her walking down the driveway. Then he saw another dark figure joining her. They seemed to speak for a short time, but it was too far for him to hear what they were saying. She pointed at him still standing in the open doorway. The other figure (he could not make out the sex) also turned. He heard their loud laughter. He shut the door and felt sick to the stomach.

She came again the following week after that, and every week after that. Now he merely went to the door, took her empty carrier and then filled it. No words passed between them, only the ritual. The quaint bow and she was gone. He bought extra groceries which he set aside for her. She did not always come on the same evening, but she never came more than once a week. She seemed to time it so that The Student was out and he was in.

Although he watched her when she left, he never saw her companion again. He started suffering from lack of sleep, was short tempered with his pupils at school and was seriously thinking of giving The Student notice and then himself moving from the flat. There was no one to whom he could speak seriously about the visits.

He told The Student about it one evening but he turned it into a joke and they both laughed. He seemed to welcome and dread her visits at the same time. He wanted to find out more about her, follow her and see where she lived. Was she married? Did she have children? Why did she have to beg? Was it only to him she came? But somehow he was afraid, afraid he might find out. He could ask her in, give her some tea and then ask questions. He was afraid of her answers.

Then one week she did not appear. Her groceries remained in the closet. The following week she did not come either. He kept her groceries in case. After she had not appeared for a month he decided to use the provisions he had bought for her. With a strange sense of fear he opened the bags and was relieved when nothing happened. He felt as if an enormous burden had dropped from his shoulders and wanted to speak to someone about it. Anyone. The Student was in his room trying in vain to study. He made some coffee and took it to The Student, standing in the doorway, attempting to keep the conversation alive.

'By the way,' The Student said, not annoyed at being disturbed, 'your girl friend turned up last week but you were out.'

'I was out?' he said, bewildered. He was eager to know more.

'I answered the door and there she was. What an ugly bitch.'

'Yes?' He hoped he didn't sound over-anxious.

'I told her to get away, clear off, hamba!' He waved his arms to indicate the action. 'She wouldn't.'

'What did you do?' His lips were trembling.

'What you should have done the first time.'

'What I should have done?'

'Yes. I took her by her black neck and frog-marched her down the driveway. Then threw her out.'

He felt a tightening across his chest. His fists balled and he felt like hitting The Student. He was shivering all over.

'She won't come again,' The Student assured him.

'You shouldn't have done that.' He tried to control his voice.

'Why the hell not?' The Student looked at him puzzled.

'You shouldn't have done that,' he repeated lamely.

'Are you sick or something?' The Student asked.

'I'm all right. Only have to get back to my books. Marking to be done.'

The Student looked at him in a strange way. Then the phone rang.

He went into his study and slumped down at the desk. He felt like crying but couldn't. He heard The Student banging the front door then the revving of the Honda engine. Long after the whine had faded away he sat at his desk just staring in the dark.

Doris Lessing
NO WITCHCRAFT FOR SALE

The Farquars had been childless for years when little
Teddy was born; and they were touched by the
pleasure of their servants, who brought presents of
fowls and eggs and flowers to the homestead when
they came to rejoice over the baby, exclaiming with
delight over his downy golden head and his blue eyes.
They congratulated Mrs Farquar as if she had achieved
a very great thing, and she felt that she had — her
smile for the lingering, admiring natives was warm
and grateful.

Later, when Teddy had his first haircut, Gideon
the cook picked up the soft gold tufts from the
ground, and held them reverently in his hand. Then
he smiled at the little boy and said: 'Little Yellow
Head.' That became the native name for the child.
Gideon and Teddy were great friends from the first.
When Gideon had finished his work, he would lift
Teddy on his shoulders to the shade of a big tree, and
play with him there, forming curious little toys from
twigs and leaves and grass, or shaping animals from
wetted soil. When Teddy learned to walk it was often
Gideon who crouched before him, clucking encourage-

ment, finally catching him when he fell, tossing him
up in the air till they both became breathless with
laughter. Mrs Farquar was fond of the old cook
because of his love for her child.

There was no second baby; and one day Gideon
said: 'Ah missus, missus, the Lord above sent this
one; Little Yellow Head is the most good thing we
have in our house.' Because of that 'we' Mrs Farquar
felt a warm impulse towards her cook; and at the end
of the month she raised his wages. He had been with
her now for several years; he was one of the few
natives who had his wife and children in the compound
and never wanted to go home to his kraal, which was
some hundreds of miles away. Sometimes a small
piccanin, who had been born the same time as Teddy,
could be seen peering from the edge of the bush,
staring in awe at the little white boy with his
miraculous fair hair and northern blue eyes. The two
little children would gaze at each other with a wide,
interested gaze, and once Teddy put out his hand
curiously to touch the black child's cheeks and hair.

Gideon, who was watching, shook his head
wonderingly, and said: 'Ah, missus, these are both
children, and one will grow up to be a Baas, and one
will be a servant,' and Mrs Farquar smiled and said
sadly, 'Yes, Gideon, I was thinking the same.' She
sighed. 'It is God's will,' said Gideon, who was a
mission boy. The Farquars were very religious people;
and this shared feeling about God bound servant and
masters even closer together.

Teddy was about six years old when he was given a
scooter, and discovered the intoxications of speed.
All day he would fly around the homestead, in and
out of flowerbeds, scattering squawking chickens and
irritated dogs, finishing with a wide dizzying arc into

the kitchen door. There he would cry: 'Gideon, look at me!' And Gideon would laugh and say: 'Very clever, Little Yellow Head.' Gideon's youngest son, who was now a herdboy, came especially up from the compound to see the scooter. He was afraid to come near it, but Teddy showed off in front of him. 'Piccanin,' shouted Teddy, 'get out of my way!' And he raced in circles around the black child until he was frightened, and fled back to the bush.

'Why did you frighten him?' asked Gideon, gravely reproachful.

Teddy said defiantly: 'He's only a black boy,' and laughed. Then, when Gideon turned away from him without speaking, his face fell. Very soon he slipped into the house and found an orange and brought it to Gideon, saying: 'This is for you.' He could not bring himself to say he was sorry; but he could not bear to lose Gideon's affection either. Gideon took the orange unwillingly and sighed. 'Soon you will be going away to school, Little Yellow Head,' he said wonderingly, 'and then you will be grown up.' He shook his head gently and said, 'And that's how our lives go.' He seemed to be putting a distance between himself and Teddy, not because of resentment, but in the way a person accepts something inevitable. The baby had lain in his arms and smiled up into his face: the tiny boy had swung from his shoulders, had played with him by the hour. Now Gideon would not let his flesh touch the flesh of the white child. He was kind, but there was a grave formality in his voice that made Teddy pout and sulk away. Also, it made him into a man: with Gideon he was polite, and carried himself formally, and if he came into the kitchen to ask for something, it was in the way a white man uses towards a servant, expecting to be obeyed.

But on the day that Teddy came staggering into
the kitchen with his fists to his eyes, shrieking with
pain, Gideon dropped the pot full of hot soup that he
was holding, rushed to the child, and forced aside his
fingers. 'A snake!' he exclaimed. Teddy had been on
his scooter, and had come to a rest with his foot on
the side of a big tub of plants. A tree-snake, hanging
by its tail from the roof, had spat full into his eyes.
Mrs Farquar came running when she heard the
commotion. 'He'll go blind,' she sobbed, holding
Teddy close against her. 'Gideon, he'll go blind!'
Already the eyes, with perhaps half an hour's sight
left in them, were swollen up to the size of fists:
Teddy's small white face was distorted by great
purple oozing protuberances. Gideon said: 'Wait a
minute, missus, I'll get some medicine.' He ran off
into the bush.

Mrs Farquar lifted the child into the house and
bathed his eyes with permanganate. She had scarcely
heard Gideon's words; but when she saw that her
remedies had no effect at all, and remembered how
she had seen natives with no sight in their eyes,
because of the spitting of a snake, she began to look
for the return of her cook, remembering what she had
heard of the efficacy of native herbs. She stood by
the window, holding the terrified, sobbing little boy
in her arms, and peered helplessly into the bush. It
was not more than a few minutes before she saw
Gideon come bounding back, and in his hand he held
a plant.

'Do not be afraid, missus,' said Gideon, 'this will
cure Little Yellow Head's eyes.' He stripped the
leaves from the plant, leaving a small white fleshy
root. Without even washing it, he put the root in his
mouth, chewed it vigorously, and then held the

spittle there while he took the child forcibly from Mrs Farquar. He gripped Teddy down between his knees, and pressed the balls of his thumbs into the swollen eyes, so that the child screamed and Mrs Farquar cried out in protest: 'Gideon, Gideon!' But Gideon took no notice. He knelt over the writhing child, pushing back the puffy lids till chinks of eye-ball showed, and then he spat hard, again and again, into first one eye and then the other. He finally lifted Teddy gently into his mother's arms, and said: 'His eyes will get better.' But Mrs Farquar was weeping with terror, and she could hardly thank him: it was impossible to believe that Teddy could keep his sight. In a couple of hours the swellings were gone; the eyes were inflamed and tender but Teddy could see. Mr and Mrs Farquar went to Gideon in the kitchen and thanked him over and over again. They felt help-less because of their gratitude: it seemed they could do nothing to express it. They gave Gideon presents for his wife and children, and a big increase in wages, but these things could not pay for Teddy's now completely cured eyes. Mrs Farquar said: 'Gideon, God chose you as an instrument for His goodness,' and Gideon said: 'Yes, missus, God is very good.'

Now, when such a thing happens on a farm, it cannot be long before everyone hears of it. Mr and Mrs Farquar told their neighbours and the story was discussed from one end of the district to the other. The bush is full of secrets. No one can live in Africa, or at least on the veld, without learning very soon that there is an ancient wisdom of leaf and soil and season — and, too, perhaps most important of all, of the darker tracts of the human mind — which is the black man's heritage. Up and down the district people were telling anecdotes, reminding each other of things that had happened to them.

'But I saw it myself, I tell you. It was a puff-adder bite. The kaffir's arm was swollen to the elbow, like a great shiny black bladder. He was groggy after half a minute. He was dying. Then suddenly a kaffir walked out of the bush with his hands full of green stuff. He smeared something on the place, and next day my boy was back at work, and all you could see was two small punctures in the skin.'

This was the kind of tale they told. And, as always, with a certain amount of exasperation, because while all of them knew that in the bush of Africa are waiting valuable drugs locked in bark, in simple-looking leaves, in roots, it was impossible to ever get the truth about them from the natives themselves.

The story eventually reached town; and perhaps it was at a sundowner party, or some such function, that a doctor, who happened to be there, challenged it. 'Nonsense,' he said. 'These things get exaggerated in the telling. We are always checking up on this kind of story, and we draw a blank every time.'

Anyway, one morning there arrived a strange car at the homestead, and out stepped one of the workers from the laboratory in town, with cases full of test-tubes and chemicals.

Mr and Mrs Farquar were flustered and pleased and flattered. They asked the scientist to lunch, and they told the story all over again, for the hundredth time. Little Teddy was there too, his blue eyes sparkling with health, to prove the truth of it. The scientist explained how humanity might benefit if this new drug could be offered for sale; and the Farquars were even more pleased: they were kind, simple people, who liked to think of something good coming about because of them. But when the scientist began talking of the money that might result, their manner showed discomfort. Their feelings over the miracle (that was how they thought of it) were so strong and deep and religious, that it was distasteful to them to think of money. The scientist, seeing their faces, went back to his first point which was the advancement of humanity. He was perhaps a trifle perfunctory: it was not the first time he had come salting the tail of a fabulous bush-secret.

Eventually, when the meal was over, the Farquars called Gideon into their living-room and explained to him that this baas, here, was a Big Doctor from the Big City, and he had come all that way to see Gideon. At this Gideon seemed afraid; he did not understand; and Mrs Farquar explained quickly that it was because of the wonderful thing he had done with Teddy's eyes that the Big Baas had come.

Gideon looked from Mrs Farquar to Mr Farquar, and then at the little boy, who was showing great importance because of the occasion. At last he said grudgingly: 'The Big Baas wants to know what medicine I used?' He spoke incredulously, as if he could not believe his old friends could so betray him. Mr Farquar began explaining how a useful medicine could be made out of the root, and how it could be put on sale, and how thousands of people, black and white, up and down the continent of Africa, could be saved by the medicine when that spitting snake filled their eyes with poison. Gideon listened, his eyes bent on the ground, the skin of his forehead puckering in discomfort. When Mr Farquar had finished he did not reply. The scientist, who all this time had been leaning back in a big chair, sipping his coffee and smiling with sceptical good-humour, chipped in and explained all over again, in different words, about the making of drugs and the progress of science. Also, he offered Gideon a present.

There was silence after this further explanation, and then Gideon remarked indifferently that he could not remember the root. His face was sullen and hostile, even when he looked at the Farquars, whom he usually treated like old friends. They were beginning to feel annoyed; and this feeling annulled the guilt that had been sprung into life by Gideon's accusing manner. They were beginning to feel that he was unreasonable. But it was at that moment that they all realized he would never give in. The magical drug would remain where it was, unknown and useless except for the tiny scattering of Africans who had the knowledge, natives who might be digging a ditch for the municipality in a ragged shirt and a pair of patched shorts, but who were still born to healing, hereditary healers, being the nephews or sons of the old witchdoctors whose ugly masks and bits of bone and all the uncouth properties of magic were the outward signs of real power and wisdom.

The Farquars might tread on that plant fifty times a day as they passed from house to garden, from cow kraal to mealie field, but they would never know it.

But they went on persuading and arguing, with all the force of their exasperation; and Gideon continued to say that he could not remember, or that there was no such root, or that it was the wrong season of the year, or that it wasn't the root itself, but the spit from his mouth that had cured Teddy's eyes. He said all these things one after another, and seemed not to care they were contradictory. He was rude and stubborn. The Farquars could hardly recognize their gentle, loveable old servant in this ignorant, perversely obstinate African, standing there in front of them with lowered eyes, his hands twitching his cook's apron, repeating over and over whichever one of the stupid refusals that first entered his head.

And suddenly he appeared to give in. He lifted his head, gave a long, blank angry look at the circle of whites, who seemed to him like a circle of yelping dogs pressing around him, and said: 'I will show you the root.'

They walked single file away from the homestead down a kaffir path. It was a blazing December afternoon, with the sky full of hot rain-clouds. Everything was hot: the sun was like a bronze tray whirling overhead, there was a heat shimmer over the fields, the soil was scorching underfoot, the dusty wind blew gritty and thick and warm in their faces. It was a terrible day, fit only for reclining on a verandah with iced drinks, which is where they would normally have been at that hour.

From time to time, remembering that on the day of the snake it had taken ten minutes to find the root, someone asked: 'Is it much further, Gideon?' And Gideon would answer over his shoulder, with angry politeness: 'I'm looking for the root, baas.' And indeed, he would frequently bend sideways and trail his hand among the grasses with a gesture that was insulting in its perfunctoriness. He walked them through the bush along unknown paths for two hours, in that melting destroying heat, so that the sweat trickled coldly down them and their heads ached. They were all quite silent: the Farquars because they were angry, the scientist because he was being proved right again; there was no such plant. His was a tactful silence.

At last, six miles from the house, Gideon suddenly decided they had had enough; or perhaps his anger evaporated at that moment. He picked up, without an attempt at looking anything but casual, a handful of blue flowers from the grass, flowers that had been growing plentifully all down the paths they had come.

He handed them to the scientist without looking at him, and marched off by himself on the way home, leaving them to follow him if they chose.

When they got back to the house, the scientist went to the kitchen to thank Gideon: he was being very polite, even though there was an amused look in his eyes. Gideon was not there. Throwing the flowers casually into the back of his car, the eminent visitor departed on his way back to his laboratory.

Gideon was back in his kitchen in time to prepare dinner, but he was sulking. He spoke to Mrs Farquar like an unwilling servant. It was days before they liked each other again.

The Farquars made enquiries about the root from their labourers. Sometimes they were answered with distrustful stares. Sometimes the natives said: 'We do not know. We have never heard of the root.' One, the cattle boy, who had been with them a long time, and had grown to trust them a little said: 'Ask your boy in the kitchen. Now, there's a doctor for you. He's the son of a famous medicine man who used to be in these parts, and there's nothing he cannot cure.' Then he added politely: 'Of course, he's not as good as the whiteman's doctor, we know that, but he's good for us.'

After some time, when the soreness had gone from between the Farquars and Gideon, they began to joke: 'When are you going to show us the snake-root, Gideon?' And he would laugh and shake his head, saying, a little uncomfortably: 'But I did show you, missus, have you forgotten?'

Much later, Teddy, as a schoolboy, would come into the kitchen and say: 'You old rascal, Gideon! Do you remember that time you tricked us all by making us walk miles all over the veld for nothing? It was so far my father had to carry me!'

And Gideon would double up with polite laughter. After much laughing, he would suddenly straighten himself up, wipe his old eyes, and look sadly at Teddy, who was grinning mischievously at him across the kitchen: 'Ah, Little Yellow Head, how you have grown! Soon you will be grown up with a farm of your own . . .'

Nadine Gordimer
SIX FEET OF THE COUNTRY

My wife and I are not real farmers — not even Lerice, really. We bought our place, ten miles out of Johannesburg on one of the main roads, to change something in ourselves, I suppose; you seem to rattle about so much within a marriage like ours. You long to hear nothing but a deep satisfying silence when you sound a marriage. The farm hasn't managed that for us, of course, but it has done other things, unexpected, illogical. Lerice, who I thought would retire there in Chekhovian sadness for a month or two, and then leave the place to the servants while she tried yet again to get a part she wanted and become the actress she would like to be, has sunk into the business of running the farm with all the serious intensity with which she once imbued the shadows in a playwright's mind. I should have given it up long ago if it had not been for her. Her hands, once small and plain and well kept — she was not the sort of actress who wears red paint and diamond rings — are hard as a dog's pads.

I, of course, am there only in the evenings and at weekends. I am a partner in a luxury-travel agency, which is flourishing — needs to be, as I tell Lerice, in order to carry the farm. Still, though I know we can't afford it, and though the sweetish smell of the fowls Lerice breeds sickens me, so that I avoid going past their runs, the farm is beautiful in a way I had almost forgotten — especially on a Sunday morning when I get up and go out into the paddock and see not the palm trees and fishpond and imitation-stone bird bath of the suburbs but white ducks on the dam, the lucerne field brilliant as window dresser's grass, and the little stocky, mean-eyed bull, lustful but bored, having his face tenderly licked by one of his ladies. Lerice comes out with her hair uncombed, in her hand a stick dripping with cattle dip. She will stand and look dreamily for a moment, the way she would pretend to look sometimes in those plays. 'They'll mate tomorrow,' she will say. 'This is their second day. Look how she loves him, my little Napoleon.' So that when people come out to see us on Sunday afternoon, I am likely to hear myself saying as I pour out the drinks, 'When I drive back home from the city every day, past those rows of suburban houses, I wonder how the devil we ever did stand it . . . Would you care to look around?' And there I am, taking some pretty girl and her young husband stumbling down to our riverbank, the girl catching her stockings on the mealie-stooks and stepping over cow turds humming with jewelgreen flies while she says, '. . . the tensions of the damned city. And you're near enough to get into town to a show, too! I think it's wonderful. Why, you've got it both ways!'

And for a moment I accept the triumph as if I *had* managed it — the impossibility that I've been trying for all my life — just as if the truth was that you could get it 'both ways', instead of finding yourself

with not even one way or the other but a third, one
you had not provided for at all.

But even in our saner moments, when I find Lerice's
earthy enthusiasms just as irritating as I once found
her histrionical ones, and she finds what she calls my
'jealousy' of her capacity for enthusiasms as big a
proof of my inadequacy for her as a mate as ever it
was, we do believe that we have at least honestly
escaped those tensions peculiar to the city about
which our visitors speak. When Johannesburg people
speak of 'tension', they don't mean hurrying people
in crowded streets, the struggle for money, or the
general competitive character of city life. They mean
the guns under the white men's pillows and the
burglar bars on the white men's windows. They mean
those strange moments on city pavements when a
black man won't stand aside for a white man.

Out in the country, even ten miles out, life is
better than that. In the country, there is a lingering
remnant of the pretransitional stage; our relationship
with the blacks is almost feudal. Wrong, I suppose,
obsolete, but more comfortable all around. We have
no burglar bars, no gun. Lerice's farm boys have their
wives and their piccanins living with them on the
land. They brew their sour beer without the fear of
police raids. In fact, we've always rather prided
ourselves that the poor devils have nothing much to
fear, being with us; Lerice even keeps an eye on their
children, with all the competence of a woman who
has never had a child of her own, and she certainly
doctors them all — children and adults — like babies
whenever they happen to be sick.

It was because of this that we were not particularly
startled one night last winter when the boy Albert
came knocking at our window long after we had gone

to bed. I wasn't in our bed but sleeping in the little dressing-room-*cum*-linen-room next door, because Lerice had annoyed me and I didn't want to find myself softening towards her simply because of the sweet smell of the talcum powder on her flesh after her bath. She came and woke me up. 'Albert says one of the boys is very sick,' she said. 'I think you'd better go down and see. He wouldn't get us up at this hour for nothing.'

'What time is it?'

'What does it matter?' Lerice is maddeningly logical.

I got up awkwardly as she watched me — how is it I always feel a fool when I have deserted her bed? After all, I know from the way she never looks at me when she talks to me at breakfast the next day that she is hurt and humiliated at my not wanting her — and I went out, clumsy with sleep.

'Which of the boys is it?' I asked Albert as we followed the dance of my torch.

'He's too sick. Very sick, *Baas,*' he said.

'But who? Franz?' I remembered Franz had had a bad cough for the past week.

Albert did not answer; he had given me the path, and was walking along beside me in the tall dead grass. When the light of the torch caught his face, I saw that he looked acutely embarrassed. 'What's this all about?' I said.

He lowered his head under the glance of the light. 'It's not me, *Baas.* I don't know. Petrus he send me.'

Irritated, I hurried him along to the huts. And there, on Petrus's iron bedstead, with its brick stilts, was a young man, dead. On his forehead there was still a light, cold sweat; his body was warm. The boys stood around as they do in the kitchen when it is

discovered that someone has broken a dish — unco-
operative, silent. Somebody's wife hung about in the
shadows, her hands wrung together under her apron.

I had not seen a dead man since the war. This was
very different. I felt like the others — extraneous,
useless. 'What was the matter?' I asked.

The woman patted at her chest and shook her head
to indicate the painful impossibility of breathing.

He must have died of pneumonia.

I turned to Petrus. 'Who was this boy? What was
he doing here?' The light of a candle on the floor
showed that Petrus was weeping. He followed me out
the door.

When we were outside, in the dark, I waited for
him to speak. But he didn't. 'Now, come on, Petrus,
you must tell me who this boy was. Was he a friend
of yours?'

'He's my brother, *Baas*. He came from Rhodesia to
look for work.'

The story startled Lerice and me a little. The young
boy had walked down from Rhodesia to look for
work in Johannesburg, had caught a chill from sleeping
out along the way, and had lain ill in his brother
Petrus's hut since his arrival three days before. Our
boys had been frightened to ask us for help for him
because we had never been intended ever to know of
his presence. Rhodesian natives are barred from
entering the Union unless they have a permit; the
young man was an illegal immigrant. No doubt our
boys had managed the whole thing successfully
several times before; a number of relatives must have
walked the seven or eight hundred miles from poverty
to the paradise of zoot suits, police raids, and black

slum townships that is their *Egoli,* City of Gold — the
Bantu name for Johannesburg. It was merely a matter
of getting such a man to lie low on our farm until a
job could be found with someone who would be
glad to take the risk of prosecution for employing an
illegal immigrant in exchange for the services of
someone as yet untainted by the city.

Well, this was one who would never get up again.

'You would think they would have felt they could
tell *us,'* said Lerice next morning. 'Once the man was
ill. You would have thought at least —' When she is
getting intense over something, she has a way of
standing in the middle of a room as people do when
they are shortly to leave on a journey, looking
searchingly about her at the most familiar objects as
if she had never seen them before. I had noticed that
in Petrus's presence in the kitchen, earlier, she had
had the air of being almost offended with him, almost
hurt.

In any case, I really haven't the time or inclination
any more to go into everything in our life that I know
Lerice, from those alarmed and pressing eyes of hers,
would like us to go into. She is the kind of woman
who doesn't mind if she looks plain, or odd; I don't
suppose she would even care if she knew how strange
she looks when her whole face is out of proportion
with urgent uncertainty. I said, 'Now I'm the one
who'll have to do all the dirty work, I suppose.'

She was still staring at me, trying me out with
those eyes — wasting her time, if she only knew.

'I'll have to notify the health authorities,' I said
calmly. 'They can't just cart him off and bury him.
After all, we don't really know what he died of.'

She simply stood there, as if she had given up —
simply ceased to see me at all.

I don't know when I've been so irritated. 'It might have been something contagious,' I said. 'God knows.' There was no answer.

I am not enamoured of holding conversations with myself. I went out to shout to one of the boys to open the garage and get the car ready for my morning drive to town.

As I had expected, it turned out to be quite a business. I had to notify the police as well as the health authorities, and answer a lot of tedious questions: How was it I was ignorant of the boy's presence? If I did not supervise my native quarters, how did I know that that sort of thing didn't go on all the time? Et cetera, et cetera. And when I flared up and told them that so long as my natives did their work, I didn't think it my right or concern to poke my nose into their private lives, I got from the coarse, dull-witted police sergeant one of those looks that come not from any thinking process going on in the brain but from that faculty common to all who are possessed by the master-race theory — a look of insanely inane certainty. He grinned at me with a mixture of scorn and delight at my stupidity.

Then I had to explain to Petrus why the health authorities had to take away the body for a post-mortem — and, in fact, what a post-mortem was. When I telephoned the health department some days later to find out the result, I was told that the cause of death was, as we had thought, pneumonia, and that the body had been suitably disposed of. I went out to where Petrus was mixing a mash for the fowls and told him that it was all right, there would be no trouble; his brother had died from that pain in his chest. Petrus put down the paraffin tin and said, 'When can we go to fetch him, *Baas?*'

'To fetch him?'

'Will the *Baas* please ask them when we must come?'

I went back inside and called Lerice, all over the house. She came down the stairs from the spare bedrooms, and I said, '*Now* what am I going to do? When I told Petrus, he just asked calmly when they could go and fetch the body. They think they're going to bury him themselves.'

'Well, go back and tell him,' said Lerice. 'You must tell him. Why didn't you tell him then?'

When I found Petrus again, he looked up politely. 'Look, Petrus,' I said. 'You can't go to fetch your brother. They've done it already — they've *buried* him, you understand?'

'Where?' he said slowly, dully, as if he thought that perhaps he was getting this wrong.

'You see, he was a stranger. They knew he wasn't from here, and they didn't know he had some of his people here so they thought they must bury him.' It was difficult to make a pauper's grave sound like a privilege.

'Please, *Baas,* the *Baas* must ask them.' But he did not mean that he wanted to know the burial place. He simply ignored the incomprehensible machinery I told him had set to work on his dead brother; he wanted the brother back.

'But, Petrus,' I said, 'how can I? Your brother is buried already. I can't ask them now.'

'Oh, *Baas!*' he said. He stood with his bran-smeared hands uncurled at his sides, one corner of his mouth twitching.

'Good God, Petrus, they won't listen to me! They can't, anyway. I'm sorry, but I can't do it. You understand?'

He just kept on looking at me, out of his knowledge that white men have everything, can do anything; if they don't, it is because they won't.

And then, at dinner, Lerice started. 'You could at least phone,' she said.

'Christ, what d'you think I am? Am I supposed to bring the dead back to life?'

But I could not exaggerate my way out of this ridiculous responsibility that had been thrust on me. 'Phone them up,' she went on. 'And at least you'll be able to tell him you've done it and they've explained that it's impossible.'

She disappeared somewhere into the kitchen quarters after coffee. A little later she came back to tell me, 'The old father's coming down from Rhodesia to be at the funeral. He's got a permit and he's already on his way.'

Unfortunately, it was not impossible to get the body back. The authorities said that it was somewhat irregular, but that since the hygiene conditions had been fulfilled, they could not refuse permission for exhumation. I found out that, with the undertaker's charges, it would cost twenty pounds. Ah, I thought, that settles it. On five pounds a month, Petrus won't have twenty pounds — and just as well, since it couldn't do the dead any good. Certainly I should not offer it to him myself. Twenty pounds — or anything else within reason, for that matter — I would have spent without grudging it on doctors or medicines that might have helped the boy when he was alive. Once he was dead, I had no intention of encouraging Petrus to throw away, on a gesture, more than he spent to clothe his whole family in a year.

When I told him, in the kitchen that night, he said,

'Twenty pounds?'

I said, 'Yes, that's right, twenty pounds.'

For a moment, I had the feeling, from the look on his face, that he was calculating. But when he spoke again I thought I must have imagined it. 'We must pay twenty pounds!' he said in the faraway voice in which a person speaks of something so unattainable that it does not bear thinking about.

'All right, Petrus,' I said, and went back to the living-room.

The next morning before I went to town, Petrus asked to see me. 'Please, *Baas*,' he said, awkwardly handing me a bundle of notes. They're so seldom on the giving rather than the receiving side, poor devils, that they don't really know how to hand money to a white man. There it was, the twenty pounds, in ones and halves, some creased and folded until they were soft as dirty rags, others smooth and fairly new — Franz's money, I suppose, and Albert's, and Dora the cook's, and Jacob the gardener's, and God knows who else's besides, from all the farms and small-holdings round about. I took it in irritation more than in astonishment, really — irritation at the waste, the uselessness of this sacrifice by people so poor. Just like the poor everywhere, I thought, who stint themselves the decencies of life in order to insure themselves the decencies of death. So incomprehensible to people like Lerice and me, who regard life as something to be spent extravagantly and, if we think about death at all, regard it as the final bankruptcy.

The servants don't work on Saturday afternoon anyway, so it was a good day for the funeral. Petrus and his father had borrowed our donkey cart to fetch the coffin from the city, where, Petrus told Lerice on their return, everything was 'nice' — the coffin waiting for them, already sealed up to save them from what must have been a rather unpleasant sight after two weeks' interment. (It had taken all that time for the authorities and the undertaker to make the final arrangements for moving the body.) All morning, the coffin lay in Petrus's hut, awaiting the trip to the little old burial ground, just outside the eastern boundary of our farm, that was a relic of the days when this was a real farming district rather than a fashionable rural estate. It was pure chance that I happened to be down there near the fence when the procession came past; once again Lerice had forgotten her promise to me and had made the house uninhabitable on a Saturday afternoon. I had come home and been infuriated to find her in a pair of filthy old slacks and with her hair uncombed since the night before, having all the varnish scraped off the living-room floor, if you please. So I had taken my No. 8 iron and gone off to practise my approach shots. In my annoyance, I had forgotten about the funeral, and was reminded only when I saw the procession coming up the path along the outside of the fence towards me; from where I was standing, you can see the graves quite clearly, and that day the sun glinted on bits of broken pottery, a lopsided homemade cross, and jam jars brown with rain water and dead flowers.

I felt a little awkward, and did not know whether to go on hitting my golf ball or stop at least until the whole gathering was decently past. The donkey cart creaks and screeches with every revolution of the wheels, and it came along in a slow, halting fashion somehow peculiarly suited to the two donkeys who drew it, their little potbellies rubbed and rough, their heads sunk between the shafts, and their ears flattened back with an air submissive and downcast; peculiarly suited, too, to the group of men and women who came along slowly behind. The patient ass. Watching, I thought, you can see now why the creature became a Biblical symbol. Then the procession drew level with me and stopped, so I had to put down my club. The coffin was taken down off the cart — it was a shiny, yellow-varnished wood, like cheap furniture — and the donkeys twitched their ears against the flies. Petrus, Franz, Albert, and the old father from Rhodesia hoisted it on their shoulders and the procession moved on, on foot. It was really a very awkward moment. I stood there rather foolishly at the fence, quite still, and slowly they filed past, not looking up, the four men bent beneath the shiny wooden box, and the straggling troop of mourners. All of them were servants or neighbours' servants whom I knew as casual, easygoing gossipers about our lands or kitchen. I heard the old man's breathing.

I had just bent to pick up my club again when there was a sort of jar in the flowing solemnity of their processional mood; I felt it at once, like a wave of heat along the air, or one of those sudden currents of cold catching at your legs in a placid stream. The old man's voice was muttering something; the people had stopped, confused, and they bumped into one another, some pressing to go on, others hissing them to be still. I could see that they were embarrassed, but they could not ignore the voice; it was much the way that the mumblings of a prophet, though not clear at first, arrest the mind. The corner of the coffin the old man carried was sagging at an angle; he seemed to be trying to get out from under the weight of it. Now Petrus expostulated with him.

The little boy who had been left to watch the
donkeys dropped the reins and ran to see. I don't
know why — unless it was for the same reason people
crowd around someone who has fainted in a cinema
— but I parted the wires of the fence and went
through, after him.

Petrus lifted his eyes to me — to anybody — with
distress and horror. The old man from Rhodesia had
let go of the coffin entirely, and the three others,
unable to support it on their own, had laid it on the
ground, in the pathway. Already there was a film of
dust lightly wavering up its shiny sides. I did not
understand what the old man was saying; I hesitated
to interfere. But now the whole seething group
turned on my silence. The old man himself came over
to me, with his hands outspread and shaking, and
spoke directly to me, saying something that I could
tell from the tone, without understanding the words,
was shocking and extraordinary.

'What is it, Petrus? What's wrong?' I appealed.

Petrus threw up his hands, bowed his head in a
series of hysterical shakes, then thrust his face up at
me suddenly. 'He says, "My son was not so heavy". '

Silence. I could hear the old man breathing; he
kept his mouth a little open, as old people do.

'My son was young and thin,' he said at last, in
English.

Again silence. Then babble broke out. The old man
thundered against everybody; his teeth were yellowed
and few, and he had one of those fine, grizzled,
sweeping moustaches that one doesn't often see
nowadays, which must have been grown in emulation
of early Empire builders. It seemed to frame all his
utterances with a special validity, perhaps merely
because it was the symbol of the traditional wisdom

of age — an idea so fearfully rooted that it carries still something awesome beyond reason. He shocked them; they thought he was mad, but they had to listen to him. With his own hands he began to prise the lid off the coffin and three of the men came forward to help him. Then he sat down on the ground; very old, very weak, and unable to speak, he merely lifted a trembling hand towards what was there. He abdicated, he handed it over to them, he was no good any more.

They crowded round to look (and so did I), and now they forgot the nature of this surprise and the occasion of grief to which it belonged, and for a few minutes were carried up in the astonishment of the surprise itself. They gasped and flared noisily with excitement. I even noticed the little boy who had held the donkeys jumping up and down, almost weeping with rage because the backs of the grown-ups crowded him out of his view.

In the coffin was someone no one had ever seen before: a heavily built, rather light-skinned native with a neatly stitched scar on his forehead — perhaps from a blow in a brawl that had also dealt him some other, slower-working injury which had killed him.

I wrangled with the authorities for a week over the body. I had the feeling that they were shocked, in a laconic fashion, by their own mistake, but that in the confusion of their anonymous dead they were helpless to put it right. They said to me, 'We are trying to find out,' and 'We are still making inquiries.' It was as if at any moment they might conduct me into their mortuary and say, 'There! Lift up the sheets; look for him — your poultry boy's brother. There are so many black faces — surely one will do?'

And every evening when I got home, Petrus was waiting in the kitchen. 'Well, they're trying. They're still looking. The *Baas* is seeing to it for you, Petrus,' I would tell him. 'God, half the time I should be in the office I'm driving around the back end of the town chasing after this affair,' I added aside, to Lerice, one night.

She and Petrus both kept their eyes turned on me as I spoke, and, oddly, for those moments they looked exactly alike, though it sounds impossible: my wife, with her high, white forehead and her attenuated Englishwoman's body, and the poultry boy, with his horny bare feet below khaki trousers tied at the knee with string and the peculiar rankness of his nervous sweat coming from his skin.

'What makes you so indignant, so determined about this now?' said Lerice suddenly.

I stared at her. 'It's a matter of principle. Why should they get away with a swindle? It's time these officials had a jolt from someone who'll bother to take the trouble.'

She said, 'Oh.' And as Petrus slowly opened the kitchen door to leave, sensing that the talk had gone beyond him, she turned away, too.

I continued to pass on assurances to Petrus every evening, but although what I said was the same and the voice in which I said it was the same, every evening it sounded weaker. At last, it became clear that we would never get Petrus's brother back, because nobody really knew where he was. Somewhere in a graveyard as uniform as a housing scheme, somewhere under a number that didn't belong to him, or in the medical school, perhaps, laboriously reduced to layers of muscle and strings of nerve?

Goodness knows. He had no identity in this world anyway.

It was only then, and in a voice of shame, that Petrus asked me to try and get the money back.

'From the way he asks, you'd think he was robbing his dead brother,' I said to Lerice later. But as I've said, Lerice had got so intense about this business that she couldn't even appreciate a little ironic smile.

I tried to get the money; Lerice tried. We both telephoned and wrote and argued, but nothing came of it. It appeared that the main expense had been the undertaker, and after all he had done his job. So the whole thing was a complete waste, even more of a waste for the poor devils than I had thought it would be.

The old man from Rhodesia was about Lerice's father's size, so she gave him one of her father's old suits, and he went back home rather better off, for the winter, than he had come.

Ahmed Essop
THE HAJJI

When the telephone rang several times one evening
and his wife did not attend to it as she usually did,
Hajji Hassen, seated on a settee in the lounge, cross-
legged and sipping tea, shouted: 'Salima, are you
deaf?' And when he received no response from his
wife and the jarring bell went on ringing, he shouted
again: 'Salima, what's happened to you?'

The telephone stopped ringing. Hajji Hassen
frowned in a contemplative manner, wondering where
his wife was now. Since his return from Mecca after
the pilgrimage, he had discovered novel inadequacies
in her, or perhaps saw the old ones in a more
revealing light. One of her salient inadequacies was
never to be around when he wanted her. She was
either across the road confabulating with her sister,
or gossiping with the neighbours, or away on a
shopping spree. And now, when the telephone had
gone on assaulting his ears, she was not in the house.
He took another sip of the strongly spiced tea to
stifle the irritation within him.

When he heard the kitchen door open he knew that
Salima had entered. The telephone burst out again in

a metallic shrill and the Hajji shouted for his wife. She hurried to the phone.

'Hullo . . . Yes . . . Hassen . . . Speak to him? . . . Who speaking? . . . Caterine? . . . Who Caterine? . . . Au-right . . . I call him.'

She put the receiver down gingerly and informed her husband in Gujarati that a woman named 'Caterine' wanted to speak to him. The name evoked no immediate association in his memory. He descended from the settee and, squeezing his feet into a pair of crimson sandals, went to the telephone.

'Hullo . . . Who? . . . Catherine? . . . No, I don't know you . . . Yes . . . Yes . . . Oh . . . now I remember . . . Yes . . . '

He listened intently to the voice, urgent, supplicating. Then he gave his answer: 'I am afraid I can't help him. Let the Christians bury him. His last wish means nothing to me . . . Madam, it's impossible . . . No . . . Let him die . . . Brother? Pig! Pig! Bastard!' He banged the receiver onto the telephone in explosive annoyance.

'O Allah!' Salima exclaimed. 'What words! What is this all about?'

He did not answer but returned to the settee, and she quietly went to the bedroom.

Salima went to bed and it was almost midnight when her husband came into the room. His earlier vexation had now given place to gloom. He told her of his brother Karim who lay dying in Hillbrow. Karim had cut himself off from his family and friends ten years ago; he had crossed the colour line (his fair complexion and grey eyes serving as passports) and gone to cohabit with a white woman. And now that he was on the verge of death he wished to return to the world he had forsaken and to be buried under

Muslim funeral rites and in a Muslim cemetery.

Hajji Hassen had, of course, rejected the plea, and for good reason. When his brother had crossed the colour line, he had severed his family ties. The Hajji at that time had felt excoriating humiliation. By going over to the white Herrenvolk, his brother had trampled on something that was vitally part of him, his dignity and self-respect. But the rejection of his brother's plea involved a straining of the heartstrings and the Hajji did not feel happy. He had recently sought God's pardon for his sins in Mecca, and now this business of his brother's final earthly wish and his own intransigence was in some way staining his spirit.

The next day Hassen rose at five to go to the mosque. When he stepped out of his house in Newtown the street lights were beginning to pale and clusters of houses to assume definition. The atmosphere was fresh and heavy, and he took a few deep breaths. The first trams were beginning to pass through Bree Street and were clanging along like decrepit yet burning spectres towards the Johannesburg City Hall. Here and there a figure moved along hurriedly. The Hindu fruit and vegetable hawkers were starting up their old trucks in the yards, preparing to go out for the day to sell to suburban housewives.

When he reached the mosque the Somali muezzin in the ivory-domed minaret began to intone the call for prayers. After prayers, he remained behind to read the Koran in the company of two other men. When he had done the sun was shining brilliantly in the courtyard onto the flowers and the fountain with its goldfish.

Outside the house he saw a car. Salima opened the

door and whispered, 'Caterine'. For a moment he felt irritated, but realising that he might as well face her he stepped boldly into the lounge.

Catherine was a small woman with firm fleshy legs. She was seated cross-legged on the settee, smoking a cigarette. Her face was almost boyish, a look that partly originated in her auburn hair which was cut very short, and partly in the smallness of her head. Her eye-brows, firmly pencilled, accentuated the grey-green glitter of her eyes. She was dressed in a dark grey costume.

He nodded his head at her to signify that he knew who she was. Over the telephone he had spoken with aggressive authority. Now, in the presence of the woman herself, he felt a weakening of his masculine fibre.

'You must, Mr Hassen, come to see your brother.'

'I am afraid I am unable to help,' he said in a tentative tone. He felt uncomfortable; there was something so positive and intrepid about her appearance.

'He wants to see you. It's his final wish.'

'I have not seen him for ten years.'

'Time can't wipe out the fact that he's your brother.'

'He is a white. We live in different worlds.'

'But you must see him.'

There was a moment of strained silence.

'Please understand that he's not to blame for having broken with you. I am to blame. I got him to break with you. Really you must blame me, not Karim.'

Hassen found himself unable to say anything. The thought that she could in some way have been responsible for his brother's rejection of him had never occurred to him. He looked at his feet in awkward silence. He could only state in a lazily recalcitrant tone: 'It is not easy for me to see him.'

'Please come Mr Hassen, for my sake, please. I'll never be able to bear it if Karim dies unhappily. Can't you find it in your heart to forgive him, and to forgive me?'

He could not look at her. A sob escaped from her, and he heard her opening her handbag for a handkerchief.

'He's dying. He wants to see you for the last time.'

Hassen softened. He was overcome by the argument that she had been responsible for taking Karim away. He could hardly look on her responsibility as being in any way culpable. She was a woman.

'If you remember the days of your youth, the time you spent together with Karim before I came to separate him from you, it will be easier for you to pardon him.'

Hassen was silent.

'Please understand that I am not a racialist. You know the conditions in this country.'

He thought for a moment and then said: 'I will go with you.'

He excused himself and went to his room to change. After a while they set off for Hillbrow in her car.

He sat beside her. The closeness of her presence, the perfume she exuded stirred currents of feeling within him. He glanced at her several times, watched the deft movements of her hands and legs as she controlled the car. Her powdered profile, the outline taut with a resolute quality, aroused his imagination. There was something so businesslike in her attitude and bearing, so involved in reality (at the back of his mind there was Salima, flaccid, cowlike and inadequate) that he could hardly refrain from expressing his admiration.

'You must understand that I'm only going to see my brother because you have come to me. For no one else would I have changed my mind.'

'Yes, I understand. I'm very grateful.'

'My friends and relatives are going to accuse me of softness, of weakness.'

'Don't think of them now. You have decided to be kind to me.'

The realism and the commonsense of the woman's words! He was overwhelmed by her.

The car stopped at the entrance of a building in Hillbrow. They took the lift. On the second floor three white youths entered and were surprised at seeing Hassen. There was a separate lift for non-whites. They squeezed themselves into a corner, one actually turning his head away with a grunt of disgust. The lift reached the fifth floor too soon for Hassen to give a thought to the attitude of the three white boys. Catherine led him to apartment 65.

He stepped into the lounge. Everything seemed to be carefully arranged. There was her personal touch about the furniture, the ornaments, the paintings. She went to the bedroom, then returned and asked him in.

Karim lay in bed, pale, emaciated, his eyes closed. For a moment Hassen failed to recognize him: ten years divided them. Catherine placed a chair next to the bed for him. He looked at his brother and again saw, through ravages of illness, the familiar features. She sat on the bed and rubbed Karim's hands to wake him. After a while he began to show signs of consciousness. She called him tenderly by his name.

When he opened his eyes he did not recognize the
man beside him, but by degrees, after she had repeated
Hassen's name several times, he seemed to understand.
He stretched out a hand and Hassen took it, moist
and repellent. Nausea swept over him, but he could
not withdraw his hand as his brother clutched it
firmly.

'Brother Hassen, please take me away from here.'

Hassen's agreement brought a smile to his lips.

Catherine suggested that she drive Hassen back to
Newtown where he could make preparations to
transfer Karim to his home.

'No, you stay here. I will take a taxi.' And he left
the apartment.

In the corridor he pressed the button for the lift. He
watched the indicator numbers succeeding each other
rapidly, then stop at five. The doors opened — and
there they were again, the three white youths. He
hesitated. The boys looked at him tauntingly. Then
suddenly they burst into deliberately brutish laughter.

'Come into the parlour,' one of them said.

'Come into the Indian parlour,' another said in a
cloyingly mocking voice.

Hassen looked at them, annoyed, hurt. Then
something snapped within him and he stood there,
transfixed. They laughed at him in a raucous chorus
as the lift doors shut.

He remained immobile, his dignity clawed. Was
there anything so vile in him that the youths found it
necessary to maul that recess of self-respect within
him? 'They are whites,' he said to himself in bitter
justification of their attitude.

He would take the stairs and walk down the five
floors. As he descended he thought of Karim. Because
of him he had come there and because of him he had

been insulted. The enormity of the insult bridged the gap of ten years when Karim had spurned him, and diminished his being. Now he was diminished again.

He was hardly aware that he had gone down five floors when he reached ground level. He stood still, expecting to see the three youths again. But the foyer was empty and he could see the reassuring activity of street life through the glass panels. He quickly walked out as though he would regain in the hubbub of the street something of his assaulted dignity.

He walked on, structures of concrete and glass on either side of him, and it did not even occur to him to take a taxi. It was in Hillbrow that Karim had lived with the white woman and forgotten the existence of his brother; and now that he was dying he had sent for him. For ten years Karim had lived without him. O Karim! The thought of the youth he had loved so much during the days they had been together at the Islamic Institute, a religious seminary though it was governed like a penitentiary, brought the tears to his eyes and he stopped against a shop window and wept. A few pedestrians looked at him. When the shop-keeper came outside to see the weeping man, Hassen, ashamed of himself, wiped his eyes and walked on.

He regretted his pliability in the presence of the white woman. She had come unexpectedly and had disarmed him with her presence and subtle talk. A painful lump rose in his throat as he set his heart against forgiving Karim. If his brother had had no personal dignity in sheltering behind his white skin, trying to be what he was not, he was not going to allow his own moral worth to be depreciated in any way.

When he reached central Johannesburg he went to the station and took the train. In the coach with the blacks he felt at ease and regained his self-possession. He was among familiar faces, among people who respected him. He felt as though he had been spirited away by a perfumed, well-made, wax doll, but had managed with a prodigious effort to shake her off.

When he reached home Salima asked him what had been decided and he answered curtly, 'Nothing'. But feeling elated after his escape from Hillbrow he added condescendingly, 'Karim left of his own accord. We should have nothing to do with him.'

Salima was puzzled, but she went on preparing supper.

Catherine received no word from Hassen and she phoned him. She was stunned when he said: 'I'm sorry but I am unable to offer any help.'

'But . . . '

'I regret it. I made a mistake. Please make some other arrangements. Goodbye.'

With an effort of will he banished Karim from his mind. Finding his composure again he enjoyed his evening meal, read the paper and then retired to bed. Next morning he went to mosque as usual, but when he returned home he found Catherine there again. Angry that she should have come, he blurted out: 'Listen to me, Catherine. I can't forgive him. For ten years he didn't care about me, whether I was alive or dead. Karim means nothing to me now.'

'Why have you changed your mind? Do you find it so difficult to forgive him?'

'Don't talk to me of forgiveness. What forgiveness, when he threw me aside and chose to go with you? Let his white friends see to him, let Hillbrow see to him.'

'Please, please, Mr Hassen, I beg you . . . '

'No, don't come here with your begging. Please go

away.'

He opened the door and went out. Catherine burst into tears. Salima comforted her as best she could.

'Don't cry Caterine. All men hard. Dey don't understand.'

'What shall I do now?' Catherine said in a defeated tone. She was an alien in the world of the non-whites. 'Is there no one who can help me?'

'Yes, Mr Mia help you,' replied Salima.

In her eagerness to find some help, she hastily moved to the door. Salima followed her and from the porch of her home directed her to Mr Mia's. He lived in a flat on the first floor of an old building. She knocked and waited in trepidation.

Mr Mia opened the door, smiled affably and asked her in.

'Come inside, lady; sit down . . . Fatima,' he called to his daughter, 'bring some tea.'

Mr Mia was a man in his fifties, his bronze complexion partly covered by a neatly trimmed beard. He was a well-known figure in the Indian community. Catherine told him of Karim and her abortive appeal to his brother. Mr Mia asked one or two questions, pondered for a while and then said: 'Don't worry, my good woman. I'll speak to Hassen. I'll never allow a Muslim brother to be abandoned.'

Catherine began to weep.

'Here, drink some tea and you'll feel better.' He poured tea. Before Catherine left he promised that he would phone her that evening and told her to get in touch with him immediately should Karim's condition deteriorate.

Mr Mia, in the company of the priest of the Newtown mosque, went to Hassen's house that evening. They found several relatives of Hassen's

seated in the lounge (Salima had spread the word of
Karim's illness). But Hassen refused to listen to their
pleas that Karim should be brought to Newtown.

'Listen to me Hajji,' Mr Mia said. 'Your brother
can't be allowed to die among the Christians.'

'For ten years he has been among them.'

'That means nothing. He's still a Muslim.'

The priest now gave his opinion. Although Karim
had left the community, he was still a Muslim. He had
never rejected the religion and espoused Christianity,
and in the absence of any evidence to the contrary it
had to be accepted that he was a Muslim brother.

'But for ten years he has lived in sin in Hillbrow.'

'If he has lived in sin that is not for us to judge.'

'Hajji, what sort of a man are you? Have you no
feeling for your brother?' Mr Mia asked.

'Don't talk to me about feeling. What feeling had
he for me when he went to live among the whites,
when he turned his back on me?'

'Hajji, can't you forgive him? You were recently in
Mecca.'

This hurt Hassen and he winced. Salima came to
his rescue with refreshments for the guests.

The ritual of tea-drinking established a mood of
conviviality and Karim was forgotten for a while.
After tea they again tried to press Hassen into
forgiving his brother, but he remained adamant. He
could not face Catherine without looking ridiculous.
Besides he felt integrated now; he would resist anything that negated him.

Mr Mia and the priest departed. They decided to
raise the matter with the congregation in the mosque.
But they failed to move Hassen. Actually his
resistance grew in inverse ratio as more people came
to learn of the dying Karim and Hassen's refusal to

forgive him. By giving in he would be displaying
mental dithering of the worst kind, as though he were
a man without an inner fibre, decision and firmness
of will.

Mr Mia next summoned a meeting of various
religious dignitaries and received their mandate to
transfer Karim to Newtown without his brother's
consent. Karim's relatives would be asked to care for
him, but if they refused Mr Mia would take charge.

The relatives, not wanting to offend Hassen and
also feeling that Karim was not their responsibility,
refused.

Mr Mia phoned Catherine and informed her of
what had been decided. She agreed that it was best
for Karim to be amongst his people during his last
days. So Karim was brought to Newtown in an
ambulance hired from a private nursing home and
housed in a little room in a quiet yard behind the
mosque.

The arrival of Karim placed Hassen in a difficult
situation and he bitterly regretted his decision not to
accept him into his own home. He first heard of his
brother's arrival during the morning prayers when the
priest offered a special prayer for the recovery of the
sick man. Hassen found himself in the curious
position of being forced to pray for his brother. After
prayers several people went to see the sick man,
others went up to Mr Mia to offer help. Hassen felt
out of place and as soon as the opportunity presented
itself he slipped out of the mosque.

In a mood of intense bitterness, scorn for himself,
hatred of those who had decided to become his
brother's keepers, infinite hatred for Karim, Hassen
went home. Salima sensed her husband's mood and
did not say a word to him.

In his room he debated with himself. In what way should he conduct himself so that his dignity remained intact? How was he to face the congregation, the people in the streets, his neighbours? Everyone would soon know of Karim and smile at him half sadly, half ironically, for having placed himself in such a ridiculous position. Should he now forgive the dying man and transfer him to his home? People would laugh at him, snigger at his cowardice, and Mr Mia perhaps even deny him the privilege: Karim was now *his* responsibility. And what would Catherine think of him? Should he go away somewhere (on the pretext of a holiday) to Cape Town, to Durban? But no, there was the stigma of being called a renegade. And besides, Karim might take months to die, he might not die at all.

'O Karim, why did you have to do this to me?' he said, moving towards the window and drumming at the pane nervously. It galled him that a weak, dying man could bring such pain to him. An adversary could be faced, one could either vanquish him or be vanquished, with one's dignity unravished, but with Karim what could he do?

He paced his room. He looked at his watch; the time for afternoon prayers was approaching. Should he expose himself to the congregation? 'O Karim! Karim!' he cried, holding on to the burglar-proof bar of his bedroom window. Was it for this that he had made the pilgrimage — to cleanse his soul in order to return into the penumbra of sin? If only Karim would die he would be relieved of his agony. But what if he lingered on? What if he recovered? Were not prayers being said for him? He went to the door and shouted in a raucous voice: 'Salima!'

But Salima was not in the house. He shouted again

and again, and his voice echoed hollowly in the rooms. He rushed into the lounge, into the kitchen, he flung the door open and looked into the yard.

He drew the curtains and lay on his bed in the dark. Then he heard the patter of feet in the house. He jumped up and shouted for his wife. She came hurriedly.

'Salima, Salima, go to Karim, he is in a room in the mosque yard. See how he is, see if he is getting better. Quickly!'

Salima went out. But instead of going to the mosque, she entered her neighbour's house. She had already spent several hours sitting beside Karim. Mr Mia had been there as well as Catherine — who had wept.

After a while she returned from her neighbour. When she opened the door her husband ran to her. 'How is he? Is he very ill? Tell me quickly!'

'He is very ill. Why don't you go and see him?'

Suddenly, involuntarily, Hassen struck his wife in the face.

'Tell me, is he dead? Is he dead?' he screamed.

Salima cowered in fear. She had never seen her husband in this raging temper. What had taken possession of the man? She retired quickly to the kitchen. Hassen locked himself in the bedroom.

During the evening he heard voices. Salima came to tell him that several people, led by Mr Mia, wanted to speak to him urgently. His first impulse was to tell them to leave immediately; he was not prepared to meet them. But he had been wrestling with himself for so many hours that he welcomed a moment when he could be in the company of others. He stepped boldly into the lounge.

'Hajji Hassen,' Mr Mia began, 'please listen to us. Your brother has not long to live. The doctor has seen him. He may not outlive the night.'

'I can do nothing about that,' Hassen replied, in an audacious matter-of-fact tone that surprised him and shocked the group of people.

'That is in Allah's hand,' said the merchant Gardee. 'In our hands lie forgiveness and love. Come with us now and see him for the last time.'

'I cannot see him.'

'And what will it cost you?' asked the priest who wore a long black cloak that fell about his sandalled feet.

'It will cost me my dignity and my manhood.'

'My dear Hajji, what dignity and what manhood? What can you lose by speaking a few kind words to him on his death-bed? He was only a young man when he left.'

'I will do anything, but going to Karim is impossible.'

'But Allah is pleased by forgiveness,' said the merchant.

'I am sorry, but in my case the circumstances are different. I am indifferent to him and therefore there is no necessity for me to forgive him.'

'Hajji,' said Mr Mia, 'you are only indulging in glib talk and you know it. Karim is your responsibility, whatever his crime.'

'Gentlemen, please leave me alone.'

And they left. Hassen locked himself in his bedroom and began to pace the narrow space between bed, cupboard and wall. Suddenly, uncontrollably, a surge of grief for his dying brother welled up within him.

'Brother! Brother!' he cried, kneeling on the carpet

beside his bed and smothering his face in the quilt. His memory unfolded a time when Karim had been ill at the Islamic Institute and he had cared for him and nursed him back to health. How much he had loved the handsome youth!

At about four in the morning he heard an urgent rapping. He left his room to open the front door.

'Brother Karim dead,' said Mustapha, the Somali muezzin of the mosque, and he cupped his hands and said a prayer in Arabic. He wore a black cloak and a white skull-cap. When he had done he turned and walked away.

Hassen closed the door and went out into the street. For a moment his release into the street gave him a feeling of sinister jubilation, and he laughed hysterically as he turned the corner and stood next to Jamal's fruitshop. Then he walked on. He wanted to get away as far as he could from Mr Mia and the priest who would be calling upon him to prepare for the funeral. That was no business of his. They had brought Karim to Newtown and they should see to him.

He went up Lovers' Walk and at the entrance of Orient House he saw the night-watchman sitting beside a brazier. He hastened up to him, warmed his hands by the fire, but he did this more as a gesture of fraternization as it was not cold, and he said a few words facetiously. Then he walked on.

His morbid joy was ephemeral, for the problem of facing the congregation at the mosque began to trouble him. What opinion would they have of him when he returned? Would they not say: he hated his brother so much that he forsook his prayers, but now that his brother is no longer alive he returns. What a man! What a Muslim.

When he reached Vinod's Photographic Studio he pressed his forehead against the neon-lit glass showcase and began to weep.

A car passed by filling the air with nauseous gas. He wiped his eyes, and looked for a moment at the photographs in the showcase; the relaxed happy, anonymous faces stared at him, faces whose momentary expressions were trapped in film. Then he walked on. He passed a few shops and then reached Broadway Cinema where he stopped to look at the lurid posters. There were heroes, lusty, intrepid, blasting it out with guns; women in various stages of undress; horrid monsters from another planet plundering a city; Dracula.

Then he was among the quiet houses and an avenue of trees rustled softly. He stopped under a tree and leaned against the trunk. He envied the slumbering people in the houses around him, their freedom from the emotions that jarred him. He would not return home until the funeral of his brother was over.

When he reached the Main Reef Road the east was brightening up. The lights along the road seemed to be part of the general haze. The buildings on either side of him were beginning to thin and on his left he saw the ghostly mountains of mine sand. Dawn broke over the city and when he looked back he saw the silhouettes of tall buildings bruising the sky. Cars and trucks were now rushing past him.

He walked for several miles and then branched off onto a gravel road and continued for a mile. When he reached a clump of blue-gum trees he sat down on a rock in the shade of the trees. From where he sat he could see a constant stream of traffic flowing along the highway. He had a stick in his hand which he had picked up along the road, and with it he prodded a crevice in the rock. The action, subtly, touched a chord in his memory and he was sitting on a rock with Karim beside him. The rock was near a river that flowed a mile away from the Islamic Institute. It was a Sunday. He had a stick in his hand and he prodded a crevice and the weather-worn rock flaked off and Karim was gathering the flakes.

'Karim! Karim!' he cried, prostrating himself on the rock, pushing his fingers into the hard roughness, unable to bear the death of that beautiful youth.

He jumped off the rock and began to run. He would return to Karim. A fervent longing to embrace his brother came over him, to touch that dear form before the soil claimed him. He ran until he was tired, then walked at a rapid pace. His whole existence precipitated itself into one motive, one desire, to embrace his brother in a final act of love.

His heart beating wildly, his hair dishevelled, he reached the highway and walked on as fast as he could. He longed to ask for a lift from a passing motorist but could not find the courage to look back and signal. Cars flashed past him, trucks roared in pain.

When he reached the outskirts of Johannesburg it was nearing ten o'clock. He hurried along, now and then breaking into a run. Once he tripped over a cable and fell. He tore his trousers in the fall and found his hands were bleeding. But he was hardly conscious of himself, wrapped up in his one purpose.

He reached Lovers' Walk, where cars growled around him angrily; he passed Broadway Cinema, rushed towards Orient House, turned the corner at Jamal's fruitshop. And stopped.

The green hearse, with the crescent moon and stars emblem, passed by; then several cars with mourners

followed, bearded men, men with white skull-caps on
their heads, looking rigidly ahead, like a procession
of puppets, indifferent to his fate. No one saw him.

Lionel Abrahams
THE OTHER WINDOWS

In the old house once, Moh walked him to a corner
of the garden where there was a little rockery in a
loop of the pathway. It was a journey to America,
she had told him. 'Let's go to America and see all the
wonders.'

She had walked him around the rockery twice,
then stood him between the stones on the lowest
of the three dry beds.

And that was a journey.

America?

America?

The three rings of stones were mysterious: on one
stone a paint-smear of dried moss, the withered
trumpet of an iris leaf dangling through a gap from the
top bed to the one below, and, amid the paperiness,
the vibrating flamepoint of an untwisting purple bud.
The house, from this new angle, the verandah and the
windows, looked different, and the garden so big and
strange . . .

It was hardly twenty steps to America.

But approaching the Children's Hospital, seeing the
red brick building loom and stretch behind the

wrought-iron top of the long street wall, entering the tall gates, he was dizzy and frightened as if he were the pink child on a navy blue moulded plaque high on one blank facade, and hung over an empty silence nearly as deep as the one where the sky was that cold colour. The car, as it came through the gates, commanded importantly, 'Husssh . . . !' anxiously continuing the sound while it crossed the gravelled area and pushed into a parking space. The garden — lawn, palm and path — to be glimpsed down one side beyond a corner of the building, was empty, square and still. The hospital's rows of sliding windows were like solemn eyes half-closed while the least possible noise was being made.

A part of the building had a steep tiled roof. They crossed its polished black stoep, and glass swing-doors let them into the hospital smell, into the bareness of hushed waiting-rooms whose white walls turned all the brisk and timid murmurings to echoes, and pale-grey corridors leaping with a squeal of rubber, radiator by radiator, into the gloom, into the depths of the building.

Somewhere in the chill he felt kisses. Somewhere through the hum and rustle of the uniformed people's quiet hurrying he called out, and everything that Moh and Daddy said became knotted into, 'Soon, darling! Soon . . .'

Soon?

It was a sound that came of itself, echoing off the smooth high walls . . . and they were gone.

He was on a rubber-wheeled trolley passing along a corridor with glimpses of white rooms. He saw as he passed another waiting trolley with a boy lying on it, and someone in white was stroking his hair. 'Well, Joseph Anthony, are you back again?' she said, with terrible kindness.

At last there was a bed. He snatched at sleep.

How long was he in that little room? Two days? Twice they came with the smell of methylated spirits and a steady purple flame and a needle which drew a drop of stinging blood from his thumb.

Then he was in a vast room with rows of beds.

He lay and listened to other children talking about things he did not know yet: Dinky Toys and Meccano sets and operations and visiting. He saw them looking at comics and throwing things from bed to bed, and opening strange round boxes out of which poured heaps of smooth sticks and wooden rounds that they built into windmills. Across such spaces would he dare to call back to them? He did, a little, reaching out from the wide silence of watching and waiting on what was happening to him.

He felt even through his sleep the stiffness of his bed and starchy sheets. And he wakened to the lights breaking into the last of the night with the first wash, with the splashing, the protesting and crying of the children, the strong impatient movements of the nurses and their low-voiced conversation with each other across their work.

That was every day. And so was the unacceptable taste of the meals that came in deep bowls, and the comedy when the canvas-clothed Zulus came to move all the beds out of place and thumpingly polish the floor.

But there were also the things that happened only once. A day when a man came into the ward with a bunch of whispering bright balloons and there was one for him, yellow, and real under his hand and threatening. And once he was awake when it was dark, late, later even than eight o'clock. There was a sound of snoring far across the ward. And from away, away in the midst of the stillness came the thin crying of a baby. Crying, but so deeply lost that there was nothing to do.

And then, coming through the door into the ward slowly like two more strangers but bursting toward him when they saw where he was, Moh and Daddy with him again for the first visiting time — just a few minutes that seemed far, far off as soon as they were over. He had something sweet to eat. He swam in the music of Moh's voice reading the Sunday comics to him. Mavis and Becky's names, when Daddy spoke about them, sounded like people he had never seen. He lay sticky and trembling afterwards, until the nurses came, brisk with thermometers and basins, and tumbled him to smooth his bed. Another visiting time Moh and Daddy told him about a lorry. It had run up the pavement and bumped their fence and their wall. How did that look? he wondered, how did *that* look? The fence was broken. That was terrible, fearful! They left him a book that had a black cat on the cover. No, the soft flat book was shaped like a cat, it *was* a black cat, cut out. When it opened there were two black cats. All the pages inside were white cats.

But more mysterious, what he longed most of all to know about was the other windows.

One morning he sat in his bed and looked through a window in front of him into the dewy first of the daylight. Perhaps a screen had been moved away, or a blind was lifted, or it was when the Zulus moved his bed. Suddenly, across a straight cool garden with beds of cannas, he saw part of a red-brick building facing him, and in it was a row of windows. They were windows with white, perfect frames and plain white curtains looped up around the dimness beyond.

Perhaps he saw them yet another time, or even twice more, and perhaps figures behind them. Once, while he stared, one of the children in the ward stretched up to a window-sill and shouted loudly across the garden, and in one of those windows something white flickered and a tiny joyous voice rang back. Who were the happy people there, what kind of place could it be that they were in, in the shadowiness behind those windows? If he waited and watched closely enough and long enough, perhaps he would find out.

But the day came when he was taken up from his bed and dressed in his clothes to go home at last. Going home was so exciting that he wanted, whenever he had to speak, to shout instead and laugh at something. He was wheeled along unrecognisable passages and into a lift, the door closed, and when it opened there was a different place outside, a strange green vestibule decorated with photographs, where Daddy was waiting. Yet they came out at the same glassed swing doors at the tile-roofed porch of the hospital. Beyond the polished black stoep was the gravelled area and Daddy's motor car with Mavis inside standing behind Daddy's seat, very shy.

Reaching home, the new house in the new half-built street, he saw the deep tracks of the wheels in the damp earth of the pavement, and the fence with bent supports, still sagging against the verandah wall. That was what the lorry had done. There. There! And he saw the veld behind the houses, fresh green on the overcast day, and the grass on the pavement, flat like ragged rugs but heaping up high along the fence. Somewhere, perhaps in that grass, there were crickets chirping, and from down in the veld came the clank and creak of the windmill.

Inside the house everything was so small! And there were kittens. He peered through the gloom to see the new kittens, weird, weird, in the laundry-basket behind the bathroom door. And the rooms were all *tiny*. How did they all get into this kitchen? Moh and Daddy and Mavis and the baby and he and the table and chairs and the stove and the sink? And there was the light hanging down!

But at night in bed waiting for sleep he was filled again with the mystery of those windows at the hospital — with all the mysteries of the whole hospital which flooded into his feelings like smells of polish and spirits and disinfectants, but most of all with the mystery of the windows across the garden that were as remote as the pattern of white canals on a planet.

Mbulelo Mzamane
MY OTHER COUSIN, SITHA

Just how I happened to fall for the paraffin one,
week in and week out, still puzzles me. I never
approved of Sitha's weekly disappearance. I loathed
Slakes, the fellow who always hijacked her. I simply
couldn't understand why she preferred him to her
other boyfriend, Martin, who didn't land her in the
same trouble. But come Friday and I became an
accessory, as it were, after the fact.

When my father was transferred to Johannesburg,
my mother remained with relatives in Brakpan, in
order to be near the Far East Rand Non-European
Hospital where she worked. She only came home
when she was day-off. My father worked in the vast
parish of Moroka, which has since been divided into
four parishes. The main church in Senaoana, where he
also had his office, was a good distance from home.
When he was not in his office, he was doing parish
visits, on a bicycle. Most of the time, therefore, we were
left to our own devices. Being the eldest among us,
my cousin Sitha then became the mistress of the house.
We enjoyed so much freedom that I seldom went to
school. On the few occasions when I did, it was

because I had a rock group which practised daily, after lessons.

On Fridays, when Sitha returned from school, she made fire and placed the pots on the stove. Then she instructed my sisters, who remained playing outside, to watch over the pots — which meant we often ate charcoal-flavoured food for supper. She vanished into the bathroom to wash, as though she hadn't washed in the morning before going to school, and emerged with shiny legs and a face masked in Butone. Because I have such a passion for music, I duly resented being dragged from under my pile of records to accompany her to the shops.

'Sabelo, get the paraffin container ready, we're going to the shops,' she'd say.

We bought our groceries from Khanyile's General Dealers. Tat' uKhanyile, the proprietor, was our church warden. We were more than just important customers, we behaved like virtual shareholders. We helped Bhut' Plum, who ran the shop, supervise the lady who baked fatcakes at the back of the store; we checked to see if the customers had collected in sufficient numbers in the shop and, if they had, served them ourselves, shovelling malted toffees and sharps into our pockets as we did so. When we were sent to buy anything, we behaved as at a self-service supermarket and then paid or kept the money, as our fancy dictated. Sitha considered herself above the racket and so let us steal whatever we'd been sent to buy, while she retained the money.

On Fridays, when we went to buy paraffin, I left Sitha on the verandah of the shop, overlooking the Moroka West taxi rank, sauntered in, bided my time, filled up the tin with paraffin and then came out. Invariably, I'd find Slakes already with her.

Slakes belonged to a group which appropriately called itself The Black Swine. They wore black and white fung kong shoes, rustler suits and black skull-caps with elongated tailpieces, rather like the devil's tail. They ruled with an iron hand over White City, which had the only high school, serving more than ten townships. That put all of us who attended the school, from Naledi to Mofolo, at the mercy of the Black Swine. For the girls, salvation lay in falling in love. Just how much free will counted in Sitha's case, and how much she was swayed by intimidation, just to what extent she became Slakes's willing victim, I can't tell. There were many girls in her position. My own girlfriend, Puni, from whom I'd had to part, used to argue that she had no alternative. I couldn't believe that when I caught her putting her hand, voluntarily, round Kali's shoulders — he wasn't wielding any knife blade that I could see. She told me that it was all flattery, that she had to make the affair look authentic, for the safety of us both. I thought differently. I rather thought my safety lay in breaking with her, if I didn't want my jaws socked. However, since the boys had virtually nothing to offer the Black Swine, not even some token resistance, our fate was more or less sealed. We paid sixpence, every Monday, as protection fee. As the Black Swine had no system of accounting, one had to pay this fee as often as it was demanded, which was on every school day and sometimes twice a day. Occasionally, Slakes rescued me, but most of the time his shifty eyes just passed me over.

'Take it home,' Sitha would say. 'I won't be long.'

I'd take the paraffin home.

She'd disappear until Sunday evening when she came back to get her gym-dress pressed, in readiness for school. I couldn't understand why she took so much trouble over her gyms, since she wasn't a regular at school. I was only prevented from reporting the matter to my father by the fact that I wasn't such a model of attendance either.

My father is very long-suffering. But when he gets angry, you thank your ancestors you aren't on the receiving end. He never fails to point out that even our Lord wasn't averse to using the whip, and applies the maxim himself with apostolic zeal. In Sitha's case, he first tried every possible method to reform her. He pleaded with her and sometimes adopted a very menacing tone; he begged her to show some consideration for his public image; he appealed to her not to jeopardise her own future; he reasoned with her, threatened her, but all to no avail.

One Friday afternoon he returned home much earlier than usual. We'd already left for the shops. He changed into his great overcoat, although the evening temperature in December was very high, and followed us. I bumped into him, on my way back home, at the corner near the Nazarene church.

'Where's she?' he asked.

'Tata?' I still have the habit of pretending deafness and incomprehension when I'm at a loss for an answer. I expected my father to repeat his question, instead of which he fixed me with an unnerving stare. I hated to betray Sitha. 'I left her talking to some friends.'

'Where?'

'Outside Khanyile's.'

'What friends?'

'Some gentlemen . . . '

He didn't wait for my reply. I knocked into a small boy, pushing a tyre, as I craned my neck to catch my father's disappearing figure. He vanished into a thick crowd around the taxi rank. I knew then that Sitha had had it.

He mingled with the crowd but kept a close watch on the couple, who were holding hands on the stoep outside the shop. In due course, Sitha and Slakes took a taxi. My father also got into an empty one and ordered the driver to trail the one in which Sitha and Slakes were travelling.

I can only fill in the rest from my father's report: at the crossroads in White City the taxi in front stopped, and the one behind drove on a few blocks before stopping. With his coat collar raised to the level of his ears, my father followed them to a house in White City. Since he only wanted to find out where they were going, he turned at the gate of the house they'd entered and went for the police.

They were in bed when he returned in the black maria, accompanied by about ten policemen from the Moroka police station. They had little trouble in persuading Slakes to open the door. In fact, he had hoped to satisfy their enquiries at the door, and opened it with only a blanket around his body. The police squadron barged in, my father at the tail end.

What followed was, strictly speaking, illegal — but the police realized just how necessary it was for my father to let off steam a bit, and so they let it continue for a while. From under his greatcoat he produced a sjambok. One of my father's few boasts is the expert way in which he used to fight with sticks as a boy, looking after cattle in the Transkei. I once witnessed his expertise in Brakpan the day he thrashed Don, who was regarded by all who knew him as the boss of the township. Don was an indiscriminate bully who thrived on the cautious nature of township folk. He could close a function, be it a stokvel or a church bazaar, merely by telling everybody to leave the premises. But my father had never heard of Don before their encounter at a party to celebrate the christening of a daughter of one of my father's parishioners. Don descended on the gathering like a Philistine and demanded liquor. When he was told that there was none, he ordered the host to close the party. My father was so furious that he slipped into one of the bedrooms, unobserved, and returned with a stick. He gave Don a beating which remained the talk of the township long after we'd left Brakpan. The thrashing Slakes received that evening left him with welts the size of hose-pipes. No doubt worse damage would have been done if, at a certain stage, the police had not thought it fit to intervene. When he decided to turn to Sitha, the police again threw themselves between them.

Sitha and Slakes were marched into the black maria in their birthday suits, with only their blankets around them. Dad carried her clothes in a bundle, under his armpit. They drove them to the police station, where the police went through the motions of taking statements. After more intimidation, they were released and told they'd hear from the police as soon as a day had been fixed for their trial. There was to be no trial but the whole show was calculated to act as a repellent, which it did. Slakes was released and told to make himself scarce. The police drove Sitha and my father home.

Thanks to the township telegraphic system, the following morning the story was all over the place. For days afterwards, Slakes elicited giggles wherever he appeared. His swaggering walk had lost a bit of its former bounce, I noticed.

We became a complete family again, from Friday to Friday. Even my mother eventually transferred from the Far East to Baragwanath Hospital.

At this time, the happiest man alive was undoubtedly Martin.

Martin had matriculated at Lovedale Institution. He worked as a dispatch clerk at some factory in Doornfontein. He wanted to become a lawyer and was studying for a diploma, by correspondence, through the University of South Africa. He also taught Sunday School, sang in the church choir and was generally every parent's idea of a decent young man. Naturally, he was as suited to his environment as is a specialist surgeon who suddenly finds he has to exchange positions with a village butcher.

On Saturday afternoons we attended church choir practices: my mother, Sitha and I. We even formed a double quartet with some close family friends and met on alternate Sundays, when my mother was afternoon-off. Martin, who had not the slightest respect for pitch, tune or time, was in it from the beginning. He never missed a practice. His enthusiasm made up for his tone-deafness and assured him a permanent place in the choir. Just how the grown-ups tolerated him, I couldn't understand. We'd never have considered him, even during a crisis or for comic effects, in my pop group.

My family is sharply divided into two: those who can sing and those who can't. The latter group is invariably more critical than the former. Their ears are paradoxically more faultless, and their taste more cultivated. They try to hide their inability to correct any false notes they hear by producing equally off-key guffaws. They were always present at our practices because Martin's singing gave them no end of amusement. They were untiring in their efforts to provide us with new songs, especially those with very complicated transitions. My only good memory of these practices lies in the consolatory fact that we never actually performed in public.

These choral occasions also served as amorous encounters between Martin and Sitha. To be able to check your girlfriend, as they say, at her home, before her parents, is no mean achievement. That sort of thing does not occur commonly outside our white suburbs. It is not customary, but where it occurs it is the measure of the boyfriend's acceptability.

Many a squabble between families has arisen over the issue of children in love. My younger brother, Soso, once created strained relations between my family and the Qwathis, who had several daughters, because every time he went to check, he rained such stones over their roof to summon his girl out that one evening, unable to bear it any longer, Tat' uQwathi came out in person and chased him right to the doorstep of our house. I was once punched in the face by an outraged parent who found me and his daughter locked in a tight embrace, in his sitting room. It's always best to grab your girl and disappear with her, into the bushes. You dare not risk even taking her out for a walk in a township teeming with Black Swine.

In a way, I envied Martin, who actually had supper with us every Sunday. Not that I really care much for that kind of affair. It may have class but it lacks adventure. Besides, the other family always imagines it has a permanent claim on you, a thing which makes it very difficult to break the silver cup. Still it is something to boast about when you are actually admitted to her home.

After Sunday practices, Sitha and Martin would go out for a walk. They usually went to watch soccer or to the library which was converted to a hall over weekends for ballroom dancing. They seldom strayed far from home. He always brought her back dead on time for supper.

One Sunday afternoon they invited me to accompany them to Baragwanath, to visit a sick aunt of Martin's. At Moroka West we waited in vain for a taxi and eventually decided to try Moroka Central. Near Elkah Stadium we bumped into a gang of Black Swine. It was all so unexpected there was no turning back. They simply emerged from nowhere, Slakes among them.

Fortunately they let Martin and me pass, unmolested, but Slakes stayed Sitha behind.

Martin had bought some fruit for his aunt which he and Sitha had been carrying in a paper-bag between them. The paper-bag remained with Sitha.

We walked up a steep hill to the taxi rank in silence, occasionally glancing back to see if Sitha was following.

At the taxi rank I met a schoolmate, Mafa, and we began to chat about all sorts of irrelevant matters. Half an hour later, Mafa decided to proceed on his way to the football ground, to watch a soccer derby between the local rivals, Moroka Swallows and Desert Rats. I wanted to accompany Mafa to the match but Martin pleaded with me to remain with him.

An hour passed, still no Sitha!

'It's almost past visiting time,' Martin said. 'We could at least drop the fruit at the hospital. Will you go and see if she'll give us the paper-bag?'

One of Boswell's famous acts was popping his head

in and out of a live lion's mouth. But the circus king fell victim to his own pranks. He was eaten alive by one of his own lions. I've a very well-developed survival instinct. I'm as mad as my neighbour, no worse, and equally sensitive to danger. Martin's suggestion fell on deaf ears.

We stood at the rank watching and never for a moment letting them out of sight.

Slakes decided to sit on the grass near the road. After a while Sitha followed his example.

Excited voices rose from the nearby soccer pitch. Slakes and Sitha eventually stood up and, hand in hand, decided to walk in the direction from which we'd come. That did it.

'I'm going to the ground,' I said.

'Let's get the fruit,' Martin said.

I looked him up and down and wondered where he was born.

'It's well past the visiting hour,' I said.

'Please, Sabelo, my *swaar*, what shall we say when we get home?'

'I'm not going home, at least not just yet. We can go home after the match. She'll be home by then.'

I walked resolutely across the street. Martin followed me.

The match was in the second half. My side was trailing Desert Rats by an odd goal. It was a very stiff match. Gloom enveloped the Swallows camp, until Rhee got the ball near the centre line. He dribbled past two opponents and passed the ball to Aarah who heeled it to Differ. Differ unleashed a cannonball from outside the eighteens which left the opposing goalkeeper as flat-footed as a duck. From then on it was us all the way. In the closing stages of the game Carlton intercepted a loose ball and dished it to the

evergreen Differ, who was standing unmarked inside
the opponents' eighteens. Baboon, Desert Rats'
running back, charged in and brought Differ down
with a tackle that would have been discouraged even
in rugby. The referee unhesitatingly awarded a
penalty. Desert Rats disputed his decison. Chaos
broke loose. Supporters of both teams swarmed onto
the field. Martin forgot himself and rushed on with
the rest, muttering something about 'infringement'
and 'constitution'. The referee blew his whistle to
signal the end of the match. The last we saw of him,
he was running for dear life in the direction of
Moroka police station with three youths, brandishing
glittering blades, in hot pursuit.

The players went to change into their clothes at
one corner of the field. We clustered round them,
indulging in a post-mortem of the match, as liberal
with advice as only spectators can be.

Martin was explaining the league's constitution to
someone who seemed to pay very little attention
to him.

Soon everybody began to trickle away. Martin and
I were among the last to leave.

It was almost dark when we got back home, now
trooping as solemnly as tragedians.

'What shall we say?' Martin asked, when we
reached the gate.

'Say we left her dancing at the library and went to
the football ground.'

'But we can't say that. We should have gone straight
to the police and not procrastinated. Suppose something happens to her? This chap could be hauled in
for forcible abduction and possible seduction.'

Damn the fellow with his long words and his law!

'Better say we left her at the library, if we're asked,

that is.'

Someone opened the door and terminated our argument.

'Thought I recognized your voices. Come in. Supper's almost ready. Mom was beginning to worry about your whereabouts.' Sitha held the door for us and shut it after us.

When we had mixed fruit for dessert, I didn't ask where the fruit had come from. I ate with an appetite which astonished my mother.

'You should take him out more often,' she told Martin.

I didn't choke at the remarks which followed either.

'Oh! Don't think we're ungrateful,' she continued. 'Thanks a lot for the fruit.'

Mtutuzeli Matshoba
TO KILL A MAN'S PRIDE

Every man is born with a certain amount of pride in his humanity. But I have come to believe that pride is only a mortal thing, and that there are many ways to destroy it. One sure way is to take a man and place him in a Soweto hostel.

At the mention of the word 'hostel' those who have never been near the Soweto version, or live in places where all people are treated as people, if there is any such place in the world, will immediately think of an establishment along Salvation Army lines. They would be infinitely far from the truth. A nearer comparison would be a Nazi concentration camp. North of our location lies our own Auschwitz. From its long grey structures the chimneys jut out of asbestos roofs into the sky; row upon monotonous row of low-built rough brick is packed into a triangular patch north of Mzimhlope and the adjacent Killarney, south east of Meadowlands. These three locations are separated from the hostel by one street on two sides; the third side faces the golden mine dunes across a rocky veld depression with an almost dry stream meandering in the middle from a small dam, which is more like a swamp, in Florida.

The hostel is, by conservative estimate, the home of some twenty thousand migrant labourers from all parts of Southern Africa, some of whom begin the trek as far away as Malawi and Zambia. Since the Kliptown floods at the beginning of 'seventy-seven, the families whose shanties were swept away in the deluge have been 'located' in a section of the hostel complex near Meadowlands. (This section was evacuated in 'seventy-six after certain tragic events about which I shall find the opportunity one day to tell you.) There they waited, a family to a five by three metre cubicle, until the WRAB could figure out what to do with them. Opposite Killarney a space just big enough for two soccer fields side by side was left vacant when the hostel was built. That is all the whole complex can boast by way of recreation facilities. There was also a bottle store, a beer lounge for fifty people all seated around rusty metal tables, and a *mai-mai* (sorghum beer) beerhall, an open square with benches along the walls and under a sort of continuous verandah. Along a street off the Soweto highway were prospering shops where the hostel inmates used to buy food. Today, the ruins of these buildings are ghastly monuments of the day of fire in June 'seventy-six.

It was there, in room 413, that my friend Somdali stayed. We had met at work. I had just been hired and was still keeping to myself, working at the tedious paper guillotine impatiently, with repeated glances at the clock high up on the wall. Lunch-time was forty-five minutes away and it seemed to me that Detail Die-cut Limited worked to a different time scale. The minutes were crawling, and Pieters had just come to instruct me about something I knew, for the thousandth time. Perhaps he underestimated my intelligence; but more likely he was 'breaking me in', measuring my tolerance. The die-cutting machines were whining incessantly and above their noise the maddening sound of Springbok Radio screeched out of a small home-made soundbox hanging from the whitewashed concrete roof which was supported by colossal, whitewashed cylindrical pillars. The walls too were whitewashed. The thirty or so factory 'girls' were working noisily at their tables behind me, chattering and giggling as if trying to outdo the machines and the radio.

Tea-break, my first there, had been an ordeal of eyes studying me from behind large mugs and the tins that were used as teacups. Fortunately, the 'girls' had their own tea-room, otherwise it would have been worse. There were sixteen 'boys', including myself, round the long unvarnished table. I was sitting at the far side, a pungent toilet door behind me — not the type that you sit on, but a hole in the floor for squatting over. I could never bring myself to use it during all the eight months I spent working there. The tea was the only thing the firm could offer. You bought your own bread and anything that you could afford to go with it. Since I hadn't known that, and hadn't had a cent in my pocket when I was taken on in the morning, I was not eating. After being tipped by a neighbour who worked next door to Detail that one 'boy' had severed his fingers with the guillotine and there might be a 'space', I had borrowed a twenty cent piece for the train ticket and rushed there. So now I sat at the end of the table, not knowing what to do with my hands and feeling like a specimen for human study and contemplation while the others were hurriedly eating their first meal of the day. The 'girls' were chatting at the tops of their voices in the other room. One of the 'boys' suggested that John had cut his fingers on purpose to get workers' insurance money. They talked about it until the buzzer sounded after fifteeen minutes.

At lunch I had nowhere to go. I decided to familiarise myself with the neighbourhood. It was one of those rusty industrial outskirts of town where one sees no one but grease-stained overall-clad mechanics and handy-men. Nothing but trucks and vans off-loading semi-processed goods. Our firm was at the southern end of Mooi street, under a maze of highways, with Heidelberg road forming a T with Mooi street, and running into mine dunes. I followed Mooi street in the direction of Carlton Centre. I had an hour, a hungry hour to kill. Not that my empty stomach worried me; well, it worried me only because it was an uncomfortable sensation which could not be totally ignored. Someone was walking beside me. His tall shadow had fallen in line with mine. Both of us had our hands in our pockets. I moved aside to give him way to pass but he did not.

'Hawu, sawubona mfowethu.' He extended his massive hand to greet. It was one of the 'boys' from the firm; tall, receding forehead, smooth dark skin and one eye. In the one eye and the wide grin I could read recognition, although I had never seen the man myself. His Elmer skipper that was no longer its original white but brownish, and the flimsy dark trousers that came to just above his naked ankles, were worn without any thought of physical decoration, but only to cover the body. I gave him my hand.

'Seems you don't recognise me, but I know you. I have seen you at Mzimhlope.' He was telling the truth. I felt slightly embarrassed at not knowing a man

who knew me. It's always like that. Anyway he did
not know me by name either. 'I can't even recognise
you. Let alone place you,' I answered, also showing
my teeth.

'My name is Somdali. I also stay at Mzimhlope,' he
said by way of introduction.

'Mzimhlope? Which side?' I was asking with due
regard for his feelings, not wishing to make him feel
awkward. I had already placed him in 'Auschwitz'
from his appearance and the way he spoke with a
deep Zulu accent. People born and bred in Soweto
speak every language in a characteristic way.

'The northern side of the station,' and seeing that
he had finally to divulge the guarded domicile, he
amassed enough courage to tell me, 'in the hostel.'

'Oh, I see. My name is Mtutu. I stay in . . . in the
location.'

'Yes. I have seen you there, when I'm going to and
from the station.' They hold a servitude, a right of
way in the location and are hardly worth a second
glance from the location residents, except maybe the
dark night's children who never fail to collect the
dues on Fridays and month-ends, or the fallen women
who provide the hostelers with female company for
sale.

I did not have anything to say. We went a few
paces before he continued. 'You were lucky to arrive
first. One guy cut his fingers with the guillotine
yesterday. That thing needs to be operated with
care, it's dangerous. You've filled that guy's space.'
I did not comment. 'They're going to teach you
the machines too.' I let him go on. 'But you won't
be paid before you're registered. They first take a
person on trial.'

That was interesting. 'How long is the trial?'

'Two, three weeks — Pieters decides. But ag, it's only a way to get free labour out of the people they employ before they register them. Pieters is the owner of the firm. He takes the good-looking girls away in his VW station wagon 'to clean his house' before he registers them. You should see him among the girls — acts like a bull that has been kept alone for months, when it is released among a herd of cows. Some of the girls are married. When their husbands want to talk to them on the phone, or come looking for them at lunch or after work, he refers to them as 'boyfriends'. Otherwise he has a little sense of humour when he has not got out on the wrong side of his bed in the morning. His assistant is aloof and has an affair with one of the two Indian girls in the office.'

'How much is the starting pay?'

'Twenty-five rand a week. Thirty for those who have been with the firm over three years. The women, I don't know.'

He told me a little more about himself, that he had come from Mondlo near Vryheid in Natal to work in Johannesburg with a forged pass eight years before, that he had been with Detail for two years and (he must have guessed I was curious to know) that he had lost his eye in a stick-fight competition when he was a teenager, an unfortunate accident for which no-one could be blamed. 'Your mouth is dry. You must be hungry.'

'I'm used to it, mfo. Don't worry,' I said politely.

'Say it again, mfowethu. We are all used to it at one time or another of our lives. But I have fifty cents here. Let's go buy some magewu.'

That was how I struck up a friendship with the man from the hostel. At the end of the first week he lent me money to buy a weekly ticket, gave me cigarettes every day without being asked; we ate and talked together during lunch and entrained together at Mzimhlope and Faraday Stations.

Tell me — who could deny such a man friendship? I could see that people we met who knew me always wondered what I was up to with a 'country boy', but I knew better. However I never invited him home — what could I invite him for? To remind him that he also had a family he was denied? And it was not until after I had been registered that he invited me to the hostel 'just to see where I live'.

Registration for work is such an interesting example of a way of killing a man's pride that I cannot pass it by without mention. It was on Monday, after two weeks of unrewarded labour and perseverance, that Pieters gave me a letter which said I had been employed as a general labourer at his firm. I was to take the letter to the notorious 80 Albert Street. Monday is usually the busiest day there because everybody wakes up on this day determined to find a job. They end up dejected, crowding the labour office for 'piece' jobs.

That Monday I woke up elated, whistling all the way as I cleaned the coal stove, made fire to warm the house for those who were still asleep, and took my toothbrush and washing rags to the tap outside the toilet. The cold water was revivifying as I splashed it over my upper body. I greeted 'Star', also washing at the tap diagonally opposite my home. Then I took the washing basin, half-filled it with water and went into the lavatory to wash the rest of me. When I had finished washing and dressing I bade them goodbye at home and set out, swept into the torrent of workers rushing to the station. Somdali had reached the station first and we waited for our trains with the hundreds already on the platform. The guys from the location prefer to wait for trains on the station bridge. Many of them looked like children who did not want to go to school. I did not sympathize with them. The little time my brothers have to themselves, Saturday and Sunday, some of them spend worshipping Bacchus.

The train schedule was geared to the morning rush hour. From four in the morning the trains had rumbled in with precarious frequency. If you stay near the road to the hostel you are woken up by the shuffle of a myriad footfalls long before the first train. I have seen these people on my way home when the nocturnal bug has bitten me. All I can say is that an endless flow of resolute men, hastening in the inky, misty morning down Mohale street to the station, is an awesome apparition.

I had arrived ten minutes early at the station. The 'ninety-five' to George Goch passed Mzimhlope while I was there. This train brought the free morning stuntman show. The daredevils ran along the roof of the train, a few centimetres from the naked cable carrying thousands of electric volts, and ducked under every pylon. One mistimed step, a slip — and reflex action would send his hand clasping for support. No comment from any of us at the station. The train shows have been going on since time immemorial and have lost their magic.

My train to Faraday arrived, bursting along the seams with its load. The spaces between the adjacent coaches were filled with people. So the only way I could get on the train was by wedging myself among those hanging on perilously by hooking their fingers into the narrow runnels along the tops of the coaches, their feet on the door ledges. A slight wandering of the mind, a sudden swaying of the train as it switched lines, bringing the weight of the others on top of us, a lost grip — and another labour unit would be abruptly terminated. We hung on for dear life until Faraday.

In Pieters's office. Four automatic telephones, two scarlet and two orange coloured, two fancy ashtrays, a gilded ball-pen stand complete with gilded pen and chain, two flat plastic trays, the one on the left marked IN and the other one OUT, all displayed on the bland face of a large highly-polished desk. Under my feet a thick carpet that made me feel like a piece of dirt. On the soft opal green wall on my left a big framed 'Desiderata' and above me a ceiling of heavenly splendour. Behind the desk, wearing a short cream-white safari suit, leaning back in a regal flexible armchair, his hairy legs (the pale skin of which curiously made me think of a frog's ventral side) balanced on the edge of the desk in the manner of a sheriff in an old-fashioned western, blue-eyed, slightly bald, jackal-faced overlord.

'You've got your pass?'

'Yes, mister Pieters.' That one did not want to be called baas.

'Let me see it. I hope it's the right one. You got a permit to work in Johannesburg?'

'I was born here, mister Pieters.' My hands were respectfully behind me.

'It doesn't follow.' He removed his legs from the edge of the table and opened a drawer. Out of it he took a small bundle of typed papers. He signed one of them and handed it to me. 'Go to the pass office. Don't spend two days there. Otherwise you come back and I've taken somebody else in your place.'

He squinted his eyes at me and wagged his tongue,

trying to amuse me the way he would try to make a baby smile. That really amused me, his trying to amuse me the way he would a baby. I thought he had a baby's mind.

'Esibayeni'. Two storey red-brick building occupying a whole block. Address: 80 Albert street, or simply 'Pass Office'. Across the street, half the block (the remaining half a parking space and 'home' of the homeless methylated spirit drinkers of the city) taken up by another red-brick structure. Not offices this time, but 'Esibayeni' (at the kraal) itself. No question why it has been called that. The whole black population of Johannesburg above pass age knows that place.

Like I said, it was full on a Monday, full of wretched men with defeated eyes sitting along the gutters on both sides of Albert Street, others grouped where the sun's rays leaked through the skyscrapers, and the rest milling about. When a car driven by a white man went up the street pandemonium broke loose as men, I mean dirty slovenly *men*, trotted behind it and fought to give their passes first. If the white person had not come for that purpose they cursed him until he went out of sight. Occasionally a truck or van would come to pick up labourers for a piece job. The clerk would shout out the number of men that were wanted for such and such a job, say forty, and double the number would be all over the truck before you could say 'stop'. None of them would want to miss the cut, which caused quite some problems for the employer. A shrewd businessman would take all and simply divide the money he had laid out among the whole group, as it was left to him to decide how much to pay for a piece job. Everybody was satisfied in the end — the temporary employer having his work done in half the time he had bargained for, and each of the labourers with enough for a ticket back to the pass-office the following day, and maybe ten cents worth of dish-water and bread from the oily restaurants in the neighbourhood, for three days. Those who were smart and familiar with the ways of the pass-office handed their passes in with twenty and/or fifty-cent pieces between the pages. This gave them first preference, and they could choose the better jobs.

The queue to 'Esibayeni' was moving slowly. It snaked about thirty metres around the corner of Polly street. It had taken me more than an hour to reach the door. Inside the ten-foot wall was an asphalt rectangle, longitudinal benches along the opposite wall in the shade of narrow tin ledges, filled with bored-looking men, toilets on the lower side of the rectangle, facing wide bustling doors. It would take me another three hours to reach the clerks. If I finished there just before lunch-time, it would mean that I would not be through with my registration by four in the afternoon when the pass office closed. Fortunately I had twenty cents and I knew that the blackjacks who worked there were nothing but starving leeches. One took me up the queue to four people who stood before a snarling white boy. Those whose places ahead of me in the queue had been usurped wasted their breath grumbling.

The man in front of me could not understand what was being bawled at him in Afrikaans. The clerk gave up explaining, not prepared to use any other language than his own. I felt that at his age, about twenty, he should be at RAU learning to speak other languages. That way he wouldn't burst a vein trying to explain everything in one tongue just because it was his. He was either bone-headed or downright lazy or else impatient to 'rule the Bantus'.

He took a rubber stamp and banged it furiously on one of the pages of the man's pass, and threw the book into the man's face. 'Go to the other building, stupid!'

The man said, 'Thanks,' and elbowed his way to the door.

'Next! Wat soek jy?' he asked in a bellicose voice when my turn to be snarled at came. He had freckles all over his face, and a weak jaw.

I gave him the letter of employment and explained in Afrikaans that I wanted E and F cards. My use of his language eased some of the tension out of him. He asked for my pass in a slightly calmer manner. I gave it to him and he paged through. 'Good, you have permission to work in Johannesburg right enough.' He took two cards from a pile in front of him and laboriously wrote my pass numbers on them. Again I thought that he should still be at school, learning to write properly. He stamped the cards and told me to go to room six in the other block. There were about twelve other clerks growling at people from behind a continuous U-shaped desk, and the space in front of the desk was overcrowded with people who made it difficult to get to the door.

Another blackjack barred the entrance to the building across the street. 'Where do you think you're going?'

'Awu! What's wrong with you? I'm going to room six to be registered. You're wasting my time,' I answered in an equally unfriendly way. His eyes were bloodshot, as big as a cow's and as stupid, his breath was fouled with 'mai-mai', and his attitude was a long way from helpful.

He spat into his right hand, rubbed his palms together and grabbed a stick that was leaning against the wall near him. 'Go in,' he challenged, indicating with a tilt of his head, and dilating his gaping nostrils.

His behaviour perplexed me, more than angering or dismaying me. It might be that he was drunk; or was I supposed to produce something first, and was he so uncouth as not to tell me why he would not allow me to go in? Whatever the reason, I regretted that I could not kick some of the 'mai-mai' out of the sagging belly, and proceeded on my way. I turned to see if there was anyone else witnessing the unnecessary aggression.

'No, mfo. You've got to wait for others who are also going to room six,' explained a man with half his teeth missing, wearing a tattered overcoat and nothing to cover his large, parched feet. And, before I could say thanks: 'Say, mnumzane, have you got a cigarette on you? Y'know, I haven't had a single smoke since yesterday.'

I gave him the one shrivelled Lexington I had in my shirt-pocket. He indicated that he had no matches either. I searched myself and gave the box to him. His hands shook violently when he lit and shielded the flame. 'Ei! Babalaaz has me.'

'Ya, neh,' I said, for the sake of saying something. The man turned and walked away as if his feet were sore. I leaned against the wall and waited. When there were a good many of us waiting the gatekeeper grunted that we should follow him inside to another bustling 'kraal'. That was where the black clerks shouted out the jobs at fifty cents a piece or more, depending on whether they were permanent or temporary. The men in there were fighting like mad to reach the row of windows where they hand in their

passes. We followed the blackjack up a sloping
cement way rising to a green double door.

There was nowhere it wasn't full at the pass-office.
Here too it was full of the same miserable figures that
were buzzing all over the place, but this time they
stood in a series of queues at a long counter like the
one across the street, only this one was L-shaped
and the white clerks behind the brass grille wore ties.
I decided that they were of a better class than the
others, although there was no doubt that they also
had the same rotten manners and arrogance. The
blackjack left us with another one who told us which
queues to join. Our cards were taken and handed to a
lady filing clerk who went to look for our records.

I was right! The clerks were, at bottom, all the
same. When I reached the counter I pushed my pass
under the grille. The man who took it had close-
cropped hair and a thin sharp face. He went through
my pass checking it against a photostat record with
my name scrawled on top in a handwriting that I did
not know.

'Where have you been from January until now,
September?' he said in a cold voice, looking at me
from behind the grille like a god about to admonish a
sinner.

I have heard some funny tales, from many tellers,
when it comes to answering that question. See if you
recognise this one:

CLERK: Heer, man. Waar was jy al die tyd, jong?
            (Lord, man. Where have you been all the
            time, jong?)
MAN: I . . . I was mad, baas.
CLERK: Mad!? You think I'm your uncle, kaffer?

KAFFER: No baas, I was mad.

CLERK: Jy . . . jy dink . . . (and the white man's mouth drops open with no words coming out.)

KAFFER: (Coming to the rescue of the baas with an explanation) At home they tell me that I was mad all along, baas. 'Strue.

CLERK: Where are the doctor's papers? You must have been to hospital if you were mad! (With annoyance.)

KAFFER: I was treated by a witchdoctor, baas. Now I am better and have found a job.

Such answers serve them right. If it is their aim to harass the poor people with impossible questions, then they should expect equivalent answers. I did not, however, say something out of the way. I told the truth. 'Looking for work.'

'Looking for work, who?'

'Baas.'

'That's right. And what have you been living on all along?' he asked, like a god.

'Scrounging, and looking for work.' Perhaps he did not know that among us blacks a man is never thrown to the dogs.

'Stealing, huh? You should have been caught before you found this job. Do you know that you have contravened section two, nine, for nine months? Do you know that you would have gone to jail for two years if you had been caught, tsotsi? These policemen are not doing their job anymore,' he said, turning his attention to the stamps and papers in front of him.

I had wanted to tell him that if I had had a chance

to steal, I would not have hesitated to do so, but I
stopped myself. It was the wise thing to act timid in
the circumstances. He gave me the pass after stamping
it. The blackjack told me which corridor to follow. I
found men sitting on benches alongside one wall and
stood at the end of the queue. The man in front of
me shifted and I sat on the edge. This time the queue
was reasonably fast. We moved forward on the seats
of our pants. If you wanted to prevent them shining
you had to stand up and sit, stand up and sit. You
could not follow the line standing. The patrolling
blackjack made you sit in an embarrassing way.
Halfway to the door we were approaching, the
man next to me removed his upper clothes. All the
others nearer to the door had their clothes bundled
under their armpits. I did the same.

We were all vaccinated in the first room and moved
on to the next one where we were X-rayed by some
impatient black technicians. The snaking line of
black bodies reminded me of prisoners being searched.
That was what 80 Albert Street was all about.

The last part of the medical examination was the
most disgraceful. I don't know whether it was
designed to save expense or on some other ground of
expediency, but on me it had the effect of dishonour.
After being X-rayed we could put on our shirts and
cross the corridor to the doctor's cubicle. Outside
were people of both sexes waiting to settle their own
affairs. You passed them before entering the cubicle,
inside which sat a fat white man in a white dust-coat
with a face like an owl, behind a simple desk. The
man who had gone in ahead of me was zipping up his
fly. I unzipped mine and stood facing the owl behind
the desk, holding my trousers with both hands. He
tilted his fat face to the right and left twice or thrice.

'Ja. Your pass.'

I hitched my trousers up while he harried me to give him the pass before I could zip my trousers. I straightened myself at leisure, in spite of his 'Gou, gou, gou!' My pride had been hurt enough by exposing myself to him, with the man behind me preparing to do so and the one in front of me having done the same, a row of men of different ages parading themselves before a bored owl. When I finished dressing I gave him the pass. He put a little maroon stamp somewhere in amongst the last pages. It must have meant that I was fit to work.

The medical examination was over and the women on the benches outside pretended they did not know. The young white ladies clicking their heels up and down the passages showed you they knew. You held yourself together as best as you could until you vanished from their sight, and you never told anybody else about it.

'Maar, my friend. Why don't you come with me to the hostel one day? Just to see where I stay, and meet some of the guys who come from Natal with me. Are you afraid?' Somdali asked as we went through the barriers at Faraday station.

It was the third week after I had been to the pass office. I was even beginning to get used to the twenty-five rand and few cents in a brown envelope that the Indian lady bookkeepers in the office had given me, and which made me feel very ashamed each time I received it. I felt like a dupe when I had to go to the office to sign for chicken feed after working honestly for a whole week and taking Pieters's scorn without any complaint. He seemed to think that we, the

workers, depended on him for a living — and to forget
that he, in turn, depended on our labour for his easy
life. Maybe this was because he knew that the greater
demand was for jobs, for work, not for labour.
Everybody was at his mercy. Somdali had been right
about the bull-like behaviour of our boss. He behaved
like a sheikh in a harem. None of the women liked it,
but they had to hide their disapproval as long as they
wanted to remain working. We only gritted our teeth
and let him continue.

I could not refuse Somdali's invitation. It was not
an invitation to a cocktail party but it was an
invitation right enough. Such are the invitations of
the simple. Apart from the fact that he was my friend,
in the evenings I usually had nothing to do at home
but listen to the hysterical screams of my sisters'
babies, while being asked to shift this way and that in
the doll's house. And the hostel was no longer
dangerous: 'seventy-six had come and gone. Before
Somdali invited me there, the hostel was to me a
place I knew of and didn't know about. I knew it
must be hell to live there — family men without
families, married men without wives. That was how I
had seen it, and that was where my concern ended.
But when it comes to the misery of life one has to
partake to really understand. The deepest pangs
of the man caught up in squalor are never really felt
from a safe distance. Most people shrink from
experiencing what it feels like to be down, licking
the base of the drain. Somdali's invitation was my
chance to get to the core of hostel life.

In order for you to understand why I had never
cared about the hostel, I think a brief description of
how I viewed the hostel from afar will be necessary.
At first the security of the hostel was tight, with

watchmen at every gate, preventing outsiders from entering the premises. Perhaps someone still had a little conscience, and wished to try and hide the shameful place. As time went on this security slackened until there was free traffic between the location and the hostel, although only men went there — it would have been sheer madness for a woman to go into that encampment of deprived men. Even then it was mainly the location drunks who went in after the poisonous brew of yeast, brown bread, brown sugar and water — mbamba, skokiaan and other variations of the same thing which they consumed there out of sight of the people of the location. We only went there to sell something — a watch maybe, the hostelers being ever prepared to 'snatch a bargain' — or to use the showers and quickly return to the location.

The few inmates with a venturesome spirit or having relatives 'outside', most of whom had been discovered there in the Golden City by the tracing of lineage, went out to mix with the location people. Black people seem to believe that they are all related to each other in this way. This way you can never be lost, wherever you go, because everybody with the same surname or clan-name as you is regarded as a relative and is obliged to you. Others formed bands who invaded the location at night solely to rape and kill, so that there was someone lying dead somewhere in the small location once in every week. This gave the hostel people a formidableness that made it difficult to befriend them or to sympathise with their terrible lot.

The bulk of the inmates chose to stay 'inside' at weekends, filling in the emptiness of their lives with alcohol and traditional song that brought them nostalgia for the places of their birth, the barren

hopelessness of which had driven them to gather
scraps in the human jungles of Johannesburg. Murder
was also rife inside. Dehumanized people lose their
concern for life: 'We live like hogs, wild dogs or any
other neglected animals. The pets of abeLungu live
better than we,' Somdali would say to me on a day
when he was in a really depressed mood. Normally
he never complained.

'Okay Somdali, I'll go with you today. It's still
early,' I said and saw that he was pleased.

At the station a man named Joe, who was already
quite familiar with Somdali from dice games in the
hostel, joined us. Somdali and Joe were friends, only
that was rather costly to the former. What kept them
going was that Somdali provided beers. Innocent
Somdali was not aware of the exploitation and
derived great satisfaction from living with amajita, as
he would say. There was no need to wise him up. I
could not help laughing inside when I heard Joe
promising to get Somdali a woman and to lead the
latter to a 'spot'. The expeditions always ended up
with both of them drunk and Somdali claiming that
he had been pickpocketed at the 'spot', but not sore
about it, perhaps considering it as part of the sacrifice
of learning to live Soweto-style. The three of us went
up Mohale street with the wave of countless people,
turned down Carr street and fifty metres later crossed
the new Soweto highway where it started skirting
Mzimhlope.

We entered the first 'street' to our left. It was the
first time that I had been to the hostel to visit
someone (I had gone there on impersonal matters)
and naturally my senses were sharp. The first thing
that told you you were in a different place was the
smell hanging in the air, the stench of rotting rubbish,

urine, dirty water and neglected toilets, an unhygienic mucky atmosphere that almost made you puke. If you've ever been near a pigsty, then you have the right idea. Not that I rate the location much better, but at least the location smells of life, not neglect. As we went deeper into the hostel I was disgusted to think that it was humans who let other humans live like that, in the lowest state of dereliction: and yet their sweat fuelled the economy of the country to keep it going. The so-called last bastion against roving Marxism; a bastion of men scraping small sooty enamel pots to cook the tomatoes, onions and mealie meal they had in plastic carriers. A bastion of men wasting away on skokiaan, a bastion of men washing overalls in the water-troughs; a bastion of men walking in the open in their underpants. Don't count me in, and count Somdali out too.

The first dormitory was fifty short paces long. Three doors. A gap. Another pile of brownish, greyish bricks and undulating asbestos on top, this time the toilets. Six basins in a row in an enclosure with no door and the wall going only halfway up so that a passerby could see a person sitting inside. Adjacent to this: high narrow troughs, apparently to wash dishes in. Behind this: low, deep cement troughs for washing clothes in. The longitudinal half of this place an empty room with eight showers. A man was vigorously rubbing soap on his naked glistening body under one of them. The long dormitories alternated with the toilets. A man obeying the call of nature in the middle of the night had to walk outside for not less than fifteen paces — well, like in the location. The wise thing to do was to be armed when going to the toilet.

There had been an attempt to make the place

homely, maybe when it was still new. Peach trees
lined our way on both sides and through the gaps
between the buildings I saw that there were garden
patches with wilting plants, mostly maize and
potatoes. The grass behind and between the buildings
grew waist high. The stench was unbearable.

At length, after jumping and stepping around the
puddles, we came to where Somdali stayed. He
pushed the metal door inwards without knocking.
The noise it made put our teeth on edge. He went in
ahead and as we followed, my foot sank into stagnant
water just in front of the door. There was a buzz of
agitated insects.

When you go into a place where people are living,
you expect to find something, at least, which
indicates that this is so. But in the hostel you are
utterly disheartened. The door opened into a
medium-sized room. The floor was bare, dust-laden
cement. Near the wall facing the door, which had two
squares cut into it for windows that had never been
cleaned since the hostel was built, were two tables
made of cement slabs on metal stilts coming out of
the floor. The benches on opposite sides of the tables
were also made of cement slabs resting on sewerage
pipes. Two old men in denim overalls sat at one table
talking in a dull murmur and apparently drinking
from a plastic container between them. They did not
even raise their eyes to see who was coming in. Against
the side walls were long steel cabinets from which the
green paint had peeled long ago and which rust now
covered almost completely. They extended from the
front wall half the length of the side walls to two
openings on the left and right. The walls were not
plastered and the asbestos roof rested on rafters that
were coated with thick layers of soot and spider-webs.

The soot might have come from a brazier during winter.

We followed Somdali to the opening on the right, into a closet for four people sleeping in the corners. The first opening led to another, into a closet exactly the same as the one we had passed, except that it was the last and had only one opening to it. Eight men on either side of the central room, which meant sixteen men to one door and, there being three doors in the long dormitories, forty-eight men to one unit fifty paces long. There is absolutely no privacy there. You sleep in your corner of the closet, on the door-like lid of a brick kist in which you are supposed to keep your possessions, a metre from the man next to you and the men below you.

The last closet was full of men huddled around a small one-plate stove hardly a foot high from which a thin battered chimney pipe rose to a small hole in the roof. The sun was setting and it was cold in the 'house', although the middle of summer was not long gone. Worn, dirty shreds and blankets were heaped on the wooden lids and from the smutty rafters hung all sorts of dust-covered rags, jackets, overcoats, jerseys and whatever you may care to name. There was even a bicycle suspended with a wire, and two electric guitars. A smell of rotting food, sweat and the coal-smoke from the miniature stove stifled the air. Suddenly the naked bulb blinked alive and shed a light that made the room eerie, casting darkness in the corners.

'This is my bed, majita, make yourselves at home,' Somdali said and took off his jacket which he added to the clothes hanging near his 'bed'. We sat on the kist, Joe settling down beside me without showing any sign of surprise at the unspeakable living conditions. As I said, he was used to personal visits to the hostel. As for me, I was shocked.

After hanging his coat Somdali turned to greet the others. When we had come in they had just glanced at us and resumed their conversation. The African way of entering the company of others is for the new-comer to announce himself by greeting first. It is the 'umthakathi' (wizard) who arrives unseen. 'Sonibonani ekhaya (Good evening at home).'

'Awu, Somdali! You are back from esiLungwini. Athin'ama Bhunu? (What do the Boers say?)' They greeted him enthusiastically, as if they were noticing Somdali for the first time.

'What can they say, but continue to give us the scorpion's bite? Er, madoda, I have brought you a friend of mine that I work with . . . ' and he introduced me, starting with my first name and inserting the possessive preposition 'ka' before my surname. 'Well, this skelm Joe you know.'

One man held my hand and introduced himself. The others followed suit. I counted eight of them. Somdali came to sit next to me. 'You seem not to be at ease, my friend. Relax. You must be shocked by this stable when you see it for the first time. You'll get used to it, mfowethu.'

'Let's hope I will. But I doubt it,' I replied.

'This is our reward for working for the whites. They don't care how you live, as long as you turn up for work the following day,' said Somdali bitterly.

'They don't know. Otherwise they'd be ashamed of themselves,' I answered, thinking that no normal human being could consciously tolerate other people living that way.

'You think so?' Somdali seemed to disagree. 'What do you say of the very idea of building such a place, of removing men from their families after taking their livestock and what little land they had, and burying them in filth? Is that not meant to kill a man's pride in himself?'

I understood what Somdali meant. Before I could make that known in so many words he went on, with gall in his voice, 'If you take a man, a married man, from his wife it's tantamount to castrating him. A bullock is castrated to make it strong for labour purposes.'

'Yes, Somdali is right, ndodana (son).' It was old Khuzwayo, the grey-head sexagenarian Somdali had told me was like a father to them in their labour camp dens. 'Come nearer boy, I want to see you when I talk to you. Fana, sit yourself somewhere.' Fana stood up from the tin of paint he was sitting on. I replaced him beside the old man. The little stove was beginning to glow on the sides, a solitary pot filling its whole face and boiling furiously. The heat-wave was too much for me, so I shifted a little back-ward. The old man also positioned himself to look directly into my face. His Bushman-like features were attractive.

'Ya, ndodana ka . . . ? (Yes, son of?)' I answered him by finishing his greeting with my name. I did this twice before he heard me well. 'You defend abeLungu by saying they do not know? Now, my boy, tell me this: is this — the way we live, all of us blacks — our rightful legacy from the ancestors, or from Tixo who made heaven and earth?' He paused, looking at me. 'Or is it an apportionment that our conquerors think fit for us?'

'It is the latter, baba,' I replied without certainty, as I did not know what old Khuzwayo was getting around to. Everybody was listening. Doubtless they were all sensitive about the question of their status in the social stratification. They knew that a man could not sink lower down than they were, and the only way they could let off steam was by damning the system that degraded them. To them every white man stood for the forces that held them down with their faces in the muck of the hostel. In other words, their hopelessness bred a volcanic racism.

'That is right, my boy. You are following my words well. You see, they have laid claim to everything that you can turn your eyes to see. If everything had gone according to their desires they would have owned even us black people, to till the soil for them until the end of the world. But one human being cannot be owned by another. And since they are unable to own us, all they lack is a way to justify genocide. You can remove a man from the face of a piece of paper, scratch his name out and pretend that he does not exist, but you cannot remove him physically from the face of the earth without murdering him. For he is born here and so he dies here, fighting perhaps for the one square metre he owns in the world. For man was created by Nkulunkulu so that he might avail himself of that which umhlaba (earth) was made to give. Man was not created to divide for others that which is bad and to keep that which is good for himself. We all die in the end and leave everything as we found it when we were born.'

'Ya. The old man is right, mfowethu. No man is ordained to determine the fate of another. If he has, by some vile means, usurped the other's right to self-determination, then peace is disturbed. When peace is disturbed it is always a sign that someone who is dissatisfied is trying to get his rightful share from the world.' So said the man who had introduced himself

as Bongani. I had tried to vindicate their oppressors
and they assailed me from all directions.

I attempted to manoeuvre out of the spot I was in
by explaining exactly what I had meant. 'What I
intended to say was that the majority of whites do
not know how you live because the whole rotten
situation is camouflaged. The harsh enforcement of
the inhumane laws that result in such conditions
produces a calm of sorts, and this deceives them into
thinking that everybody is satisfied except a few
anarchists and agitators who must be weeded out. I
think that the people are very apt when they refer to
the police as "the camouflage" these days, because
they camouflage black vexations with brute violence
— and whenever there is a marked "calm" the whites
are made to believe that all is peaceful. Whatever the
cause of strife was, it has been settled and things are
under control. The means by which this has been
brought about are made light of, or deliberately and
unscrupulously suppressed. A counterfeit peace is
produced for them. They don't know what is going
on "in their own backyard". That's what I meant.'

They seemed satisfied with my clarification, for no
one attacked me after that.

Old Khuzwayo had taken to me. He slapped my
shoulder amicably. 'You know, my son, you know.
For a moment I thought that you were lost. Your
explanation takes my mind back to the end of the
Second World War. When the time came to ask the
German nation why they had allowed people to be
decimated in front of their eyes, they shamefully
claimed that they had not known what was taking
place until it was too late to do anything about it but
stand up in defence of the sovereignty of their
country. It did not help them any because everybody

was against them. Their country was divided among
their enemies because they allowed some fanatics to
control their destiny. Blind obedience and gullibility
are suicidal.'

I stayed longer than I had intended with Somdali
and his mates. Bongani, who had been cooking —
boiling an assortment of old vegetables into a thick
soup — cut our topic short by announcing supper.
Each man dived to where he kept his spoon and, at
the drop of an eyelid, I was alone in front of the
small stove. Even Khuzwayo had been surprisingly
swift for his age. Joe came from the shadows to sit on
the old man's plastic milk crate.

I saw why they had been so fast in their reactions
to Bongani's call. They all ate together from the
steaming pot. Three loaves of bread were placed on a
sheet of paper that was spread on the dusty floor.
They broke pieces from the loaves and scooped from
the pot with their spoons. You could see that they
were racing, each wanting to down more soup and
pieces of bread than the next man. I don't wish to
insult those brothers of ours, but have you ever seen
the deadly excitement of a predator after making a
killing? They even fought over space.

'Damn it, Fana, don't push!' snarled one of them.

'Give me space. How do you think I'll reach the
pot?' retorted Fana with a full mouth.

'You're cheeky, you Fana. One day I'll beat it out
of you,' the other one threatened.

Old Khuzwayo ruled for peace. 'Awu, don't fight
over food like puppies, boys. You're spoiling everybody's meal. And while you're busy fighting, the
food is getting finished.'

Supper over, Somdali sent Fana to buy him 'mai-
mai' from the opposite dormitory. Bongani went to

wash the pot and the spoons in the sink outside.
Another one took a broom to sweep where they had
been eating. 'No, boy. You'll sweep tomorrow
morning. The dust will take time to settle down,' said
Somdali, preventing him. He collected only the
crumbs they had made. There was a certain organis-
ation in the way they lived. The young ones did the
chores.

When Bongani returned he removed the guitars
from their perches and gave one to Fana. They
connected the guitars to an amplifier with a PM 10
and strummed for some seconds. Then, with extraordinary dexterity, they played a moving 'mbaqanga'
(a fast African beat that is still a favourite with
country people). The sound of an electric guitar in
that gloomy lair, with the men sitting around the
small stove and listening sorrowfully to the melodious
twangs, the overhanging dust-covered rags, the bicycle,
the shadows cast by the dim, stained light bulb,
mesmerised me in a way which I fail to find words to
describe. Somdali was drinking his beer in slow sips.
He passed the can to the next man, who took a few
draughts and also passed it on. If you did not want
to drink you gave the can to the man beside you. The
music paused while Bongani and Fana drank. They
started another song immediately after that.

'What's the time, Somdali?' I asked, thinking that
at home they would be wondering why I had not
returned from work. I was three hours late already.

'I don't know, my friend. You want to go now?
Madoda, any of you got a watch?' None had, so one
of the younger men had to go and ask the time in the
opposite house, and bring another can of beer.

'Yes, ndoda, I should be running away before my
people decide to go looking for me at the police-

stations.' It was after nine. I bade everybody good-
night and stood to go. Joe did the same. Somdali
took us out. 'So you've seen where I stay, my friend.
Hope you come by yourself when you've got time. So
long.'

'Sweet, Somdali. See you tomorrow morning,' I
said, and we parted.

As we came out of the gaping fence onto the highway, I remarked about our visit to Joe.

'You know, Joe, I've never spent such a long time
in the hostel. Jesus, man, these people live like
animals. To travel the whole distance from where
they come from to stay like this!'

'Ya. It's bad, sonny. Think of the many other such
places in Soweto alone. How many are there? Let's
see — it's this one, Dube, Nhlazane, Merafe, Nance-
field,' counted Joe.

'And Diepkloof. All about the same size. Hundreds
of thousands of disgruntled men, leaving hundreds of
thousands of starving families in the so-called home-
lands. That's not counting us location people, because
we're not much better off than the hostel residents
except in that we are allowed a temporary sojourn
with our families.'

'Not counting the rest of South Africa either. It's
not only Johannesburg. All over the country there are
people who have uprooted from normal family life
to slave in the cities. Take Somdali's bitterness and
multiply it about twenty million times and see if you
don't arrive at a very sad and volcanic state of affairs,'
said Joe, and I silently agreed with him.

At home I thought about the hostel before I dozed
off. The more I recalled all the details of my visit the
more I felt depressed. My last thought was that the
world was still too far from perfection and that those

who hoped for world peace at this point in time were building castles in the air.

It would not be the last time I visited Somdali. Something about the dirt and the desolation of the hostel attracted me strongly towards the place. Instead of going there for vice, like many of the location people, I went there out of sympathy with my friends and maybe that is why I felt so strongly about the way they lived. What's more, sharing the emptiness of the life of Somdali and his comrades filled, for me, the listless evenings on street corners, outside the shops and at the station. Every day we gave vent to our feelings and it was amazing how therapeutic the exercise was for me. It gave me the satisfaction of knowing much more about life than those who prefer the escapism of artificiality.

As I continued going there, I discovered that song was the only solace of those lonely people. At least two days a week they sang traditional choral music. After supper they would assemble in the adjoining closet and start singing with the conscientiousness of a stage group rehearsing for a fête. Hearing this, Mbobo and others would come from the opposite house and join in the singing. Some of the songs were performed with graceful dances, so elegantly carried out that I wondered where they could all have learnt the same paces. When they sang, it was from the core of their souls, their eyes glazed with memories of where they had first sung those lyrics; and interruptions were not tolerated. Sometimes I was so moved by their music that I yearned to join them, and because I did not know the songs I sailed away in my mind for paradises that I conjured up, where people sang their troubles away. After an evening of invigorating talk and untainted African traditional

song I went away feeling as if I had found treasure
in a graveyard. Those men might be buried there in
the labour camps, but they are still people and,
because they live in the throes of debasement, human
adaptability has given them a most simple and
practical approach to life, and none of the illusions of
people who live comfortable lives or strive only for
that throughout their time on earth, never achieving
it but ending up drowning their frustrations in the
pleasures of the flesh, half-immersed in intoxicants
and half out of their minds half the time, until their
humanity rots inside them. I would rather depend
on a poor man for help, because a rich man, never
having known hunger himself, will let you go away
with an empty stomach.

The weekends were most exciting. They made me
think of words I heard from a friend (I don't know
where he picked them up). He would look at some of
the people we worked with, who came from the rural
areas and say, 'You can take the man out of the
country, but you can never take the country out of
the man.' On Friday the dreariness was stirred by a
din that reached a crescendo on Sunday afternoon.

A typical weekend went like this: after looking in
at home on Friday, I would go up to the hostel in the
company of Joe or some of the guys who went there
to augment their scanty paypackets with Soweto's
favourite game of chance, shooting craps (dice).
Somdali was a loyal worshipper of Bacchus. I would
find him sitting like a lord in the shadows of his kist
with two or three bottles of beer between his legs, the
rest of a whole crate inside the multi-purpose 'bed'.
When I came in he would greet me like a long-lost
friend, as if we had not been together only an hour or
so before.

'Aah, son of my mother! You came just in time. Borrow a mug from one of our brothers here and let us drink to our ancestors. Bongani, give him something to drink with.'

'Here, Somdali. You're drinking the sweat of your brow? Is this what you have been working for, the whole week?' I would reply jokingly, and accept the mug that Bongani handed to me.

'Of course — what do you think? It's Friday today; everybody drinks white man's beer and feels rich. Come on, use your mouth for what it should be used now, not for preaching.'

When Joe was with me, he did not wait to be invited, but took a container and gulped down as much as he could before Somdali protested that he was drinking as if it was his last day on earth.

Meanwhile, the game would be warming up in the main room. 'Five I do, five I do . . . Eê, pop! Eê, six three!' we would hear them singing out with great gusto. On that evening the stove would burn itself to ashes with no one tending it. Fridays they did not dine together. Everyone ate an almost substantial meal in one of the city 'chesanyamas' and returned to the hostel replete. Old Khuzwayo never returned at weekends because of the boisterousness, which was too much for his aged nerves. He slept in the sky slums on the roof of the Golden City. When we felt that the game was hot enough, we went in for the gambit. Sometimes we won and at other times we lost, but mostly we lost. The foolish lost their whole pay envelopes there and it was such a pity to watch them begging to be advanced more money, only to lose that as well. Depending on the amount of money involved, it was possible for the game to last the whole night. The winners never hung around the game long, but went off to drink their crumpled scoops in one of the countless haunts of vice. When you are poor there is no form of entertainment that you can afford to drown your misfortunes in besides over-indulgence of one kind or another.

At Msomi's you got everything: cigarettes, dagga, any concoction you wanted, and the profligate women whose sole source of income was peddling themselves to the famished hostel men. The latter were only too eager to part with a little hard-earned cash for the company of anything in skirts, no matter what she was like. Msomi's traffic in vice was booming and there was no fear of interference from the police, any sign of whom in the hostel invoked among the inhabitants a primordial bloodlust. Stoning and hacking to death of 'sellout intruders', as they referred to them, occurred from time to time.

When it got late I went home or somewhere else in the location. The difference was striking. In the location the presence of womenfolk and children contributed a certain amount of warmth and a reason for living; a man's delight is a loving woman and growing children.

Saturday morning was always a drab spectacle. Many woke up with a whole day to themselves. Before the beerhall was destroyed, everybody swarmed there to sink what had remained of their Friday earnings in beer. There was nothing else they could do. When the bar went up in flames the Msomis saw a chance to go into business supplying their hostel mates with debauchery. However, even before that, as soon as the sun surfaced in the east on Saturdays, everybody came out of their lairs to soak up the mild morning beams. They made me think of a plague-stricken concentration camp although I had never seen

one. That is why when I learnt of Auschwitz, the
Nazi camp in Poland, I simply dubbed the hostel 'our
Auschwitz'. Grim-looking men sat or stood against
the wall drinking from tins at every house. Some did
their washing at the troughs and others clustered
together playing dice. Door-to-door merchants had
their colourful goods draped over their shoulders and
arms with the rest of their stocks in bulging paper
bags. The clothing they sold ranged from men's under-
wear to overcoats, and even female garments which
were bought and locked away until such time as
the buyer took them home to present to his family.
The street vendors would be preparing their make-
shift shops to start selling everything from sheep
entrails to chicken pieces that hummed with green
flies, while the rib-cages of mongrels kept themselves
at a safe salivating distance. As the day got older, the
tempo would increase to a fast drunken frenzy until
the night came to cover it all up.

Then, on Sunday, a sleeping social consciousness,
underlined by a strong traditional inclination, showed
itself. The men drank together according to their
places of origin. Don't mistake this for a reflection of
tribalism. It was only their recollection of how they
used to spend their Sundays in the different country
areas they came from — not necessarily Sundays, but
those days that were traditionally set aside for social
gatherings where the young and nimble entertained
their elders with dances to the sound of tom-toms
and songs which were sung by the great-grandfathers
and handed down from father to son.

Sunday morning was no different from a Saturday
except that you could see that something important
was being prepared for. The few converts wore their
'Zionist' uniforms of blue on snow-white and clutch-

ed their staffs and bibles to join other worshippers in
the locations. Groups of dancers wearing distinctive
garb left the hostel singing, whistling, waving their
dancing sticks and pausing at every busy street corner
to treat the location people to some dancing and
singing. The disappointing part was that many location
people regarded it as backwardness. 'You'll never see
whites doing such things where they stay,' they
would say. Why should the whites do them? Mos
they're not black like I am. And who told you that
your whites are the measuring standard of right and
wrong? I wanted to ask the critics but chose not to
because I knew their minds had been stolen from
them in order to 'civilize' them. Other groups came
from other hostels to ours in the same fashion, their
sorrows forgotten for a while.

At two in the afternoon, after preparing themselves,
the groups went out to the 'market-place' (an open
space near where the beerhall used to be and where
most of the vendors sold their assortments of goods).
The first sound of the tom-tom and the flutes of the
Pedis brought people to watch from all corners of the
hostel.

The baPedi formed a line and swayed gracefully
from side to side, blowing their flutes in typical
fashion while others played the drums of diminishing
size, the biggest of them made out of paraffin drums
and the smallest the size of a gallon of paint.

A most exciting entertainment was provided by the
foot-stomping Zulus. They dressed in traditional attire
and danced to the sound of a single drum with
amazing rhythm. They sat or knelt in formations of
four, five or six, according to the size of the competing
groups, clapping hands in unison with the drum and
singing or humming in high spirits. They kept them-

selves going with long draughts from a big black clay vessel which was refilled from large plastic containers. The competitors took the 'stage' like waves, those in front vigorously stomping the ground with their tyre sandals until you thought you could feel it vibrating. Their feet rose above their heads and came down thunderously. Endurance and physical fitness is basic to the African 'ballet', and a weakling does not waste his time going on the stage. As I say, the dance was performed with superb rhythm. If you missed a step you were penalized by having to leave the stage to await your partners, and your group lost points for that.

The drum, the clapping hands, the songs, shouts of 'Usuthu!' and the rising and falling legs went on and on, the muscular and wiry black bodies glistening with sweat until sunset, when the sun would lie on Meadowlands like a glowing half-circle, and the smoke from the chimneys would blanket the slumbering Soweto.

Njabulo Ndebele
THE MUSIC OF THE VIOLIN

Vukani was doing homework in his bedroom when voices in the living room slowly filtered into his mind. He lifted his head to look up, as if to focus his ears. No. He could not recognise the voices. Now and again the hum of conversation was punctuated with laughter. Then he grew apprehensive, the continuing conversation suddenly filling him with dread. He tried to concentrate on his work: 'Answer the following questions: How did the coming of the whites lead to the establishment of prosperity and peace among the various Bantu tribes? . . . ' But the peace had gone from his mind. The questions had become a meaningless task. Instinctively, he turned round to look at his music stand at the foot of his bed. Yesterday he had practised some Mozart. Then he saw the violin leaning against the wall next to the stand. Would they come to interrupt him? He felt certain they would. He stood up, thinking of a way of escape.

There was another peal of laughter from the living room, and Vukani wondered again who the visitors were. As he opened the door slowly, he was met by another thunderous roar. Escape would be impossible.

He had to go through the living room and would
certainly be called by his mother to be introduced to
the visitors, and then the usual agony would follow.
A delicate clink of cups and saucers told Vukani that
the visitors had been served with tea. Another roar.
His father and the male visitor were laughing. He
knew now that the visitors were a man and a woman,
but he did not recognise their voices. Growing curious,
he opened the door by another inch or so, and saw
the woman visitor, who sat close to where the passage
to the bedrooms began. Vukani's mother, still in
her white nursing uniform, sat close to the woman
visitor in another heavily cushioned chair. They were
separated by a coffee table.

'I couldn't make it at all to the meeting last
Saturday,' said Vukani's mother.

'Which meeting?' asked the woman.

The men laughed again.

'Don't you laugh so loudly,' Vukani's mother
shouted.

'You see,' Vukani's father was saying, 'I had caught
the fellow by surprise, the way I like to catch them.'

'That's the only way to ensure that the work gets
done,' said the other man.

'Indeed,' agreed Vukani's father.

'So?' asked the other man.

'So I said: "Show me the students' garden plots." I
saw a twitch of anguish across his face. But he was a
clever fellow, you see. He quickly recovered and said:
"Of course Sir, of course, come along." So we went.
There was a wilderness around the school. These bush
schools: I wouldn't have been surprised if a python
had stopped us in our tracks. So, after about two
hundred yards of walking, and all the wilderness
around us, I began to wonder. So I said to this teacher:

"Mr Mabaso," — that was the fellow's name — "these plots, they are quite far, aren't they?" "We're just about there, Sir," he said.'

'Man alive!' exclaimed the other man. 'This story is getting hot. Let me sip one more time.' There was silence while the man sipped his tea. Vukani's mother also lifted her cup to her lips. The women were now listening too.

'So,' continued Vukani's father, 'we walked another two hundred yards and I turned to look at the man. "We're just about there, Sir." '

Everybody laughed. 'You see, the fellow was now sweating like a horse.'

'So?' asked the woman visitor, laughing some more. She was wiping her eyes with a tissue.

'Then this fellow, Mabaso, shows me a hill about a mile away and says: "We're going there, to that hill, Sir, the plots are behind it. You see, Sir, I figured that since the wind normally hits the hill on the side we are looking at now, I should have the plots on the leeward side to protect the plants." What bosh!'

There was more laughter and the male visitor said, in the middle of it: 'Beatrice, give me some Kleenex, please.' His wife stood up and disappeared from Vukani's view. She returned. Vukani heard the blowing of a nose. It must have been the man.

'Please don't laugh, fellow Africans,' said Vukani's father. 'The man is a genius. What's this poem by the English poet? The man blushes unseen in the wilderness. He knew I would not go any further. So I really have no proof that there were no garden plots.'

'Of course there weren't any,' asserted Vukani's mother.

'Of course there weren't,' everybody agreed.

'You school inspectors,' said the male visitor, 'have

real problems with these bush schools.'

'You haven't heard anything yet,' agreed Vukani's father. 'We just can't get it into these teachers' heads that we have to uplift the black nation. And we cannot do that through cheating and laziness. We will not develop self-reliance that way. That fellow was just not teaching the students gardening, and that is dead against government policy.' Vukani shut the door. In spite of himself, he had been amused by the story. He went back to the desk and tried to continue with the homework. He could not. What about going out through the window? No. That would be taking things too far. He wondered where Teboho, his sister was. Probably in her bedroom.

Teboho and their mother were getting involved in too many heated exchanges these days. Their mother tended to make too many demands on them. Vukani wished he could go and talk to Teboho. They had grown very close. Then he suddenly became frantic again and went to the door. He had to escape. When he opened the door, slightly again, it was the woman named Beatrice who was talking.

'You just don't know what you missed, you,' she was saying. The men laughed again.

'Please, you men!' appealed Vukani's mother. But they laughed once again.

'Do you want us to leave you and go to the bedroom?' threatened Vukani's mother. 'And you know if we go in there we won't come out.'

'Peace! Peace!' shouted Vukani's father. 'Peace, women of Africa!'

Then he lowered his voice as he continued to talk to the other man.

'What have I missed?' asked Vukani's mother, eagerly.

'Well, you just don't know what you've missed,' said Mrs Beatrice, pulling the bait away from the fish.

'Please don't tease me.'

'I want to do just that,' said Mrs Beatrice, clapping once and sitting forward in her chair, her legs thrust underneath. She kept on pulling her tight-fitting skirt down over her big knees. But after each effort, the skirt slipped back, revealing the knees again.

'You women are on again about the Housewives' League,' interrupted Vukani's father.

'Day in and day out,' supported the other man.

'Of course yes!' said Mrs Beatrice with emphatic pride.

'Forget about these men,' pleaded Vukani's mother, 'and give me a pinch of the story.'

'Mother-of-Teboho, you really missed,' Mrs Beatrice started. 'A white woman came all the way from Emmarentia, a high-class exclusive suburb, to address the meeting on Jewish recipes. Came all the way to Soweto for that. It was wonderful.'

'Was it not Mrs Kaplinsky?'

'As if you knew!'

'Eh, please, give me! Give me!' shouted Vukani's mother with great excitement, clapping her hands repeatedly. 'I'm fetching my pen, I'm fetching my pen. Give me those recipes.' But she did not leave to go and fetch her pen.

'I'm selling them, dearie. Business first, friendship after.' They laughed.

'*Ei*! Women and food!' exclaimed the other man.

'What! We cook for you,' retorted his wife.

'Exactly,' concurred Vukani's mother. 'More tea?'

'No thanks, dearie.'

'Hey you men, more tea?' But the men were already back to their conversation. Vukani's father

answered while laughing, suddenly coming into
Vukani's view as he brought his empty cup to the
coffee table that separated the women.

'No thanks,' he was saying, 'No thanks . . . he he he
hehehehe . . . that was a good one . . . no thanks . . .
what a good one.' Then he took out a handkerchief
from the pocket of his trousers, wiped his eyes, wiped
his whole face, and then wiped his lips. 'A jolly good
evening, tonight.' Then he went back to his chair,
disappearing from Vukani's view.

'Thanks for the tea,' said the other man, blowing
his nose.

'Teboho!' called Vukani's mother. 'Please come
and clear up here!'

Teboho appeared carrying a tray. She had on
denim jeans and a loose blouse.

'That was a nice cup of tea, Teboho,' said the other
man. Teboho smiled shyly. 'When are you going back
to varsity?'

'We have six more weeks,' replied Teboho.

'You are lucky to have children who are educating
themselves, dearie,' said Mrs Beatrice.

'Oh, well,' said Vukani's mother shrugging her
shoulders, as Teboho disappeared into the kitchen.
There was silence.

'Sometimes these South African Jews sicken me,'
said the other man reflectively.

'Why?' the two women asked.

'Well, they're hypocrites! I mean look, they say
they were killed left and right by the Germans, but
here they are helping the Boers to sit on us.'

'How can you say such a thing?' asked his wife.
'People like Mrs Kaplinsky are very good friends of
ours. Some of her best friends are Africans.'

'Because she gives you recipes?'

'Food, my dear husband, belongs to mankind, not just to one race.'

'Yes, exactly,' agreed Vukani's mother, 'like art, literature and things. Completely universal.'

'Well . . . ' said the man, but he did not pursue the matter further.

'In fact this reminds me,' said Vukani's mother with sudden enthusiasm, her eyes glittering, 'instead of sitting here talking politics, we should be listening to some music. Have you heard my son play? He plays the violin. A most wonderful instrument!'

'Yes,' said Vukani's father, 'you know . . . '

Vukani swiftly shut the door, shutting out the living room conversation with an abruptness that brought him sharply to himself as he moved to the centre of the room. He began to feel very lonely and noticed that he was trembling. It was coming now. He looked at the history homework on the desk, then looked at the reading lamp with its circular light which seemed to be baking the open pages of the books on the desk with its intensity, while the books looked as if they were waiting for that delicate moment when they would burst into flame. Then he thought of Doksi his friend. He wondered where he was and what he was doing at that moment. Friday evening? Probably watching his father cutting the late evening customers' hair and trimming it carefully while he murmured a song as always. Doksi had said to Vukani one day that when he was a grown-up, he would like to be a barber like his father. And Doksi did love hair. Vukani remembered his favourite game: a weekly ritual of hair burning. Every Saturday afternoon Doksi would make a fire out in the yard and when it was burning steadily, toss knots of hair into it. The hair would catch fire with a crackling

brilliance that always sent him into raptures of
delight. He never seemed to mind the smell of the
burning hair. One Saturday after his bonfire Doksi
had said, while making the sign of the cross over the
smoking fire: 'When God had finished burning hair
he thought that it was good.' Vukani had playfully
accused him of sacrilege. But Doksi, suddenly looking
serious, had said, 'Dead things catch fire.' Now
Vukani was suddenly fascinated by a desire to see the
books on the desk aflame. Perhaps he should lower
the lamp, bringing it closer to the books. It was a silly
idea but he lowered the lamp all the same. But the
papers shone defiantly with a sheen. It was futile.
Then he saw his violin again, and felt the sensation
of fear deep in his breast.

He looked at the violin with dread, as something
that could bring both pain and pleasure at once. It was
like the red dress which Miss Yende, their class
teacher in Standard Four, occasionally wore. She had
once said to the class: 'When I wear this red dress,
children, know that I shall not stomach any nonsense
that day. Know that I shall expect sharp minds: I
shall expect quick responses to my questions, and I
shall expect absolute seriousness. And I shall use the
stick with the vengeance of the God of the Old
Testament.' That dress! It was a deep, rich velvety red
that gave the impression that the dress had a flowery
fragrance. Yet, because it also signalled the possibility
of pain, it had a dreadful repulsiveness.

Vukani tried to brace himself for the coming of the
visitors. It was always like that. Every visitor was
brought to his room, where he was required to be
doing his school work or practising on the violin.

Then he had to entertain these visitors with violin
music. It was always an agonising nuisance to be an

unwilling entertainer. What would happen if he
should refuse to play that night? He knew what his
mother would say. It was the same thing all the time.
His eyes swept round the room. He was well provided
for. There was the beautiful desk on which he did his
work; bookshelves full of books, including a set of
the *Encyclopaedia Britannica*; a reading lamp on the
desk; two comfortable easy chairs; a wardrobe full of
clothes; his own portable transistor radio; a violin and
a music stand; a chest full of games: Monopoly, chess
and many others. His mother never tired of telling
him how lucky he was. 'There is not a single boy in
the whole of Soweto, not even here in Dube, who has
a room like yours. This room is as good as any white
boy's. Isn't it exactly like Ronnie Simpson's? You
yourself, you ungrateful boy, saw that room when we
visited the Simpsons in Parktown North. Kaffir
children! That's what. Always ungrateful!'

What did all this really mean to him when it
brought so much pain? Vukani remembered what
teacher Maseko had said at assembly one morning:
'Children, I would rather be a hungry dog that runs
freely in the streets, than a fat, chained dog burdened
with itself and the weight of the chain. Whenever the
white man tells you that he has made you much better
off than Africans elsewhere on this continent, tell him
he is lying before God!' There were cheers that
morning at assembly, and the children had sung the
morning's hymn with a feeling of energetic release:

> *I will make you fishers of men*
> *Fishers of men*
> *Fishers of men*
> *I will make you fishers of men*
> *If you follow me.*

Three weeks later, teacher Maseko was fired. The

Principal had made the announcement at morning
assembly. He spoke in Afrikaans, always. Concluding
the announcement, he said: 'Children, a wandering
dog, that upsets garbage bins and ejects its dung all
over the place, is a very dangerous animal. It is a
carrier of disease and pestilence, and when you see it,
pelt it with stones. What should you do to it?'

'Pelt it with stones!' was the sombre response of
the assembled children that morning. Vukani had
wondered whether teacher Maseko was that dog. But
how could anybody pelt teacher Maseko with stones?

Vukani heard another roar of laughter from the
living room. But why did his mother have to show off
at his expense like this? That Friday, as on all
Mondays, Wednesdays and Fridays, he had carried his
violin to school. The other children at school never
got used to it. It was a constant source of wonder and
ridicule. 'Here's a fellow with a strange guitar!' some
would say. Others would ask him to play the current
township hits. It was so every day. Then one day his
violin disappeared from class while he went out to
the boys' toilet. He was met with stony faces when
after school he pleaded for its return. Everybody
simply went home and there was no sign of the violin.
What would he say to his music teacher in town? What
would he say to his mother? When he went out of the
classroom, he found Doksi waiting for him. They
always went home together, except on the days when
Vukani had to go to town for his music lessons after
school. 'Doksi,' he said, 'I can't find my violin.
Somebody took it.'

'These boys of shit!' Doksi cursed sympathetically.
He had not waited for details. He knew his friend's
problem. 'Do you suspect anybody?'

'I can't say,' replied Vukani. 'The whole class

seems to have ganged up on me. There are some things that always bring them together.' 'Even Gwendoline?' asked Doksi, with a mischievous smirk on his face. Gwendoline was the frail, brilliant, beautiful girl who vied with Vukani for first position in class. Vukani had always told Doksi that he would like to marry that girl one day. And Doksi would always say: 'With you it's talk, talk all the time. Why don't you just go to this girl and tell her you love her? Just look at how she looks at you. She's suffering, man!'

'Look,' said Vukani, 'this is no time for jokes. My violin is lost.'

'The trouble with you, Vukani, is that you are too soft. I would never stand this nonsense. I'd just face the whole class and say, "Whoever took my violin is a coward. Why doesn't he come out and fight?" I'm sure it was taken by one of those big boys whom everybody fears. Big bodies without minds. They ought to be working in town. Just at school to avoid paying tax. But me, they know me. They know what my brothers would do. My whole family would come here looking for the bastards.' Most of the children had gone now. Only those whose turn it was to clean the classrooms remained.

'Let's go and tell the Principal,' suggested Vukani. The Principal was one of those Vukani had entertained one day in his bedroom. He was a friend of his father's. 'But maybe we shouldn't,' said Vukani, changing his mind.

'Let's go and find out from the girls sweeping your classroom,' suggested Doksi. They went back. The girls were singing loudly and the room was full of dust. 'Leave it to me,' said Doksi. There were four girls in there. Gwendoline and Manana were as old as

Doksi and Vukani. The other two girls, Topsana and
Sarah were older. Much older.

'Hey, you girls!' shouted Doksi, squaring his
shoulders and looking like a cowboy about to draw.
'Where is the bloody violin?' The bigger girls simply
laughed.

'And who are you, toughie?' asked Sarah, pushing
a desk out of the way for Topsana to sweep.

'Hey you, Vukani,' called Topsana, 'I want to
soothe your heart. I've long been waiting for this
moment. Come and kiss me.' The smaller girls giggled,
and Vukani regretted that they had come back. 'I
mean it,' said Topsana. 'I know who took your violin.
It's safe. You'll find it at home. I made them promise
to take it there. There now, I want my kiss. I want to
kiss the inspector's son.'

Doksi turned to the younger girls, 'Hey you, what
is the joke? What's there to laugh at?'

'Hha!' protested Manana, sweeping rather purpose-
fully. 'We have a right to laugh.'

'I can show you a thing or two,' Doksi said. 'Punch
you up or something.'

'Doksi,' appealed Vukani, 'please let's go.' Doksi
clearly felt the need for retreat, but it had to be done
with dignity. He addressed all the girls with a sweep
of his hand, 'You are all useless. One of these days I'll
get you. Come on, Vukani, let's go.'

The walk home for Vukani had been a long one.
Better not to tell the parents. If Topsana had been
telling the truth, then he should wait. Nobody asked
him about the violin. But he would never forget the
morning following that day when his mother stormed
into his bedroom, black with anger. She had simply
come in and pulled the blankets off him. She glared
at him, holding the violin in one of her hands. Vukani

had felt so exposed — as if his mother was about to hit him with the violin. It was very early in the morning. His mother was already dressed up in her uniform, ready to go to work. If she was on day duty, she had to leave very early for the hospital.

'Vukani!' she was shouting. 'What desecration is this? What ultimate act of ungratefulness is this? Is this to spite me? Is this an insult? Tell me before I finish you off!'

'What's happening, Dorcas?' Vukani saw his father entering the bedroom. 'Can you believe this? I found this violin on the doorstep outside as I was leaving for work. Can you believe this?'

'Vukani,' said his father. 'What on earth could have made you do such a thing?'

'I didn't put it there, *Baba*,' Vukani replied.

'Nonsense,' shouted his mother, 'you have the nerve to tell your parents a lie.'

'Wait a minute, dear, maybe we should hear what he has to say.' Vukani had nothing to say. The deep feeling of having been wronged could only find expression in tears. He heard the violin land next to him and he recoiled from its coldness. He also heard his mother leave, saying that he was crying because of his sins. She never knew what had happened.

But that had been a year ago. Today he had been humiliated again in public, and there were people in that living room who wanted to humiliate him again. Right inside his home. It was all because of this violin. The homework had made him forget the latest ordeal for a while. The homework was like a jigsaw puzzle; you simply looked for pieces which fitted. All the answers were there in the chapter. You just moved your finger up and down the page until you spotted the correct answer. There was no thinking

involved. But now it was all gone. It was not South
African History, the story of the coming of the
white man he was looking at, he was now faced with
the reality of the violin.

There was that gang of boys who always stood
under the shop verandah at Maponya's shopping
complex. They shouted, 'Hey, music man!' whenever
he went past their 'headquarters' on his way home to
Dube. That very Friday they had done more than
shout at him from a distance. They had stopped him
and humiliated him before all those workers who
were returning from work in town.

'Hey, music man,' the one who seemed to be their
leader had called. Vukani, as a rule, never answered
them. He just walked on as if he had not heard
anything. But that afternoon, as he was coming up
from Phefeni station, and was turning round the
corner to go down towards the AME church, it was
as if the gang had been waiting for him.

'Hey, music man!' This time it was a chorus. Out
of the corner of his eye, Vukani saw two boys detach
themselves from the gang. He dare not turn to look.
He had to act unconcerned. He tried to quicken his
steps as imperceptibly as possible.

'Music man! Don't you know your name?' They
were behind him now. Crossing the street had been
no problem for them. They simply walked into the
street and cars came to a screeching halt. They were
the kings of the township. They just parted the traffic
as Moses must have parted the waves of the sea.
Vukani wanted to run but he was not going to give
himself away. If he ran and they caught up with him,
they could do a lot of harm to him. He had had that
feeling of wanting to take advantage of something
weaker than himself when he found a stray dog trying

to topple a garbage bin. If the dog had stood its
ground and growled, he would have been afraid. But
the dog had taken to its heels, tail tucked between
legs, and Vukani had been filled with the urge to run
after the dog, catch it, and beat it to death. A fleeing
impala must excite the worst destructive urge in a
lion. Vukani had once seen a film in which a lion
charged at a frightened impala. There had been a
confidence in the purposeful strides of the lion, as
if it felt this was just a game that would surely end
with the bringing down of the prey.

A hand grabbed Vukani's collar behind and jerked
him violently to a halt. The leader of the gang came
round and faced him. He held Vukani by the knot of
his tie. He was short but heavily built. He had puffed
up cheeks with scars on them. His bloodshot eyes
suggested the violence in him. He must have been
four or five years older than Vukani.

'Spy!' the leader cursed, glaring at Vukani. 'So you
are special! So we had to cross the street and risk
death in order to talk to you. You don't know your
name, music man? Every day we greet you nice and
you don't answer. Because you think you are being
greeted by shit. By scum, hey? Why, spy? Are we
shit?'

'Ja! Just answer that,' said the fellow behind, 'are
we shit?' Vukani tried to free his neck.

'Shit!' screamed the leader, 'we just wanted to talk
to you nice-nice. That's all. We just wanted to dance
to your music a little. Dance to your guitar a little.
But no. You don't even look at us. Do we smell,
music man? Do we smell?' There was a crowd of
workers now who were watching the spectacle quietly.

'Shake him up, Bhuka!' was the chorus from the
rest of the gang about thirty yards away at the shop.

'What are you rogues doing to this poor boy?' asked an old lady who had a bundle of washing on her head.

'Shut up!' said Bhuka. 'Go and do your white man's washing, he'll want it tomorrow.' Some of the crowd laughed at this.

'Dogs of the street! Don't talk like that to your mother. Whose child are you?'

'I'm your child,' said Bhuka with a certain flourish. This time more of the crowd laughed.

'He's the child of his mother!' said the boy behind Vukani. None laughed at that one. He was in the shadow of his leader.

'You are laughing,' said the woman, bravely addressing the crowds. 'You are laughing at this boy being harassed and you are laughing at me being insulted by these street urchins. I could be your mother and this could be your son. *Sies!* You rogues, just let decent people be.' The woman then left, taking Vukani's hopes with her. But she unsettled Bhuka slightly. He had to move his prey to safer ground. Too many lesser animals could be a disturbance. He tightened his grip around Vukani's tie, pulling him across the street towards the 'headquarters'. Vukani looked at the fist below his chin, and saw that it had a little sixth finger. There were two shining copper bangles round the wrist. Part of the crowd left but another part wanted to see the game to its end. They followed the trio to the shop. The gang had then completely encircled Vukani.

'Do you have a sister?' Bhuka snapped. Vukani had trouble breathing now. Bhuka realised this and loosened the grip. Vukani thought of Teboho at home. If she came here she would fight for him. 'I asked you a question. Do you have a sister?' Vukani nodded. 'Hey man, talk!'

'Is your voice precious? His master's voice!'

'Yes,' answered Vukani in a whisper.

'I want to fuck her. Do you hear? I want to eat her up thoroughly. Do you hear? Tell her that.' Bhuka then paused and jerked Vukani to and fro so that Vukani's head bobbed. He then stopped and glowered at Vukani. 'And what song will you play when I am on top of her?' There was a festive laugh from the crowd. Bhuka looked round in acknowledgement. 'Tell me now, can you play *Thoko Ujola Nobani?*' It was a current hit.

Vukani felt tears in his eyes. He blinked many times to keep them in. Why couldn't they just leave him alone. That day would be final, he would simply tell his parents that he did not want to play the violin again. If they still insisted, he would run away from home. 'Please, leave me alone,' he heard himself say.

'I asked you. Can you play *Thoko Ujola Nobani?*'

Vukani shook his head.

'Why, music man?'

'I'd have to see it written first. I can't just play it like that.'

'Next time you pass here you must know that song. And come with your sister!' Then he gave Vukani a shove in the chest, and Vukani reeled backwards and fell on his back. But he still held onto the violin. 'Next time we greet you nice-nice, you must greet nice-nice.' Vukani got up timidly and hurried away, glancing backwards occasionally. Somehow he felt relieved. It could have been worse. The stories he had heard about the violence of this gang were simply unbelievable. He felt deep inside him the laughter that followed him as he slunk away. Just after passing the AME church, he saw the rubbish heap that people had created at the corner and wished he was brave enough to throw the violin there.

'My son,' his mother had said one day when Vukani had complained about the harassment he suffered as a result of the violin, 'you should never yield to ignorance.'

'But maybe you should buy me a piano,' Vukani had said. 'I can't carry that in the street.'

'If Yehudi Menuhin had listened to fools, he wouldn't be the greatest living violinist. A violin you have, and a violin you shall play.'

That's how it had ended. But his agony had continued three times a week.

Then the door opened. 'Here he is!' said Vukani's mother as she led the visitors in. His father took the rear. Vukani blankly looked at the homework: Question Three: Who introduced the European type of education among the Bantu . . . ? But Vukani felt only the solid presence of four people behind him.

'Vuka,' said his mother, 'I did not hear you practise today.' It was not clear from her voice whether she was finding fault with her son or was just trying to say something by way of introduction. Vukani turned round and smiled sheepishly. They all looked at him as if they expected him to defend himself, their eyes occasionally going to the table as if to see what he was doing.

'Are you doing your homework, son?' asked the male visitor.

'E!'

'Good, hard-working boy!' he said, patting him on the shoulder. And Vukani felt in that hand the heaviness of condescension.

'He's a very serious-minded boy,' added his mother with obvious pride.

'You are very happy, dearie, to have a child who loves school,' commented Mrs Beatrice.

'And here is my Mozart's violin,' said Vukani's father, pointing at the violin against the wall. He took the case, opened it and took out the violin.

'Vuka!'

'Ma!'

'These visitors are the mother and father of Lauretta. Do you know her?'

'No, I don't think I do,' said Vukani, shaking his head.

'But you are at the same school together. Surely you know Lauretta, the daughter of Doctor Zwane? Stand up to greet them.'

Vukani then remembered the girl, who was well known at school for her brilliance. She was two classes ahead of Vukani. But Vukani wondered if she could beat Gwendoline. Vukani greeted the visitors and went back to his seat.

'Vuka, you will play the visitors something, won't you? What will you play us?' asked his mother. Vukani looked at the violin in his father's hands. He was explaining to Dr Zwane the various kinds of violins.

'This type,' he was saying, 'is very rare. You do not find it easily these days. Not at all.'

'It must have been very expensive,' observed Dr Zwane appreciatively, 'one can judge from its looks.'

'Five hundred and fifty rands down,' butted in Vukani's mother, 'made to specifications. You just tell them how you want it and they just make it. This is special.'

'One has to pay to produce a Mozart,' said Vukani's father with finality.

'We had Lauretta start on ballet recently,' said Mrs Zwane, as if suggesting that they were also doing their duty. 'I'm happy to note that she seems to be doing well. All these things have to be taught at school. You school inspectors have a duty to ensure that it happens.'

'Indeed,' agreed Vukani's father. 'But do you think the Boers would agree? Never. Remember they say Western Civilisation is spoiling us. So we have to cultivate the indigenous way of life.' The conversation was stopped by Vukani's mother.

'Okay now.' She clapped her hands. 'What will you play us?'

Vukani's father brought the violin to him. He took it with his visibly shaking hands. He saw the red, glowering eyes of Bhuka that afternoon. He heard the laughter of people in the streets. He remembered being violently shaken awake by his angry mother one morning. He remembered one of his dreams which came very frequently. He was naked in the streets and people were laughing. He did not know how he had come to be naked. It always occurred that way. He would be naked in the streets and people would be laughing. Suddenly he would reach home and his mother would scold him for bringing shame to the family. But the dream would always end with him leaving home and flying out into the sky with his hands as wings.

Vukani found that he had instinctively put the violin on his left shoulder. And when he became aware, he felt its irksome weight on him. What did people want of him? He did not want to play. He did not want to play. And for the second time that day, he felt the tears coming to his eyes and again he blinked repeatedly to keep them from flowing. This was the time.

'Mama!'

'Yes, son.' But Vukani did not go on.

His mother continued: 'Why don't you play some selections from Brahms? You know some extracts from his only violin concerto? Perhaps Mozart? Yes Mozart. I know that sometimes one is in the mood for a particular composer. What about Liszt? Where are your music books? There is something on the music stand: what is it? Ahh! it's the glorious beautiful Dvorak. Tum tee tum!' She shook her head, conducting an imaginary orchestra. 'Come up and play some of this Dvorak.'

Vukani wanted to shout, but his throat was completely dry. He wanted to sink into the ground. He tried to swallow. It was only dryness he swallowed and it hurt against the throat. Standing up would be agonising. His strength and resistance were all gathered up in his sitting position. All that strength would be dissipated if he stood up. And he would feel exposed, lonely and vulnerable. The visitors and his parents soon noticed that there was something amiss.

'What is it, Vuka?' asked his mother. 'Is there something wrong?'

'Nothing wrong, ma.' He had missed his opportunity. Why did he fear? Why did he not act decisively for his own good? Then he felt anger building up in him, but he was not sure whether he was angry with himself or with his parents — together with the visitors whose presence was now forcing him to come to terms with his hitherto unexpressed determination to stop doing what brought him suffering. At that moment there was a dull explosion from the kitchen, of something massive suddenly disintegrating into pieces. There was silence for a while. Then Vukani's mother muttered: 'The bloody street girl has done it again.' And she stormed out of the bedroom. Her voice could be heard clearly in the kitchen: '*Awu*, Lord of the heavens! My . . . my expensive . . . my precious . . . my expensive . . . this girl has done it again. Teboho, has the devil got into you again? Do you have to break something every day?' Vukani's mother was now shrieking with anger. 'Do you know what? Maybe you don't. I gave Mrs Willard three hundred rands to bring me this set from Hong Kong when she went there on holiday. And I have told you countless times that you should be extra careful when you handle those dishes. Such care doesn't cost much. How many households in the whole of Johannesburg, white and black, can boast of owning such a set — a genuine set? But you, you refuse to appreciate that. Don't just stand there . . . '

'Mama, can you please just stop that,' said Teboho in a voice that sounded urgently restrained.

'Is that how you are talking to me?'

Then Teboho's voice seemed to lose all restraint: 'You don't want to listen to anybody, you just come in shouting.' The voice was loud and defiant.

'Is that how they teach you to talk to your parents at the university?'

'Mama, that is not the point.'

'Are you arguing with me?'

'The point is that you have been showing more interest in your dishes and your furniture than in your children.'

'What?'

'I'm not going to say anything more.'

'Slut! That's what you are! What decent girl would talk like that to her mother?'

'Mama, will you stop.' There was the sound of a

slap. Another explosion. Lighter this time — perhaps a glass.

'I'm leaving this house,' screamed Teboho. Then the door to her room banged shut, rattling some cutlery. Vukani's father was about to leave for the kitchen when he met his wife at the door. She grinned at the visitors.

'I'm sorry for that unfortunate diversion. Children can be destructive. Since Teboho went to that university in the north, she has come back with some very strange ideas. Opposes everything. Defiant. Yesterday she said I was a slave of the things I bought; that the white man had planned it that way. To give us a little of everything so that we can so prize the little we have that we completely forget about the most important things in life, like our freedom. I won't have that nonsense in my house. Fancy, doing all that rubbish when the visitors are here. I've had enough. I felt I had to remind that girl that I was her parent. I wonder what all this showing-off is for?'

'One can never know with children, dearie,' observed Mrs Zwane.

'Indeed!' said her husband.

'Well, Vuka,' said Vukani's father, 'can you heal our broken spirits?'

'Yes,' agreed his mother. 'We have been waiting for too long.'

Vukani thought of his sister. He wanted to go to her. They were very lonely. Their parents disapproved of some of their friends. Even Doksi. His mother had said he should have friends of his own station in life. What would a barber's son bring him? This had brought Vukani and Teboho very close. He decided then that he would not let his sister down. But could he? He thought of smashing the violin against the wall

and then rushing out of the house. But where would
he go? Who did he know nearby? The relatives he
knew lived very far away. He did not know them all
that well anyhow. He remembered how envious he
would be whenever he heard other children saying
they were going to spend their holidays with their
relatives. Perhaps with a grandmother or an uncle. He
remembered that he had once asked his mother when
they were ever going to visit his uncle. His mother had
not answered him. But then there was that conversation between his parents.

'By the way,' asked Vukani's mother, 'when did
you say your sister would be coming?'

'Next month.' There was a brief silence and then
his father continued, 'Why do you ask? I have been
telling you practically every day.'

'I was just asking for interest's sake.'

'Well,' said the father, putting down the *Daily Mail*
and picking up the *Star,* 'I just feel there is more to
the question than casual interest.'

'You think so?'

'Yes, I think so.' There was silence.

'Relatives,' the mother came out, 'can be a real
nuisance. Once you have opened the door, they come
trooping in like ants. We cannot afford it these days.
Not with the cost of living. These are different times.
Whites saw this problem a long time ago. That is why
they have very little time for relatives. The nuclear
family! That's what matters. I believe in it. I've
always maintained that. If relatives want to visit, they
must help with the groceries. There I'm clear, my
dear. Very clear.'

Vukani's father had said something about 'whites
are whites; blacks are blacks' but Vukani's aunt never
came. Nobody ever said anything about her. Doksi

liked to say: 'It's nice to have many relatives. Then when you are in trouble at home, you can always hide with one of them. And your father will go from relative to relative looking for you. When he finds you, he will be all smiles trying to please the relatives.'

'Vukani!' called his mother. 'We are still waiting, will you start playing now.'

Vukani stood up slowly and walked round to the music stand. Then he faced his mother and something yielded in him.

'Ma, I don't want to play the violin any more.' There was a stunned silence. Vukani's mother looked at her husband, a puzzled expression on her face. But she quickly recovered.

'What?' she shouted.

'I don't want to play the violin any more.' Vukani was surprised at his steadiness.

'This is enough!' screamed his mother. 'Right now . . . right now. You are going to play that violin right now.'

'Now you just play that instrument. What's going on in this house?'

His father's voice put some fear into him.

'Wait, dearie,' pleaded Mrs Zwane. 'Maybe the boy is not well.'

'Beatrice,' answered Vukani's mother, 'it's nothing like that. We are not going to be humiliated by such a little flea. Play, cheeky brute!'

'Today those boys stopped me again.' Vukani attempted to justify his stand.

'Who?' shrieked his mother, 'those dogs of the street? Those low things?'

'What's bothering him?' asked Dr Zwane. Vukani's mother explained briefly. Then turning towards her husband she said, 'As I told you the other day, he

keeps complaining that people laugh at him because
he plays the violin.'

'Jealousy,' shouted Mrs Zwane. 'Plain jealousy.
Jealousy number one. Nothing else. Township people
do not want to see other Africans advance.'

'Dear,' answered Vukani's mother, 'you are showing
them a respect they do not deserve. If you say they
are jealous, you make them people with feelings. No.
They do not have that. They are not people; they are
animals. Absolutely raw. They have no respect for
what is better than they. Not these. They just trample
over everything. Hey, you, play that instrument and
stop telling us about savages.'

Vukani trembled. He felt his head going round
now. He did not know what to do to escape from this
ordeal. The tears came back, but this time he did not
stop them. He felt them going down his cheeks and
he gave in to the fury in him: 'I do not want to play
. . . I do not want to play . . . not any more . . . ' Then
he choked and could not speak further. But what he
had already said had carried everything he felt deep
inside him. He felt free. There was a vast expanse of
open space deep inside him. He was free. He could
fly into the sky. Then he heard Dr Zwane say: 'How
difficult it is to bring up a child properly in Soweto!
To give them culture. Black people just turn away
from advancement.'

Those words seemed to build a fire in Vukani's
mother. They had sounded like a reflection on her.
She let go at Vukani with the back of her hand.
Vukani reeled back and fell on the bed letting the violin
drop to the floor. It made no noise on the carpet.
Vukani's mother lifted him from the bed and was
about to strike him again when Teboho rushed into
the bedroom and pulled her mother away from her

brother.

'Ma! What are you doing? What are you doing?' she was screaming.

'Are you fighting me?' shrieked her mother. 'You laid a hand on your mother. Am I bewitched?'

'You never think of anybody else, just yourself.'

'Teboho,' called her father. 'Don't say that to your mother.'

'Please, dearie, please,' appealed Mrs Zwane, 'there is no need for all this. How can you do this to your children?'

'*Sies*! What disgraceful children! I am a nursing sister, your father is an inspector of schools. What are you going to be, listening to savages? You cannot please everybody. Either you please the street, in which case you are going to be a heap of rubbish, something to be swept away, or you please your home which is going to give you something to be proud of for the rest of your useless life!'

'Dorcas! That's enough now!' She looked at her husband with disbelief, a wave of shock crossing her face. Then she turned towards the door and went to her bedroom, banging the door violently. There was bitter sobbing in the main bedroom. Then it turned into the wail of the bereaved.